I0685228

ABOUT THE COVER

The end result was a collaborative effort between author, Brian Smallbrook, graphic artist, Jack Taylor, and the incredibly talented digital painter, Tom Edwards of Tom Edwards Concepts and Tom Edwards Design. All artwork pertaining to this book was painted by Tom Edwards. Tom's work may be viewed online.[1]

Prior to publication, the word, "prologue," was removed from the front cover to conform with industry standards. But, yes, the entire book is a prologue.

---

[1]   https://tomedwardsconcepts.deviantart.com/; and http://tomedwardsdesign.com/

WIZARD'S RUSE

BOOK ONE
ORIGINS OF SAYZR MAGIC

B. SMALLBROOK

READ
AT YOUR
OWN RISK

Copyright © 2018 B. Smallbrook.

Artwork Design & Concept by Brian Smallbrook & Tom Edwards
Digitally Painted by Artist, Tom Edwards of Tom Edwards Concepts

Read At Your Own Risk
1603 Capitol Ave., Suite 314
Cheyenne, WY 82001
Brian Smallbrook

All rights reserved. No part of this book may be reproduced, stored, or transmitted by any means—whether auditory, graphic, mechanical, or electronic—without the signed, written permission of the author, except in the case of brief excerpts used in critical articles and reviews. Unauthorized reproduction of any part of this work is llegal and is punishable by law.

Any resemblances to any persons, living or dead, or to places, things or actual events are coincidental. If you happen to notice any such resemblances to anything outside this work it is probably just your imagination running wild.

This is a work of fiction. All of the characters, names, incidents, organizations, and dialogue in this novel are either the products of the author's imagination or are used fictitiously.

ISBN: 978-1-944199-09-8 (sc)

Because of the dynamic nature of the Internet, any web addresses or links contained in this book may have changed since publication and may no longer be valid. Any views expressed in this work are solely those of the author and do not necessarily reflect the views of the publisher, and the publisher hereby disclaims any responsibility for them.

The portrayal of different characters expressing different views is for entertainment purposes only and should not be construed as reflecting the personal views of the author, notwithstanding the dominance of a given character or the outcome of a given dialogue. Any effect, positive or negative, that this work may have on a reader is a risk assumed by the reader.

(Seriously, read at your own risk.)

Read At Your Own Risk, Publishing rev. date: 05/10/2018

This page is dedicated to the font creation community. You are a community of unsung heroes to the publishing world.

In this copy of the *Wizard's Ruse: Origins of Sayzr Magic*, the following fonts were used:

FONT PROVIDERS & CREATORS

DEMONS & DARLINGS by Sinister Fonts a/k/a Chad Savage[1]
WWFantasy Font, e.g., 🐉🐉🐉, by WindWalker64 a/k/a Angela Lane[2]
BEBASNEUE by Dharma Type and designed by Ryoichi Tsunekawa[3]
YELLOW MAGICIAN designed by Èrico Lebedenco[4]

[1] http://www.fontspace.com/sinister-fonts/demons-and-darlings; http://www.1001 fonts.com/demons-and-darlings-font.html
[2] http://www.fontspace.com/windwalker64/wwfantasy; http://web.archive.org/web/20010210195702/members.nbci.com/windwalker64/index.html
[3] https://github.com/dharmatype/Bebas-Neue
[4] https://www.1001freefonts.com/yellow-magician.font; https://www.behance.net/ericolebedenco

For the ages

. . . and for Sam.

"Perception is the illusion of reality."

~B. Smallbrook

CONTENTS

LIFESPAN OF RACES

Race	Life Expectancy
Humans	90 – 120 years
Half-elves	200 – 400 years
Dwarves	450 – 500 years
Gnomes	500 – 600 years
Elves	1,000 – 1,200 years

PRELUDE

— CHAPTER I —
A TIME BEFORE

"WHICH SIDE OF THE BARS DO YOU WANT TO BE ON?" shouted Mother as she struggled to assist the frantic bird back into its cage.

A housecat salivating for mockingbird darted in pursuit. Another one asserted itself to the front. It was a gib named Bill, and Bill loved to kill. His wild eyes gazed intently at Echo, who was now trapped inside his little prison cell. But that didn't stop the younger cats from trying.

Though they batted and swatted at the bars of the cage to no avail, the rattling broke the sound pattern and the sleep of one elven child. Echo flapped and let out a squawk.

Little T sat up on his resting mat, his dream breaking into thoughts about his morning task, a secret task, and the need to sneak away from home undetected. Beckoned by a sacred calling, the little elve emerged from his sleeping place to journey to the edge of the forest, where he would finally be free—free to explore the world on his own; free from the supervision, doubt, and distrust of adults; free from the judgment, control, and restriction of others; and, of course, free from safety.

Here the tree limbs hung like eyelashes shading the southern border of the dense wood, their branches swaying in a gentle breeze as if eyes of the East Lands blinking open to the hilled plains and flatlands beyond. Little T leaned out from a border pine and allowed the light of day to wash over his face. Out on the horizon, the endless grass plains stretched far enough to reach the sky. Just a few hundred yards out, orchards populated the landscape.

The scatter of fruit trees out in the open had their fruit browned or scarred by worms, insects, and other critters, but Little T searched until he spied a patch of trees reflecting the sweet redness in the sunlight. He hesitated at the thought of getting a lashing if he were found to have wandered off, but that was the case before he made up his mind to venture out this morning. What truly gave him pause was the distance between the protective forest and the thin spatter of tree growth out on the plains. The area was too open. He'd be so exposed. It wasn't just the stern warnings anymore. Little T felt truly afraid. "It's not safe to go out there," warned his parents and elders. But worst of all was when the bigger kids, who had grown old enough to do as they pleased, took too much pleasure in warning him not to stray from the forest.

The sum of his courage had been a stick tucked behind his beltline—a pretend knife. It made him feel important to wear what felt like a real weapon against his hip. With his false sense of security firmly in hand, his reality realized that a toy knife simply would not do.

And there it was. Settled among the litter layer of the underbrush, leaning casually against the base of one of the border pines, the silver glint of a blade called out in stark contrast to the dark leaves and damp tree bark. It was a real knife. Little T marveled at it, especially at the red, eyelike stone inlay at the base of the blade. Never before had he seen such a fancy knife. So oddly fortuitous was this discovery that he considered whether it might be a sign that his journey was meant to be, that the world recognized some importance in what he was doing. Above the knife's hilt, set within the ricasso of the blade, the slit pupil of the rubicund stone stared back at him. As his thoughtfully distant eyes scanned the grassy hillsides along the clearing's edge, they became captured prey to the green and crimson treasures ornamenting a hilltop tree.

With his bait and his bounty well in sight, Little T gripped his newfound courage and wrenched his feet forward, determined for the sake of all mankind, among all the people throughout the entire world, to possibly be the first person to eat the freshest fruit possible. He was pretty sure no one had thought of it before.

"Everyone is always pushing fresh fruit and fresh apples," he reasoned aloud, "but it's the bugs, worms, and insects that get the best stuff!"

He kept his eye on the single area of brightest red and attempted to walk straight to it, just to see if in fact those apples were the best lot on the hillside. He then focused on one toward the bottom corner of the red grouping—the ripest-looking patch. This was a sort of game he was playing . . . to test it . . . just to see.

The rumbling of staccato vibrations in the earth startled him into a sudden balance check and interrupted his game. The loud pounding was drowned out by the beating of his heart. It was an instant of shock before the little elve's paranoid brain identified the noise as belonging to the distance being made by an equally startled deer. He held his chest for a moment, then realized he'd lost sight of the crimson cluster.

After turning his narrow frame to appreciate the stretch of openness between himself and the sheltering forest, he sought but could not discern a place to hide. Even among the occasional hills that disturbed the flatlands within a few hundred yards of where the plains terminated at the forest's edge, like breaking waves on a shoreline, there presented no familiar hiding places to a simple wood elve.

In contrast, he knew the forest fairly well. "As well as any elve," he often told himself. He did know basic trends of the wood, and there were a number of places for an elven child to secrete himself away amongst the dense conifers. Some areas of the wood were so choked with trees that horsemen were forced to dismount in order to navigate through.

Yes, there were a number of tricks a native child of the wood could pull to avoid trouble—when his back was turned, an enormous hound shifted between two of the smaller hills—but out here, this child of the wood was out of his element.

Little T returned his gaze to the rolling plains, beyond a few small hills to that higher green where he thought he had been looking before, and then continued on. The parallax of growing trees hooked his attention. The closer to the apple trees he got, the larger they appeared to become. This caused some of the trees to block his view along the way. He got past them after a time and kept his attention in roughly the same direction.

"Just maybe," he mumbled, "that tree up there is the same one."

A creature crept behind, with long fang features. The reflection in its eyes foretold the next bloody feature. But the morsel didn't run. The morsel didn't hide. The tasty morsel could not read the creature's presence or its mind.

Little T paused at the base of a large roller to have a cautious look around before climbing to its peak. Then, arriving at the smooth, gray bark of an apple tree, he launched himself into its branches. As he lay belly to branch, roughly six feet off the ground, he reached out for its fruit.

One side looked perfectly ripe. The moment of truth, however, was in the turning. The smell of apples and damp leaves humidified the morning air, giving him a sense of oneness with his task. At the end of a careful turn, the apple proved pure.

Well, lookee here, he thought. He vocalized the moment. "Well, lookee here!"

He was careful not to pick the apple. After inching his body to within biting range, he blew on it and gave it a wipe. His gap-toothed smile snapped excitedly through the skin before breaching the juicy wonders inside.

Apple on stem, stem on twig, twig on branch on tree.

He had done it. A fruit had been eaten "still on the vine." Naturally, it was the sweetest he'd ever tasted.

PROLOGUE

──── Chapter 2 ────

The Ring of Fire

Twenty years later . . .

Beneath the black and quiet, moonlit stones topping a curtain wall glowed with a calming bluish hue. A barely visible line collapsed around a decorative protrusion like an unconscious snake. Slithering out of the night silence, swift constriction brought the line to life as it was pulled taut by a hidden hand.

Moments later, a hatted head surfaced. The hat was wide brimmed and worn out-of-round. With his gloved hand gripping the line and the other hanging on the edge, the climber swung his boot over the top of the wall and dragged up the rest of his body, keeping cautiously low as he came to rest along its crest.

July Taylor, historian turned renowned treasure hunter, paused momentarily to contemplate the bounty that awaited him. He elevated himself with a gradual push-up to marvel at what he could make out of the intertwining maze of curved inner walls.

"Jules!" whispered Friar Quintin, church emissary and longtime friend. "Do you see anything? Don't leave me down here all night."

July looked down to see Quintin glancing into the darkness over one shoulder and then the other, no doubt on the lookout for trouble. July beckoned the friar to join him on the wall. "Toss up your quarterstaff."

A moment later, the men took turns rappelling down the opposite side to the interior.

With a deft double pump, July uncoiled the anchoring of his whip and rewound it, returning it to his side. "There's that look on your face again," he said. "Will you relax?"

Friar Quintin looked down to the ground and shook his head. "Noble cause or not, I'll never get used to sneaking into civilized places like this. It just feels like . . . burglary."

"Well, it's too late now, so get that out of your head. We've already had this discussion—too many times." July pointed a robust thumb to his chest. "If the church wants my services, I gotta get paid. I got expenses, you know?"

"Yes, yes—"

"And if people voluntarily turned over the items requested by the church, I'd be out of a job, and you wouldn't get your bounty, either, Brother."

"I don't get paid. My order gets paid. There's a difference."

"Yeah, yeah, whatever," July said, brushing the comment aside. "You don't have to defend the principles of your order to me."

Quintin shook his head again and grumbled, "Though I walk the path of the righteous, bringing moral well-being to the common people, what does it say about me when my best friend is the one person I cannot seem to influence?"

July tugged hard on the neck of Quintin's frock, forcing him into a crouched position, and then led the way forward along the inside perimeter of the outer wall. He needed to get his bearings without straying from their only known escape. The radical curvature of the wall—and at one point its narrowing to a near four-way convergence with other parts of itself before re-expanding—caused him some disorientation. With one hand running along the stone wall, he came upon an opening. The dimensions of the archway were concealed by the night.

"Can you see anything?" asked Quintin.

July shushed his impatient partner. As they passed through it, he realized their ingress was actually an egress.

"An entrance without a door?" Quintin observed. "That does not exactly bode well for a place that would house powerful magics."

"I know," July agreed. Unable to contain his disappointment, he kicked up the dirt and threw his hat to the ground.

"It's still a very old community," offered Quintin. "Maybe there's something we can learn—"

"Don't try to placate me!" snapped July. "How are you going to explain this to our clients? You think they're going to continue to fund our expeditions after another setback like this?" July artfully swept his hat off the ground and rested his hands on his hips. He expelled cheekfuls of air as he stared up at the archway above.

"No. I know," said Quintin. "It's just that, we've worked so hard on this thing together, and for so long, that to finally realize it's all been for nothing . . ."

July stood staring at the inviting archway, reluctant to accept their blundering miscalculation. "Hang on. Hold out your quarterstaff for a moment."

Quintin did as requested.

After affixing a lantern to the end of the staff, he lit it, and took the staff from Quintin and raised the lantern high to get a closer look at the archway. "I'll be damned."

"What is it?" asked Quintin.

"Let me see those writings we bought from the Aleucians."

"The Aleucians?" Quintin shook a few scrolled pages out of a tube and handed them to July.

July understood why Quintin looked so puzzled. None of their other sources correlated or made sense of the information from the Aleucian traders. July allowed the staff to slide down through his hand until the light of the lantern illuminated the writings. His mood reinflated. "Greeted with a question," he remarked, quoting from the unfurled papers.

"Yes, 'greeted with a question,'" Quintin repeated. "Do you have a new theory about what that might mean?"

July handed the papers back to Quintin and hoisted the lantern back up to the archway. "Don't you see? It wasn't some mysterious clue in need of deciphering. It was meant to be taken literally."

Together, they mouthed the words engraved in the stone archway.

"Hey, Jules," Quintin whispered. "Does this really mean what I think it means?"

"The greatest artifacts and enchanted weapons we've ever studied were created by the ancient elvenmen. This does more than confirm that the people of this village are their direct descendants. If our research is correct, this is also their school—*the* school."

"And that would mean the School in the Sky is not the only institution of magical teachings," said Quintin. "But *this*," he added with lackluster regard, "is their version of a magic school?"

July shrugged his shoulders. "If there's one secret truth to all magic, one would think the best chance of finding it would be right here."

Like Quintin, July was a singular theorist. He was among those in his field who believed in the existence of a single truth that unlocked the secrets to the whole of all magic.

To those whose secrets, knowledge, or artifacts he was after, it might have looked like stealing. But to July, he and Quintin were merely reclaiming what rightfully belonged to their kingdom, a society favored by a God who ordained a king to rule over all of God's creation within the domain of man. Even forgotten little villages like this one benefitted greatly from a buffer of peace secured at the cost of thousands of lives by neighboring human kingdoms. It was only fitting, therefore, that such insular people living on the fringe of society be made to contribute whatever they had in the way of useful knowledge or weaponry to support such a noble cause. This was especially true of communities that were unaware of the existence or importance certain items in their possession might have in the war against evil and chaos. It was July and Quintin's job to liberate such prized items from the waste of underutilization caused by ancient, ignorant cultures. Their present mission was not at the behest of a wealthy private interest but rather upon orders of a first cardinal whose authority could be traced back to the crown.

July felt silly simply reentering the archway on foot after having previously scaled the wall. The awkward moment made him eager to find something important to get back to. With the lantern extinguished, he produced a balled-up rag and unwrapped its folds to reveal a translucent globe.

"Anything?" asked Quintin.

"I'm not sure. It's very faint."

The palest of green auras illuminated one side of the glass globe.

"This way," July said and led the way toward one of the inner wall clusters.

At fifteen feet high, the inner walls were about half the height of the great outer wall.

July peered into the darkness within one of the cloverleaf-shaped courtyards. Though slightly more intense, the green light in the globe remained faint. He swapped the globe out for the lantern to aid in their investigation. The lantern's light placed them in the middle of a crowd of devilish-looking people with every eye turned on the two men. July's lungs emptied in a startled burst, a sort of hushed scream.

Quintin's scream was far less hushed and was followed by the scream of a young boy who had been kneeling on the ground in front of a statue. They were all statues, and the devilishness, a trick of the lantern light.

Thinking quickly on his feet, July demanded, "What are you doing in here?"

The boy stood up to answer for his presence. "I'm T'Ralo. I'm a student here. I like to come here sometimes instead of going home."

"What's wrong with home?" Quintin asked him.

"Well, for one thing," the student said reluctantly, perhaps in an effort to stall, "there are parents in it."

"You have a problem with parents?" asked July.

"No. I mean, yes. I mean, you know . . . no gods, no parents, no teachers, right?"

Quintin winced. "Is that what they teach you here?"

July shot Quintin a disapproving look.

The boy named T'Ralo shrugged. "Sort of. Wait. Who are you guys?"

"We'll ask the questions," said July, who, while pointing a mini crossbow at the boy, made sure the kid got a good look at the menacing-looking metal canister with red lights down its side. "And we know what this school is. So if you know what's good for you, you'll lead us to where they keep the most powerful magic items."

"These statues are the only things magical that I know of," said the boy.

July smiled at him. "Nice try, kid, but all I see is a bunch of shaped stones."

"They change, you know," offered the boy.

"What can they change?" asked July.

"Not . . . I mean, they may not be useful for winning a battle, but they have some kind of magic. See this woman?" He pointed to a lifelike image of a woman carved in stone. He turned to face the statue, displaying genuine interest. "Earlier today, this was a statue of a man, but after midnight it changed into this woman." He knelt before the statue to read the words carved into the pedestal. "I think it has something to do with their birthdate. See here?"

"Okay, kid," July said. "So they're enchanted. But what we want you to tell us is where to find the powerful magic. Where's the weaponry?"

"But I know nothing of that. I swear to you."

"If he's a student," Quintin urged, "then ask him about the secret."

"I will try to tell you guys whatever you want," the boy said nervously. "But I know nothing about any secret."

"Do you think us fools, kid?" asked July.

"Maybe he doesn't get out much," Quintin said. "He's just some backwoods villager."

"Kingdoms have been waging wars around this secret for centuries, kid," July explained. "Wizards compete with wizards, and the Shanzi wage their anti-magic movement to root out and destroy everything to do with magic. These competitors invest entire fortunes and consume lives hunting for enchanted artifacts and magic books, in search of the all-powerful, one true source of magic. So if you want to live through the night, you might want to rack your brain for what this secret might be."

"You know, there are better students than I for such a question. But if you insist there has to be a secret, the only secret I can make sense of is the secret that there is no secret. Could that be it?"

"Perfect, kid," said July. "If there's no secret, then you should have no problem telling us about it."

"About what?"

"What is the one true source of all magic?" Quintin pressed.

The boy gave it some thought. "I think I know, but I also think you will not be happy with the answer."

"Try us," said July, pushing the crossbow closer to the boy's face.

"Nature."

"Nature?" July repeated.

"Some would say it holds secrets, but it certainly is not hidden." The boy pointed to the ground. "See?"

"No," July said. "I don't see. See what?"

The boy picked a blade of grass from the ground and offered it to

July. "Imagine us standing inside of a cosmolongous-sized blade of grass right now."

July sighed and nodded to Quintin, who swung his quarterstaff against the kid's head, knocking him to the ground unconscious.

Items of great value would likely be hidden in an underground chamber.

July was surprised by the thought, which came to him unbidden—and in the guise of an unfamiliar voice.

"What we're searching for would most likely be hidden underground somewhere," said Quintin.

July gave the friar a startled look. "Yeah," he replied. "I was thinking the same thing."

The detection globe seemed to confirm their hunch. The increasing intensity of its light led them toward the larger structures and down a short flight of stairs below the base of one of the buildings.

July produced a set of lock-picking tools and had begun to poke at the lock when the door simply swung open under the pressure of his hand.

Down the corridor to the left, they arrived at another door. It, too, was unlocked.

July placed the ignited lantern in the center of the square storage room, which revealed full shelves, chests, and cabinets. The detection globe was fully green with light, and the two men spent a few minutes rummaging through the objects on the shelves and feeling around the desks for secret compartments.

Why not try behind the cabinet?

July jumped a little. There it was again. Was he hearing things? July motioned to Quintin, who seemed to be entertaining the same idea. "Here. Give me a hand with this thing."

Positioned on either side of a tall cabinet, they gradually slid it away from the wall, revealing a small opening in the stonework.

After a brief pause, during which they exchanged stares at the dark, scary hole and then at each other, Quintin trumped July with a bearing of finality that suggested it was July's burden to lead the way.

July held the globe up to the small opening, and sure enough, its green light blazed with an even greater intensity. He looked back at Quintin and grinned. He studied the opening, found his courage, and then brushed away some spiderwebs and crawled through the hole.

On the opposite side, he found himself kneeling in grass. The hole had opened up into a small space, a mini-courtyard completely surrounded by the building they had entered, yet exposed to the night sky.

July helped Quintin through the hole and to his feet.

Under the bright green of the detection globe and in the center of the courtyard stood a four-foot-long metal spire with a red metal ring resting around its upper portion.

The treasure hunters kept their distance as they walked around the spire, circumspect. July bent down low to examine the base of the spire. Before moving any closer, he reached into a pouch for a small mound of glistening dust and blew it toward the ringed spire. Nothing.

"What do you think it is?" asked Quintin.

"I don't know, but whatever it is," July said, gesturing to the ultra-brightness of the globe of detection, "it has to be a big deal. I still haven't found any traps."

"Something of this magnitude should be well protected," said Quintin.

"I agree," a man said in the same voice that had moments earlier echoed in July's mind. "It probably should."

Spinning on his heels, July turned and faced an older man sitting on a stone bench. The man wore a layered robe and was neatly put together. July had his energy bow aimed directly at the older gentleman by the time he completed his turn.

Quintin, in position, held his quarterstaff at the ready.

"You need not fret," the man said in a reassuring voice. "Alas, I am not here to protect the ring from you. To the contrary, I was sent here to protect you from the ring. You see, the Ring of Fire was not meant for you. It was designed for use only by a sayzr—a trained seer."

"Then I'd say you're in luck," said July.

"Yeah, we have met many seers and know plenty of their ways," added Quintin. "We have studied much on the subject."

"Yes, well, it is perhaps unfortunate that the term 'seer' has a tendency to be thrown around quite loosely. But only a true seer—a sayzr—can be trained with the mental discipline required to wield an item such as the Ring of Fire."

"Why don't you tell us how it works?" said July, emphasizing the energy bow still pointed at the man's head.

"It's simple, really. The ring wearer can concentrate his thoughts on any object and cause it to burn to ashes. Some would call it a cursed item."

"Cursed, huh?" July would not allow himself to be so easily dissuaded. "Well, you know what I think? I think you are trying to play us for fools by using a seer's tricks to keep us from our bounty. Like my partner here says, we know all about seers. Why else would you offer up that information so easily?"

"In the hope that my candor would give you cause to trust me when I tell you that the chaos inside a human brain is especially prone to impulsive thoughts. Any attempt to wield that ring by a non-sayzr, especially a human, is certain to result in unintended destruction, including the destruction of yourself."

"Yeah, well, thanks for the lesson, Pops," July said. "But who said we needed to wield it? We only need to sell it. Maybe even to another wizard."

"For how much?" the old man asked.

"What?"

"Well, if all that you seek from it is to be made richer, it may be easier for me to be the one who enriches you . . . not to steal it."

"Yeah, well, my friend here needs to appraise it first. So he's just going to pick it up without putting it on. If anything bad should happen to him when he removes the ring, I'm going to empty every electrical bolt of this crossbow into your body. So is there anything you want to tell us about any traps that might be protecting the ring?"

"I already told you," the man said. "The ring does not need protection. The ring *is* the trap."

Quintin removed the Ring of Fire and held it in the palm of his trembling hand, pausing to cast an admiring gaze at the red band and its archaic inscriptions. He walked over to July and dropped the ring into his hand.

July eased his crossbow into Quintin's hands while keeping it aimed at the old man.

"You make a tempting offer, mister." July grinned at the man. "What's your name?"

"Quarternine," the man answered with an air of import. "I am a prefect here."

"Well, Prefect Quarternine, thanks for the advice. But I just decided I can probably control my thoughts well enough to make this thing work.

After all, we're both well-educated men and have a pretty good handle on what occupies our minds."

The prefect shook his head. "Your thoughts are but a chaotic storm of simultaneous impulses. You have no idea about the depths of your undisciplined nature."

July checked in with his partner. "What do you think?"

"After you use the ring against the thing you concentrate on," reasoned Quintin, "all you have to do is remove it from your finger to avoid harming anything else."

July turned to gloat at Quarternine. He allowed a knowing smile, wide and bright, to show across his face. At two inches in diameter, the Ring of Fire was quite large for a typical human finger, but when July slipped it over his first knuckle, the ring shrank to fit him.

"Oh dear, you're going to die," remarked Quarternine in an eerily polite, apologetic tone.

When nothing calamitous occurred, July opened his hands to the prefect and took a sarcastic bow.

"No better time than the present," Quintin urged.

July pointed his fist with the ringed finger at a young maple tree growing out of the soil and concentrated his thoughts. Five seconds seemed like a long time for nothing to happen. "Is there some kind of magic word—"

The tree exploded. Flaming particles of bark and splintered wood erupted in all directions.

The men ducked and shielded their eyes.

The remaining trunk burst into flames before being reduced to ash.

July quickly removed the ring and exchanged smiles with Quintin. "Hang on," he said and slid the ring back over his finger. "I gotta try something else." He turned to Quarternine. "You might want to move, old-timer."

With alert eyes wide with fear, the prefect hurried off the bench where he had been seated.

July pointed his fist at the gray stone bench and stared intensely at it. It flared up with a flash after turning bright orange, and then collapsed as if its legs were rubber before blackening and turning to ash the same as the tree.

"Ah-ha," July said to Quarternine. "I think I'm starting to get the hang of this thing. You can control the intensity of the fire just by how hard you concentrate, can't you?"

"Only a true sayzr can control its power," said Quarternine. "See to it that you do not forget that."

July pointed his fist to aim the ring at the metal spire.

"It works from your mind," reminded the prefect, who was plainly irritated. "No . . . You don't need to actually point it—"

July ignored him and pointed it.

"Ugh!" Quarternine said with a heavy sigh as the spire glowed hot before melting and burning to ash. "You should also see to it that you do not forget to remove the ring from your finger."

"Any man who can melt metal and stone to a crisp is all-powerful," said July. "The only thing I need to see to is that you stop lying to me. And you'd better start referring to me as your master, because I won't be falling for a seer's tricks."

"Yes, Master," Quarternine complied.

"And I'll see to the ruin of anyone who tries to stand in my way." July couldn't contain his exuberance. He slapped his friend on the back. "This is it, Quintin! After all these years, you and I have finally found something that can remove all the obstacles in our way. We'll have no need of our financiers anymore."

"Yes," Quintin agreed. "No more answering to sponsors or avoiding Shanzi inquisitions."

July reveled in the friar's elation. "From now on, my friend, it's just going to be you, me, and this ring."

Quintin's warm expression suddenly failed to change. The wonderment in his eyes remained, but without the subtle fluctuations of facial movement. It was as if he'd been switched off.

"Hey, you all right?"

July watched Quintin's still face turn red. Then a flaming aura around his head peeled and curled away at the picture of his happy countenance, as if parchment. Quintin's moist head went from boiling to black—and in a flash, ash.

"What? No!" July fell to his knees in horror as his loyal partner burned up before his eyes. He pointed to Quarternine. "You did this!"

"No, Master," the prefect replied. "Only the bearer of the ring directs such destruction with his thoughts."

"Use your wizardly powers to bring him back right now, or I'll use it against you next."

"Some of his particles were transformed to ash," Quarternine began. "Others were dispersed as heat and gases and have bound themselves to foreign particles on a microverse level too small for our visual capacity, my master."

"What the hell is that supposed to mean?" shouted July.

"It means I am left with nothing to work with. Assuming I even had the power to transform his particles back to their prior form, how would we ever collect them all, now that most have drifted off into the air, including the absorption of some by your very lungs?" Quarternine stepped nervously to one side. "As I told you, Master, you should see to removing the ring from your finger at once."

With his friend gone, July was not about to leave himself vulnerable to this crafty seer. "Oh, I bet you'd like that very much. Nice try, old man. But the only thing I'll see to is the destruction of you if you don't bring my friend back. I'll see to the destruction of this school and your entire village!"

"As you wish, Master. Just see to it that you do not think about your own penis while you're at it."

"Wha—?" July was taken aback. He tried brushing the idea aside with a shrug and a grin, but his eyes soon widened with concern. With his fist pointing at the grass, streaks of hot flame burned the ground. "You have ten seconds to bring Quintin back," he warned Quarternine, "or I'll destroy you."

The prefect said nothing.

July began forcing himself to concentrate on other things—anything but his own member. Ruled by sight, he was running out of places to direct his attention. He next pointed the Ring of Fire at the inner walls of the building and burned a hole through to the outside. Changing his focus distracted his thoughts away from himself. Instead, he thought about how it seemed to be working, which led him to think about how much he was avoiding thoughts about one other thing, which impulsively led him to think about that one other thing.

Once it started heating up, he was unable to think away from it. July fell to the ground, writhing in pain while frantically ripping the Ring of Fire from his finger. As soon as he was free of the ring, he pulled himself to his feet and fled up the gradual slope and through the ruined wall at top speed, screaming in terror with both hands cupped to his groin.

CHAPTER 3

SAYZR ACADEMY

Welcome to the Academy of Sayzr Magic. The inscription across the arched entryway, written in the elven tongue, translates to:

When a million men disagree with one, who is correct?

It is customary among human and elven cultures for such inscriptions to provide inspiration. How intriguing that this one appears in riddle form. For the very knowledge within this riddle is the inspiration. What is more, it imparts knowledge by asking a question. The divine significance of this will yet unfold, but for now, note that it demonstrates a contradiction that nevertheless functions and makes sense.

The riddle should not suggest a correct choice. But if you find yourself among those who impulsively favor a particular answer, it is telling you something about yourself. Chances are, you do not know what it is telling you, but you can sense, on some level, that it reveals something about you, however minuscule or insignificant. Chances are, some people in the world can tell more about you than others with that little piece of information.

But what if a person could be specially trained to derive a basic understanding of your entire life from just a scant sampling of information? The fact is, such people do exist, and such people go to school here.

The arched entrance, supported by flying buttresses, dominates the view above an otherwise undisturbed wall. Beyond the entrance, it is a fair distance to cross the forward courtyard before reaching the academic buildings, which house the classrooms, offices, and prefect quarters. Angular walls interweave to delineate multiple courtyards, each offering an explorer its own unique experience. The Hall of Heroes populates one of the side courtyards with statues commemorating little-known, ordinary people who stood for a just cause despite being made to suffer for it. It is a controversial affront to many established kingdoms, including some that are allies to this very village. Those who died for their cause or were disenfranchised, cast away, or otherwise achieved no victory or celebrity can find their home of recognition here, in the Hall of Heroes.

The worthy student eventually comes to understand that the riddle is asking you not to come with any preconceived notions or to make presumptions. You have to be open and free of influence in order to learn the sacred knowledge imparted within these walls. Sure, a million people could kill the lone dissenter or drown out his voice with their sheer numbers, but would that make them correct? To the million people it would. It is a simple lesson in perception.

> Dandelion, shine brightly,
> On whims of winds alight thee,
> From child's breath burst blind sperm,
> Sending dangling angels of silken star
> To spark the dark walls of Mother Earth.

The sanguine face of an elven child blows into a dandelion. His reflection in the water shows like a dream. In their steady descent, the dandelion seeds scatter and float, then blend and fade into heads of pupils in a classroom.

The class is psychetropes. It is run by Prefect Sparzd.

"Your assignment for this week relates to our Solstice Fair," Prefect Sparzd said to the class. "You will identify the psychetropes used in *The Puppet Master's Theatre* for at least three main characters. A bonus award will go to whoever provides the best explication of the jester character."

Matyr Brisbn raised his hand.

"Master Brisbn?" said Sparzd, calling on the eager student.

"Yes, Prefect. In the performance I attended, the jester barely had a role at all. His only appearance was less than a minute, and he spoke very few lines. So there was not enough information about him."

"I know that, Master Brisbn," said Sparzd as he began strolling around the classroom. "The whole point of learning psychetropes is so you can quickly understand people you barely know or just met. Now wake up, people. I understand the study of psychetropes is not the most popular subject among students. The very concept may be a bit cerebral—and perhaps even boring when compared with infinite transdimensional space, recycled particles, the uniform particle code—or as we like to say, the UPC—or fractal patterns—but I swear to you, psychetropes are the subtle foundation of pure magic."

Sparzd turned to face Morris Multhrobe, the plump, high-society son of the rural township governor. He held Morris's eyes as he lectured. Morris Multhrobe became visibly nervous and began to shake.

"A master of psychetropes is the *ultimate* puppet master, guiding and influencing the actions of living people." Sparzd gave Morris a look of grave disappointment and shook his head.

Morris capitulated by placing a number of food items on his desk that he had stashed away on his person.

"If done properly, the subject never even realizes he was under attack." Sparzd strolled back toward the front of the class as he ate one of Morris Multhrobe's forbidden treats. "Some wizards have attained their mastery solely by specializing in psychetropology. Now remind us: what is a psychetrope, Master Brisbn?"

"Uh," began Matyr, "a psychetrope is sort of like a classification of experiences or conditions that influence a person's character—"

"Not 'sort of like,' Master Brisbn. It *is* that. Psychetropes are the key sensory inputs that determine a person's psychological programming, categorized by their resulting effect on a person's behavior. The organization of the psychetropic spheres helps us accurately 'read' a person by allowing us to blend a multitude of these life experiences together when attempting to map out a person's psychological development." Prefect Sparzd wrote the word out on the display board. "Just like within your profile lies the psychetrope of parents who are tough on their children whenever they make a mistake or do something differently than how they would have done it, which results in your doubting yourself even when you are correct and using such noncommittal qualifiers as 'sort of like.'"

Matyr Brisbn's face turned red.

"And if you tell your parents I said as much," threatened Sparzd, "I will, of course, deny it and tell the rest of the class far worse things about you. Nevertheless, Master Brisbn is correct, and if any of you are lucky enough to make it through this course, you would do well to take advanced psychetropes, a post-graduate course exploring the influences that one psychetropic profile can have on another."

Sparzd wandered back to Morris Multhrobe and snatched the remaining food items off his desk.

"Not one of you is quite the same when you leave this classroom. You are a different person at home than when you are with your friends, and so forth." He popped a piece of sweet bread into his mouth and chewed it while staring down Morris.

Rasilla raised her hand, not wanting to be outdone by anyone in the class. "Prefect Sparzd, would it not be helpful if we also identified a number of sittropes?"

"Yes," said Sparzd. "I think Rasilla has made a valuable suggestion. In addition to the psychetropes, we should all be able to come up with at least ten sittropes that appear in the drama. You may do this by highlighting either verbal or nonverbal portrayals."

When the class let out, Matyr Brisbn saw Morris Multhrobe run for the hallway, no doubt headed straight for the governor's home. Matyr could tell that he was making a vain attempt to hide his tears. Matyr had a similar impulse to run, but given that Morris had consumed the lion's share of humiliation for the day, Matyr's was sufficiently deemphasized. With all the attention on Morris, Matyr felt safe enough to finish out the school day. Besides, the prefect's ultimate conclusion had been that Matyr had given the correct answer. This was a good day for Matyr.

With his pride intact, Matyr even summoned enough courage to approach Rasilla as she stood in the center courtyard following a fractal geometrics lab. He had been planning this for a few weeks and had just recently worked out how he would approach her and what he would say.

Rasilla was leaning against a sycamore and sharing a snack with her friend Salyndra Stamwist. Of course, she wasn't alone. Rasilla Vandono was never alone, and among groups, she was usually found at the center of attention. Adding to Matyr's competition was Bendton Dergin, who had already begun speaking with Rasilla and Salyndra. There were a couple of other boys, Phylo and T'Ralo, who dangled from the tree while attempting to make it appear as though Rasilla's presence had nothing to do with why they were there.

Just before Matyr could seize an opening in the conversation, T'Ralo plopped down from a tree limb, blocking Matyr's path to Rasilla. Matyr felt he would implode. Fortuitous relief came when Glimmer showed up and immediately shoved T'Ralo out of the way. The relief was short-lived, however, as Matyr was doubly frustrated now that the source of his relief, Glimmer, began stealing both girls' attention. Glimmer Trezpin had a knack for showing up at just the right time and capturing the moment. Actually, Glimmer Trezpin had a knack for just about everything.

Rasilla Vandono was more than a silky, black-haired beauty with uniformly spaced teeth and piercing blue eyes. She was also an overachiever. She had beauty and a drive to succeed that inspired others. If someone wanted to get Rasilla's attention, they had to excel at something. Of all the boys in the academy, the shining star in that category was Glimmer. Matyr was highly intelligent in his own right. In fact, if someone attended the Academy of Sayzr Magic, it meant they aspired to greatness with the promise to achieve it—except, perhaps, for the boy who had just been forcibly ejected by Glimmer.

Of course! thought Matyr as he mentally slapped himself for not pushing T'Ralo out of the way first. T'Ralo would have been the perfect contrast. Rasilla would have seen the exceptional Matyr next to the uninspired and indifferent T'Ralo. But instead, Glimmer now enjoyed that advantage. Glimmer had a knack for such things. *Just great,* Matyr thought. *As if Glimmer Trezpin needs an antagonist to make him look better.*

Rasilla and Salyndra laughed after Glimmer knocked T'Ralo out of the way.

"Thank you for clearing the air," said Rasilla. "He was blocking our sun."

This rattled Matyr even further, because Rasilla had just paid Glimmer a huge compliment. Glimmer and his golden locks were deemed a satisfactory substitute for the sun.

Matyr tried his approach anyway, but his momentum was gone. "Hi, everyone," he said, feeling awkward. "Hey, Rasilla. That was a tough class. Luckily, I really know my psychetropes, right?"

"Wait, what?" interrupted Salyndra. "I thought you were going to comment on our fracs lab. Psychetropes was two classes ago."

Glimmer put a patronizing hand on Matyr's shoulder and spoke through his beaming smile. "Yes. But Matyr here was right about something in that class, and we should all congratulate him on being right about something."

The girls laughed again and congratulated him.

"That's not why I brought it up," Matyr protested.

"Go on, then," Glimmer said. "We're listening."

Matyr immediately recognized Glimmer's challenge as a tactical trap, but it was too late. So well-timed and well-played was Glimmer's move, that there was no way out for Matyr. If he answered the challenge directly, it could lead to his further embarrassment in front of the girls. But if he refused it and walked away, he would expose the same embarrassing truth: that he was otherwise barren and just trying to impress Rasilla.

Matyr refused to lay down his wits, especially in front of Rasilla. Instead of slinking off to the other side of the courtyard, he attempted to outflank Glimmer by aligning himself with Bendton Dergin, whose presence was becoming dangerously close to being forgotten. "Hey, Bendton, Prefect Sparzd whipped his tongue pretty harshly at you last week, but you didn't let him get to you as badly as he'd hoped."

Bendton eagerly accepted the praise and began justifying Matyr's talk of their psychetropes class. It was working. Matyr wondered if Rasilla noticed how he had just turned the tide on the exceptional Glimmer.

Ordinarily, this would have done the trick—two against one to outmaneuver their common obstacle—but this was Glimmer Trezpin they were dealing with. Glimmer waited for the two of them to entrench each other in a sterile conversation about teachers and school, and then quietly sat down next to the girls and spoke with them in a softer tone. The group discussion had been bifurcated.

With Matyr stuck having to continue his contrived discussion, which he had initiated with Bendton only to engage Rasilla, Glimmer eventually walked off with Rasilla and Salyndra in each hand. Matyr and Bendton's awkward conversation ended abruptly as soon as the others were out of earshot.

"That was interesting," someone said from above. "Do go on." It was Phylo, who was hanging upside down from the tree and laughing at them.

"Laugh all you want," said Bendton, "but I didn't see you do much better."

"I wasn't trying to do anything. I was just hanging out in this tree, minding my own business. If Rasilla Vandono wants to hang around the same tree that I'm in, that's her business."

"Oh, sure," said Matyr. "And which of you got here first, I wonder."

"I don't know," claimed Phylo. "Maybe she was first. What's the difference? Either way, I was just minding my own business."

"If T'Ralo didn't get knocked out," Bendton said, "you'd have been right behind him."

"Now you're just being ridiculous. Everyone knows T'Ralo is the last person that anyone would follow. You're both just upset because you were made to feel foolish in front of—"

"Excuse me, gentlemen," said a gangly girl with burrs and tree sap stuck to one side of her hair, "do any of you have a snack you could share with me?"

Matyr, along with the others, just stared at her. Sissishal Haanna's white dress was marred by a pale grape stain that covered nearly half its bodice.

"Well?" She folded her arms and tapped her foot—the one with a shoe on it. Her other foot was bare. "I would appreciate it if you would, because I seem to have misplaced my snack, and I am starting to feel a little dizzy. Unless, of course, you happen to have seen my snack bag lying around anywhere?"

Unable to contain their snickering, the boys snorted.

"Have any of you seen my snack bag, perchance?"

"You lost your snack?" Matyr asked. "Your snack? What about your shoe, Sissi? Where's that?"

Sissi peered down at her feet and appeared to realize for the first time that her shoe was missing. "Oh, I just left it somewhere."

Phylo stifled a chuckle. "You mean you lost that, too?"

"No, I didn't lose it," Sissi replied defensively.

Matyr and Bendton exchanged amused glances. "Then where is it?" they asked in unison.

Sissi studied her bare foot for a moment before looking up. "Well . . . it's not on my foot. That's for sure."

The boys laughed.

Sissi straightened and placed her hands on her hips. "Well," she huffed, "if none of you *children* are going to help me with something to eat, I'm sure I can find someone at this institute gentlemanly enough who will."

"Yeah, well, good luck," said Bendton. "Snack time is nearly over."

"Humph!" Sissi raised her chin, folded her arms with an air of superiority, and then strutted away with an uneven gait.

Bare foot. Shod foot. Bare foot. Shod foot.

Phylo, Matyr, and Bendton traded grins.

T'Ralo was sitting beside a fence post on the outer edges of the courtyard when he felt Sissi's presence. He didn't bother to look up but instead continued to stare down at what had captured his attention moments earlier: a small boulder that was swarming with tiny red spiders. A small stone, in the palm of his hand, was similarly populated.

Sissi, never one to be deterred, sat down beside him, leaving scarcely an inch between them.

He continued to ignore her, but he could see in his peripheral vision that she was holding her knees and rocking herself in an agitated fashion.

"Why are you staring at that stone?" she asked him.

"There are tiny red spiders crawling around it," he said through clenched teeth. He was being careful not to drop the bright orange carrot that dangled from his mouth.

Sissi got on her hands and knees and crept over like some kind of deranged animal. With the corner of her mouth pressed against his, she bit the carrot out of his mouth. "I need this."

T'Ralo heard several kids snicker nearby, but he didn't react, other than to wipe some of Sissi's saliva from the corner of his mouth. He was well aware that Sissi had just stolen part of his lunch—and that others in the courtyard were finding the spectacle entertaining—but he was too engrossed in the tiny red spiders to make a fuss. Instead, he absentmindedly reached into his lunch sack and retrieved an apple, the last of his snack.

As soon as he bit into his juicy apple, Sissi lunged at it.

"Don't eat that!" she shouted in alarm. "Open your mouth! Open your mouth!"

That got his attention. T'Ralo opened his eyes and mouth wide, uncertain about what he was averting.

Sissi reached into his mouth, plucked out the mashed chunk of apple he had started chewing, and put it into her own mouth. "I need this, too," she explained, snatching the rest of the apple out of his hand.

"Hey!" protested T'Ralo.

"I'll bring it back when I'm done," she said.

"Fine!" he said with agitation.

Sissi picked up the carrot she had dropped on the ground and limped away with her two snacks in hand.

T'Ralo shook his head in annoyance and then turned slightly, just enough to spy where the snickering had been coming from. Several of his classmates were still hanging from the old sycamore, where he had been a few minutes earlier. Directly across from him and nearest the school building, Glimmer was performing a double backflip off a bench carved from stone. Glimmer's rapt audience, Rasilla and Salyndra, clapped and cheered.

T'Ralo was still smarting from the way Glimmer had shoved him away from the lovely Rasilla. It was bad enough all the girls admired Glimmer for his perfect muscular body, but Glimmer had the charisma to go along with it as well. It just seemed unnecessary for Glimmer to take such an active interest in preventing him from talking to Rasilla, when Rasilla clearly favored Glimmer. T'Ralo watched Sissi limp away in their direction, still compensating for her missing shoe. He thought he might derive some satisfaction if Sissi happened to interfere with Glimmer's play.

Sure enough, before Glimmer could perform another feat of acrobatic wonder, Sissi prejudiced the entire proceedings by sitting on the bench he was using as his launch pad. While she ate her newfound snacks, Sissi stared unabashedly at Glimmer's perfect, muscular arms.

The trio exchanged looks. Glimmer's sanguine cheeks revealed his embarrassment.

"You know, Sissi," Rasilla offered, "it's not considered polite to stare at people."

Sissi was unmoved and answered without taking her eyes off Glimmer. "You stare at him."

"I do no such thing," said the red-faced Rasilla.

Glimmer came to the aid of his defender. "Looking at people and staring at them are two different things, Sissi. Rasilla and I may see each other and look at each other when we are speaking, but we do not stare at each other for long periods of time."

Perfect, thought T'Ralo. This was something worth watching.

"I know what the difference is," said Sissi. "And you stare, too. You and Salyndra both stare at Rasilla the same way I do."

Despite all his natural abilities, Glimmer obviously didn't know how to handle this situation. Though he had a knack for most things, Sissi was not one of them. T'Ralo was enjoying watching the golden boy squirm.

"Wait," Salyndra said, clearly wanting to have a go at Sissi. "You stare at Rasilla, Sissi? Why would you stare at Rasilla?"

"By studying her body, I can learn more about my own."

The trio laughed nervously.

"Rasilla used to have crescent shadows, but now they appear more like quarter moons under her breasts. Rasilla's breasts have projected considerably over the past seventeen months." Sissi pulled on the loose neck of her stained bodice to examine her own chest. This was the first time she had taken her eyes off Glimmer since she'd sat down. "Mine have remained the same, and there are no shadows. But I reason that will change, and in a few more years I, too, will have shadows like Rasilla."

"My stars, Sissi!" said Rasilla, crossing her arms to cover her chest and smiling with an affected display of modesty.

"I can assure you, Sissi," said Salyndra, "Glimmer and I do not stare at Rasilla, and certainly not for those reasons, either."

"No!" insisted Sissi.

T'Ralo knew well why she was agitated. Sissi couldn't tolerate it when someone said something or labeled something incorrectly.

"I said you both stare at Rasilla the same *way* as I do, not for the same reasons," she explained. "I study her shadows to learn about my own development. You stare at her breasts because you are jealous of her, and Glimmer stares at her breasts because—"

"Okay, Sissi," Rasilla said hotly, "that's quite enough. Can we all please stop talking about my breasts?"

T'Ralo wasn't quite ready for the discussion to end, but the bell chose that moment to ring.

Returning his thoughts to the stone in hand, he imagined it as a planet and observed that all but a few of its arachnid inhabitants had abandoned it—just as they had done with the stone he attempted to hand in as his fractals lab assignment. The enduring spider appeared as nothing more than a little red dot industriously migrating from one hemisphere to the other. He wondered about it, then looked up at the emptying courtyard to observe his fellow students heading back inside to attend the last two classes of the day. If it was any reflection at all, and T'Ralo was the one migrating, he wondered to where.

— CHAPTER 4 —

CRISIS ON CAMPUS

Headmaster Ghostas peered down at Sissishal Haanna, who had just taken a student for all his snack food. "Still," he said, "she always manages to get what she wants, does she not?"

Beside him, Prefect Quarternine chuckled. "Right out of his mouth."

From his vantage point atop the main tower's observation deck at Sayzr Academy, Headmaster Ghostas enjoyed a bird's-eye view of the courtyard and his cherished students. Behind him, a series of ornately carved wooden door panels exceeding twenty inches in thickness stood at attention. In spite of their intimidating presence, something about each massive block of wood filled Ghostas with the warmth of home. In place of hinges, each of the domineering panels pivoted on a central rod so that they could be opened and closed to vent the air. In their fully opened position, in parallel, the grand doors separated the observation deck from the austere conference room, which, even suffused in daylight, exuded a cool, somber atmosphere.

"We are discussing my progeny, Magistra Haanna, I gather?"

Ghostas turned to see Prefect Sparzd entering the conference room. A flash of sunlight reflected off his decorative skullcap when he bowed to make his greeting. Other than Quarternine, there was no one Ghostas trusted more, despite Sparzd's somewhat quarrelsome nature. "Ah, Prefect Sparzd, thank you for joining us."

Ghostas and Quarternine stepped through the open doors into the conference room to join the other prefects at the long oaken table. Only a few had taken seats.

"Actually, we are discussing all the students," said Quarternine.

"We are concerned about our prospects," Prefect Moshe-djin, the eldest member of the faculty, said in a weak yet throaty voice from his usual place seated midway along the table. A single spot of black hair on his otherwise thick, gray beard bobbed in unison with his jaw, revealing the chewing action of a well-concealed mouth. He was a bit of a curmudgeon, perhaps, but Ghostas valued his keen judgment. "We have lost more students to attrition than in any years past."

"What Moshe-djin is saying," Governor Multhrobe interjected in a brusque manner, "is that we are dangerously close to running out of prospects."

"And to what do we owe the blessing of your presence here at Sayzr Academy, Governor Multhrobe?" asked Sparzd.

Ghostas, detecting a hint of animosity in Sparzd's voice, steeled himself. He had a hunch he'd be playing the role of peacemaker shortly.

"If we fail to produce sufficient numbers for a new generation of master sayzrs," the governor answered, "it is a matter that can affect the security of the entire village and the preservation of our sacred heritage."

"This has always been the case with our people," countered Sparzd. "Likewise, it has always been a matter left to the care of the Chamber Keepers, which is comprised of our present faculty and those who actively serve on the counsel of sayzrs. I am not aware of a time when that responsibility called for the involvement of political administrators."

The governor bristled. "Now see here, Prefect Sparzd. As governor of our village proper, I am responsible for managing our future course. I have every bit as much right—"

"Gentlemen, please!" interrupted Ghostas. "I will not have this important meeting compromised by upmanship or quibbling over societal roles. Now, Prefect Sparzd, while I agree with you on our traditions, Governor Multhrobe is here on my personal invitation, which I should think warrants our offering him our highest regard." He slowed his pace and leveled his tone, determined to establish a civil tenor from the outset of what he knew was an important gathering. "As always, Moshe-djin makes the salient point that these are unprecedented times, which I believe warrants my executive discretion to make exceptions to our common traditions."

Sparzd bowed again. "Of course, Headmaster Ghostas." He turned and bowed in respect to the governor. "I beg your pardon, Governor Multhrobe. It appears I have fallen prey to the customary dynamics of a classroom environment, wherein a prefect must maintain clearly delineated authority and control over his pupils. We should be grateful for any help we can summon for such grave concerns, and I would consider it both a personal and professional privilege if you would agree to remain here to assist us with all you can on this historic day concerning matters of such great import."

Ghostas knew that Sparzd was mentally manipulating the governor. Even though sayzrs are sworn to refrain from using their powers on other villagers, emergencies—and, apparently, innocuous social trifles—were the exception. In any event, it seemed to be working.

The governor appeared most pleased with Sparzd's words, albeit somewhat unbalanced by his invitation to respond to a plea. "Er, um . . . why yes, I will agree to stay and help you."

"Then I am in your debt," concluded Sparzd with another bow.

Fortunately, Ghostas thought, Sparzd was of such artful mastery that there was no chance of the governor ever realizing what had just been done to him. Ghostas nodded to his right-hand man, Quarternine, who then directed everyone's attention back to the courtyard below the observation deck. All followed but for Moshe-djin, who remained seated before a setting of fine teas and silver side plates full of mint leaves. From his position at the table, he would be able to participate in the discussion through the open doors to the observation deck.

Quarternine leaned over the partial barrier and continued where they had left off. "With less than half our usual enrollment and only a handful of prospects, it would appear Prefect Sparzd's progeny, the little Ms. Sissishal Haanna, is our most likely candidate."

A gruff moan from behind the group punctuated Prefect Quarternine's statement. It was Prefect Moshe-djin. He offered no words, just a noise. It was a mixture of throat clearing and a groan that sounded of caution and reservation.

Ghostas glanced back at Moshe-djin and then, turning, caught sight of a frowning Governor Multhrobe.

"I have to confess that I'm more than a little confused," said the governor. "You view this Sissishal Haanna as your top student, and yet you don't all seem terribly enthused by her promise as a sayzr. I've heard that she can barely communicate with others. I've heard other things, as well."

"It can get a little complicated, Maurice," said Ghostas, who, as a former schoolmate, felt comfortable calling the governor by his first name, "but we will endeavor to explain it to you."

"Well," the governor replied, "perhaps you can start by explaining why she was crawling around on all fours earlier or why she is missing one of her shoes."

"Actually, Governor, her missing shoe is part of the explanation," said Quarternine. "You see, she lost it. But I can assure you that among the geniuses here at Sayzr Academy, she is our top genius. Off the charts, really."

"Your top genius lost her shoe?" asked the governor. "And speaking of missing things, where's my son?" He gestured toward the courtyard below. "I didn't notice Morris out there today."

"I am afraid he was not feeling well and excused himself early," explained Ghostas. "He withstood until the conclusion of Prefect Sparzd's class."

The governor turned toward Sparzd. "Oh?"

"Yes, I believe it was something he ate," said Sparzd.

The governor returned to the business at hand. "Will somebody please explain the problem with your top genius?"

Ghostas deferred to Sparzd. "Prefect?"

"Yes, well," Sparzd began, "as you all know, Ms. Haanna is affectionately referred to as my progeny and with good reason. She has a great mind for psychetropes. Among the fifteen revisions of the psychetropic spheres charting the most typical determinants, there are more than sixty-six thousand classical psychetropes, including variants. Magistra Haanna is the only student—the only person—known to be able to recreate the psychetropic spheres by memory."

Ghostas studied the governor's face. Did he fully understand the ramifications of what Sparzd had just said?

"The only humor you will find in my class is the title of mastery I assign to each student," Sparzd said, continuing, "but when I refer to Sissishal Haanna as Magistra, I assure you, no sarcasm is warranted. She is as close to being a master sayzr as an early season tree is to bearing fruit. With time, and a little nurturing, it is ineluctable."

The governor nodded, but his face bore doubt. "And?"

"We do not like to speak ill of our students," offered Quarternine. "All the more so of such a gifted child."

"The fundamentals are there, Governor," Sparzd explained. "And in time, her abilities will rival my own. Indeed, I hate to admit it about such a cherished student, but there is a possibility she could turn out to be . . . dangerous."

Ghostas winced at Sparzd's use of the word *dangerous*. It was true, of course, but a controlled leak to the people, through Governor Multhrobe as their representative, was a strategy to avert hysteria, and he wasn't sure how the governor would take such a blunt assessment. Whatever the result with Magistra Haanna, the Sayzr Academy could ill afford to appear as if it withheld important information from local villagers.

Prefect Mazer spoke up. "You see, Governor, with Ms. Haanna, the issue is not whether she will become a master wizard, but rather, what kind of wizard she will become. It is a question of loyalties."

"That's the first thing I've understood since we've been at this," said Governor Multhrobe. "But why would she be disloyal to our village?"

The bell rang to signal the start of the remaining two classes of the day.

From the observation deck, Ghostas and the others watched all but one student return to class. Ghostas could tell by the expectant look on the governor's face that he was waiting for someone to explain to him why the boy remained in the courtyard.

"Magistra Haanna does not process information the same way most of us do," said Sparzd. "While we are all prone to some variation, hers is more dramatic. She does not have the same interests or motives as the typical person, and she exhibits some highly unusual characteristics."

"What sort of characteristics might those be?" asked the governor.

"For example," offered Mazer, "she hyper-focuses on certain tasks to the exclusion of others, more so than we have seen in other exceptional students. Ironically for a master of psychetropes, she is an utter failure in the area of social skills. As such, you would not want her to accompany you to your council meetings or speak at formal political events."

"Not if she's going to snatch food out of the mouths of our visiting dignitaries," Governor Multhrobe remarked wryly.

"As Prefect Mazer pointed out," Ghostas said, "the absentmindedness is something we have seen in many of our greatest minds, and most of us can relate to it on a personal level to a certain degree." He paused as the other prefects chuckled in agreement. "With Sissishal, that condition is just more pronounced. She may yet outgrow it or find some way to better adapt, as many of our former students have."

"The point is," Sparzd continued, "in order to keep her loyal, to keep her from straying down paths that may conflict with our ways, we have to keep her fulfilled in her life here in the village."

"Need to keep her happy," croaked Moshe-djin, "or keep her isolated."

Ghostas turned away from the courtyard and back toward the conference table. He watched silently as Moshe-djin, still seated alone, passed another mint leaf through the cloud of his beard over what must have been his lower lip.

"Yes," agreed Sparzd. "Fortunately, her needs are quite simple, at least for the time being."

"What keeps her happy?" asked Governor Multhrobe.

"For now," said Sparzd, "she seems fulfilled by pets, playthings, knowledge, books, and learning. She tends to find comfort in various patterns and keeping to a routine. And then there are basic needs like food, warmth, and water. But as a child becomes an adult, their needs change, and those needs can become more complex."

"And what would happen if she were not happy with what our village could provide?" asked the governor.

"She would get whatever she needed some other way or from some other place," answered Sparzd. "She could fall into the wrong hands and be used against us. She could seek out things that are inappropriate or dangerous to her or to the village order."

The governor did not look pleased. "So this child is some kind of monster we can never say no to?"

"Not necessarily," Sparzd said. "But teaching her our values, socially acceptable behaviors, and any limits in general—essentially saying no to things she might want—will be the challenge going forward."

Ghostas, concerned that Sparzd had painted too bleak a picture, moved to intervene. "We will continue to monitor her development and keep you apprised of our progress. You can be assured we already have a series of contingency plans in place, some of which I would like to discuss with you in greater detail in another meeting."

"I should think so." Governor Multhrobe shook his head and scrunched his eyes closed. "With all due respect, can't a master sayzr predict the future, particularly one with your talents, Prefect Sparzd? Isn't there some way for you to determine what type of sayzr this girl is going to make?"

"The way of the sayzr is a path to true seeing, not foreseeing," quipped Quarternine.

The others chuckled politely.

"But you are correct that such clear sight often lends itself to reliable prophecy," Quarternine added. "It's a simple matter of pattern recognition."

Sparzd spoke up. "A sayzr who specializes in psychetropes can usually tell what a person is thinking, how a person thinks, and what a person will likely do in a given situation. Armed with that knowledge, a sayzr can heavily influence a person's actions." He stepped to the edge of the observation deck to peer out over the half-wall. "Predicting the future, generally, is a different matter than predicting the specific course of a person's development. Even for a master, the latter cannot be performed reliably. What is more, the younger the subject, the more difficult the task of prediction. We can attempt to simulate by extrapolation what the psychetropic profile may be for a child once he or she reaches adulthood, but so long as an adult psychetropic profile remains in its formative stages, it is next to impossible to determine what influences might intervene throughout a young person's life that would alter and possibly determine the end result."

"With enough sayzrs," the governor said, "I presume we could adequately handle a single bad apple. So why don't we discuss that: maintaining our population of sayzrs. After all, that was to be the topic of today's meeting, was it not?"

"Indeed," agreed Ghostas. "These other students will not take as much time to go through—"

"Who is that student, anyway?" The governor pointed to the boy now truant in the courtyard—the boy they had previously witnessed being used as a buffer by Phylo, bullied by Glimmer, and having his food stolen by Sissi. "And why is he still out there instead of back in class with the others?"

"Actually, Governor, we already include him among those lost to attrition," explained Quarternine. "His is a sad case. Essentially, he does not wish to be here. He wants to learn to fight and become a soldier like so many other boys. In addition to lacking in aptitude, he fails to see the value in our teachings and often fails to turn in assignments. And what he does turn in often misses the mark. Is that not a fair statement, Prefect Mazer?"

"It is the truth," said Mazer. "Just last period, we had a lab assignment in which the students were asked to bring in examples of natural formations that exhibited a specific pattern. Well, that child found a rock crawling with red spiders. By the time he brought it into class, few of the spiders remained. He tried to insist their movement formed a pattern, which it most certainly did not. But even if it had, it would not have been the pattern requested by the assignment, which was specifically geared toward fractals."

"Who is he?" the governor repeated.

"His name is T'Ralo," said Ghostas.

"How did such a student gain acceptance to the academy in the first place?" the governor asked.

Ghostas stroked his whiskers as he contemplated the question. "As I recall, we were largely attracted to his promise by circumstantial evidence. It was as if he were somehow swept up in the primary patterns of Nature. Of course, even looking back, there always existed reason to doubt that Nature's will had him fated for some important purpose. He wasn't even central to many noteworthy events. And yet, some happenstances were just too unusual for us to discount as mere coincidence."

"What sort of events are we talking about?" the governor asked.

"The most significant, to my mind," said Ghostas, "was when the Red Bear came to our village. Mind you, T'Ralo was barely involved in that at all, and it actually followed his enrollment, so it really only served to bolster our decision. Still, it's a perfect example of the sort of thing we're talking about. And it was such an important event that to have him caught up in it in any way was difficult to ignore."

"The Red Bear? That does sound vaguely familiar to me, but I don't—"

"It had to do with an important discovery, made some twenty years ago . . ."

— Chapter 5 —

Time of the Red Bear: Discovery

Twenty years ago . . .

The call of black crows echoed through the tall oaks and pines. Scurrying squirrels chasing one another through the trees could be heard leaping along each limb. Between the branches, rays of sunlight shone down to the forest's floor and accentuated the redness of Grimby's thick hair.

He and eight other members of the Terminators stood in the middle of the woods beside a large boulder. The boulder's bare grayness seemed out of place among the tall trees and greenish flora, save the cap of moss memorializing the time it had spent resting there. The men clustered around to stare down at a narrow hole that descended inward and beneath the giant stone.

Grimby scowled at the short straw in his hand as the other men stood around him. "Wait a minute," he growled, raising a bushy eyebrow to meet their smug faces. His scowl deepened. He wanted nothing to do with this. Among the members of the Terminators, he was the one who had voted against getting involved in this hunt right from the start. "You all cheated," he accused his party members.

Roble, the party mage of the Terminators, responded first. "Either way, your size does seem to make you best suited for the job," he said, staring down at the rabbit hole beneath the base of the boulder.

"Is that so?" Grimby said, resting his fist against his hip. "You know, you're a tad blind for a so-called seer. We dwarves may be shorter than your lot, but not so small." Grimby clenched his fist and flexed a bicep. His muscular arms were as broad as Roble's legs, and covered in a thickness of hair resembling the coat of a bear. "Be thar anyone should be crawlin' down that cranny 'tis you, ya wiry wizard!"

"Grimby!" shouted Commander Murtock. "You drew your straw, short and fair."

Murtock wasn't the party leader, but he outranked everyone in the current fragment, and Grimby bemoaned having to follow his orders. Unable to contain himself, Grimby mumbled something about a useless artifact. "The only magic secrets I need is the kiss o' me blade," he said, thrusting a hand axe in the air.

"You're right about one thing," said Roble, who was still smirking as he handed a rope line to Grimby. "You are short. Short on height, short in stature, short on luck, and short on straw."

Grimby snatched the rope out of Roble's hands and tied it around his waist. "If I comes outta dis ting alive," he said, pointing to the hole, "and one day comes to outlive y'all, I'm gonna drink myself drunk and piss on yer graves!"

"And piss on our graves," the other men sang in unison, for it was not the first time Grimby had offered up this solemn promise.

"And that's my solemn promise to ya's," offered Grimby.

Being forced to burrow through the narrow tunnel like a filthy animal put Grimby in a sour mood. At one point, he tried wiping his face clean against his soiled shoulder, but that only made it worse. *It should be someone else stuck in this hole. Anyone but me*, he thought. The semblance of a self-satisfied smile appeared through his dirt-clogged beard when he imagined emerging from the hole empty-handed, just to spite the other party members who had allowed him to be chosen for this.

Despite his lack of enthusiasm, after twenty minutes of digging, Grimby unearthed a wooden case that had been wrapped in leather and buried in sand beneath the soil.

"Oh, those swindling bastards don't deserve this find," he muttered to himself.

With the end of the tunnel having opened up to a bulbous shape, Grimby managed to contort and shimmy his body around to face the way out. He tied a short line to the case and affixed it around his ankle to be towed behind.

With the case secured, Grimby tugged the rope line. No response. He grumbled and tugged the line again. "C'mon, ya backstabbing larrikins. Pull me up already." He waited for a brief moment. And then—"Bah!" He gave up on them and began making his way, crawling toward the steeper incline of the hole.

When a full minute passed without any response from above, Grimby began reeling in the lifeline for any sign of resistance. But before long, he found himself still at the bottom of a hole, holding the opposite end of the rope in his hand.

"Hu-hoa! Of all the mud-suckin', fish-cuttin' double-dealin'. You larcenous, loveless larrikins won't be gettin' away with this!" Grimby growled under his breath as he was forced to endure the ignominy of clawing his way out of the hole under his own power and with loose soil falling over his face and interfering with his breathing. At the steepest portion, where the tunneling ran near vertical, the sides gave way at his grip, causing him to slide back several feet. At the end of his fall, he spat out a mouthful of soil, followed by a mouthful of curses. But the anger in his belly, its hunger for revenge, gave him the determination to try again. He didn't want their help anymore. "Don't give 'em the satisfaction," he told himself. "And I'll be takin' double me share before giving up this box o' spoils to those inglorious, orc-lovin' bastards!"

Finally, with the worst of his arduous task behind him, Grimby made it to the last incline where he could see daylight through the mouth of the hole. He managed to put a hand over the edge of the opening and hoisted himself out onto the forest floor. Rolling over onto his back, he released a heavy breath of air.

"Orc-lovin' larrikins," he muttered, catching his breath.

He sat up and began untying the case from his ankle. He was all sweaty and covered in dirt while everyone else seemed to be enjoying a good time around a campfire. "I could have broken me leg," he complained. "I could have suffocated."

His party members gave him no response.

"You know, the whole point of a lifeline is lost if you don't anchor the other end, ya' daft fools." Grimby felt they were snickering at him with their backs turned. "Laugh it up, ya' loveless larrikins!" He walked over to directly address Murtock, who was seated with the others on a downed tree branch. He put his foot against Murtock's back and gave him a solid shove. "'Cause none ya's gonna taste these spoils 'tils I renegotiates me share o' the—"

Murtock had fallen off the branch and onto his knees, then tipped over to his side, revealing the wooden end of a spear sticking out of his throat. Grimby hopped over the downed branch to get a look at his other party members. They had all been propped up this way, skewered on wooden spears. Everyone except . . .

"Roble!" The name dripped like acid off of Grimby's tongue. He tucked the case into a strap across his chest and readied an axe in each hand. "Just the sort of skullduggery I'd expect from a sap-sucking seer." He glanced back and forth in a panic, nearer in the trees, then farther in the forest, hastening to locate the traitorous wizard. "I never trusted you!" His eyes shifted. He listened for movement. "The lives of my dear friends will not go unavenged. Why don't you show yourself, you treacherous—"

Grimby spied their party wizard high above the campfire. With arms and legs stretched wide like a star, Roble was suspended on glistening strands among the surrounding trees. Roble's eyes had been carved out of his face, and his tongue was pinned against the bottom of his chin with a small knife. It was plain to Grimby that whoever had done this had gone to the extra trouble of making Roble suffer in life and desecrating his body in death. Roble's heart dangled outside his chest, and his intestines hung down, unwound from his abdomen.

"By the Mighty Gedtor!" Grimby cried out, invoking the name of his dwarven god. "Roble, my bosom brother, my nearest and dearest friend, I will avenge your death. I will avenge all of my Terminator brothers. And in the name of the Terminators, I will terminate everyone responsible for this, even if I have to do it all myself."

Grimby thought he detected something moving in the woods. It reawoke in him a sense of imminent danger, and he immediately fell silent. His eyes shifted about warily, uncertain if he had truly seen anything. Had it been a raid that was now over, or were they still out there?

Whatever he thought he had seen among the stillness of the wood, he thought he saw it again. It was a flash movement, like the flicker of a shadow.

Grimby stood by the crackling campfire and stared back at his fallen companions who were seated before him. The dead eyes of their propped-up faces were bearing witness to his performance like an audience from hell. Grimby shuddered, then steadied himself with hand axes at the ready. He was careful not to move. He controlled his breathing and listened to the sounds of the woodland. There was nothing but stillness.

As he lowered his weapons, another flicker appeared not more than fifty yards from where he stood. But this flicker remained. A humanoid figure wearing a bright-white hooded cloak appeared from behind a tree trunk. A hundred yards to the left of it, another white cloak revealed itself. There was another, followed by a fourth one that was even nearer to Grimby. Soon, the white cloaks quietly populated the forest like a flutter of butterflies.

"Shanzi scum!" snarled Grimby. Realizing he was outnumbered, Grimby stepped backward and stood behind the fire as they advanced on his position.

"Drop the scroll, and you are free to go," echoed a voice from among the flutter.

Grimby tossed a powder sack into the fire, causing the flames to flare upward and outward in a twenty-foot radius. He then pitched a second powder sack through the intensified flames. It caught fire and sent a flaming barrier in the direction of the Shanzi. "Go suck an orc!" Grimby growled.

— Chapter 6 —

A New Concern

"T'Ralo," the governor repeated. "I know that name. I have heard my son speak of him—and not in a flattering way, I'm afraid. A 'loser,' I believe, was one of the descriptions Morris used."

"It is regrettably worse than that," said Sparzd. "A loser at least tries. We can work with that. This one does not try and does not care when he fails."

"Then what is he still doing here? Why hasn't he been permanently excused?"

"He is," Quarternine said, hesitating, "one of Sissishal Haanna's playthings that we alluded to earlier."

The governor leaned forward with a look of grave concern. "Lots of things can be a plaything: a frog, a dog, a bird, even a mole. But we cannot have a person, especially one of our own citizens, be the plaything of another citizen. Need I remind you gentlemen of our Declaration of Rights?"

"We are sensitive to every student's rights," Ghostas said.

"So then," the governor began, "what do his parents think of this . . . unorthodox arrangement?"

"They are grateful we permit him to remain," Ghostas answered, "because it keeps him from joining up with some human's army and getting killed in battle."

"Okay, fine. But aside from not getting him killed, what are we really doing to help further this child?"

"Keeping our youth alive, by itself, should be sufficient justification," croaked Moshe-djin, the soothing tea having done very little to alleviate the rasp in his voice.

"We are offering him the best education available to prepare him for the rest of his life," Ghostas added. "I'm talking about real life. Not the world seen by most outsiders, but the real world as seen by a true sayzr." He pointed to the other sayzrs in the room. "The world we know."

"A sayzr's perception training offers a tremendous advantage," Sparzd explained. "Only a true seer can see the real world. A sayzr walks the Earth among its blind populace. Even though T'Ralo is failing and rejects our teachings, he cannot help that some of the messages and insights are getting through. He may disregard the way of a sayzr today, but someday, if the need is great enough, there will be something of it within him to draw from, provided he is open to it."

The governor appeared more satisfied by Sparzd's explanation, which Ghostas had to admit sounded better than merely keeping the boy alive.

"It was actually Prefect Sparzd's idea that this student would make a good companion for our little Ms. Sissishal Haanna," said Quarternine, "although he was not quite in favor of allowing a failing and indifferent student to remain at Sayzr Academy."

"With all due respect, gentlemen," said Governor Multhrobe, "this 'plaything' plan of yours seems to have run its course, since it would appear the plaything no longer wishes to attend this institution. Which means the potential monster in Sissishal Haanna won't be happy." His mouth formed a frown as he gazed warily down at T'Ralo in the courtyard. "If a student refuses to return to class on one day, what's to prevent that student from refusing to show up to school at all on the next?"

"It appears we are in the midst of a new problem," said Ghostas. Ghostas glanced over to the table to appreciate how the steam rising from Moshe-djin's teacup became lost in the fuzz as it entered the fog of whiskers covering his chin. He had paused in the hopes that Moshe-djin would clear his throat with a quick solution, as he often did. But this time, Moshe-djin offered nothing up to Ghostas. "Governor, I regret that this has occurred during your visit. Does anyone have any suggestions for ensuring this student's continued attendance?"

"It was one thing to turn a blind eye to a failing student, Headmaster," objected Sparzd, "but now we are to bend over backward to keep a failure enrolled?"

"I do not like it any more than you do," said Ghostas. "But under the circumstances, we should explore all options."

The fog suddenly lifted, and the black spot on Moshe-djin's gray beard bobbed up and down again. "If he wants to learn to fight so badly, let us teach him more intensively."

"Our physical skills class already includes a combat and swordsmanship component," said Prefect Serren, the physical skills trainer. "Surely you do not propose we deprive our students of gymnastics, climbing, tumbling, and other skills, just to cater to this retained washout. His mere presence is enough of a distraction. He is a negative influence on our genuine students."

Ghostas held up his hand. "I believe Moshe-djin is talking about a personal trainer, a private tutor of sorts, only for fencing."

Moshe-djin rocked his body and nodded.

"I suppose we could find someone to show up for an hour or two after school," Ghostas said.

Moshe-djin coughed. "*During* school."

Ghostas walked over to the table and leaned closer to Moshe-djin. "During school?" he whispered with concern. "In place of classes?"

"He is already failing," the old man replied in his usual scratchy voice, "and dislikes his classes."

"Karmin Porris, the young apprentice of Swordmaster Geltin, could be asked," offered Quarternine, "with Master Geltin's permission. Sparzd, do you see this working?"

"I see us breaking with long-standing traditions," said Sparzd. "But yes, it would work." He seated himself at the conference table and continued reluctantly, "In fact, it would work for both of them. Magistra Haanna needs a highly tolerant friend who will indulge her unique obsessions and behaviors. She needs a T'Ralo, or someone like him, to keep her grounded and happy so that she remains . . . on our side."

Ghostas, spying the look of unease on the governor's face, turned to address the remaining prefects who were still leaning against the half-wall with the governor. "We shall table this discussion until we have spoken with Master Geltin about Karmin." He gestured for the governor to join him and the others at the conference table. "Come. Let us sit for tea and get back to the business of our dwindling class of prospects."

Chapter 7

A Time Before

. . . continued

The excitement and challenge of the little elve's journey to the orchard had served as a distraction from the dangers of the open plains. The return trip, however, left him with nothing else to focus on. The taste of apple, still sweet on his breath, offered no comfort.

Little T picked up the pace as he yearned to lessen the distance between himself and the forest.

To the west, he spotted a young wolf lowering its head and elongating its neck with a whine before disappearing behind the taller grasses. Little T's heart skipped a beat, and the courage slipped from his hand. The eye-knife came to rest as casually as whence it was found—a blade of steel lost among blades of grass. With his weapon gone, he tried taking comfort in the lone wolf acting afraid and going away, but that didn't stop his belly from feeling funny. Eyeing the distance to the border pines with great concern, the young forest dweller sped to a jog.

The same wolf coolly reappeared, accompanied by two others. On his opposite side, another wolf revealed itself. Together, the four wolves nonchalantly kept pace with him. Little T's ears felt warm and numb, as if they were filled with hot cotton, and in a panic, he ran. The wolves pursued him with apparent deliberateness. Little T heard the sound of a canine's cough followed by a silky smooth roar. The frightened child of the wood glanced to his right and saw a pack running toward him with bursts of flame igniting the grass along the way. With the edge of the Black Forest farther away than the wolves, the fire hounds closed to within about thirty yards from Little T's position.

Little T ran as fast as his little legs could carry him, but it would not be enough to reach the forest before the fire hounds took him down. He looked for a stray tree to leap into, but there was not one. He wanted to leap, leap up into a tree so the wolfies would let him go. His focus remained on the border pines. He willed the distance to the forest edge to close, and for the trees to be within his reach to climb. Here, he noticed the same illusion that occurred with the apple trees. The closer he ran toward the trees, the larger they appeared to become. With the scent of burnt grass in his nostrils, Little T's last thought was trying to imagine the trees growing even bigger, faster.

The speed at which the trees drew closer to Little T doubled, tripled. A fire hound nipped at his heels, and another coughed up a burst of flame that ignited his pant leg before each of their skulls caromed backward off the wide trunk of a pine. The fire hounds yelped in unison as Little T leapt up into a tree. He didn't stop climbing its branches until he reached the top. He could hear more yelping as he climbed, but dared not pause to look down.

When he finally reached the treetop and was able to look down, the canopy blocked his view of the action on the ground. The yelping stopped. Little T heard no more growling, no roaring fire coughs—nothing.

Tarphoon, the village taxidermist and examiner of all things dead, knocked at the front door of Little T's home just before supper. Little T's mother was tending to his burns as his father, Wymbrom, answered the door.

"I heard a fire watch group ran into a number of fire hounds along the southern clearing," Tarphoon announced.

"I hope they were able to handle them all right," Wymbrom said, unable to contain the concern in his voice.

"They didn't have to," Tarphoon replied. "They were found dead. That's how I come to learn of it."

Wymbrom frowned. "Any idea what killed them?"

Tarphoon shook his head. "But I discovered that their skulls were cracked—every one of them."

"Wait," Wymbrom said. "What brings you to our home? Why are you telling me this?" It suddenly dawned on him. "Bright stars, Tarphoon! Are you suggesting our little tyke was mixed up in this? You don't think—"

Tarphoon filled Wymbrom in on the rest. "They said the burn marks indicated a chase outside the border pines. Black spots of scorched grass were found scattered in a line rather than a single area."

Wymbrom felt his eyes swell with rage and blood rush to his face. He didn't bother to hide his anger when he turned to confront his youngest son. "What happened?" he asked with a scowl.

"Try to get to trees," Little T answered, reverting to baby talk as he sometimes did when stressed, "but trees too far. Wolfies wanna bite me."

Fire hounds, whose short breath of flame could burn trousers or set brush aflame, were a relatively new phenomenon in and around the Black Forest, but Wymbrom knew his son had never encountered them before. Although the hounds by themselves were enough to contend with, the forest fires they sometimes caused were a different menace altogether. To be sure, it was not entirely uncommon for a fire hound to be felled by the very hazard it created.

Wymbrom shook his head in frustration and turned to his wife, who looked more frightened than angry.

"What happened?" she asked her son, cupping her hands around his. "How did you get away from the wolfies?"

"The trees came."

"What do you mean, 'the trees came'?"

"They came fast . . . and I hide in the woods."

Before Wymbrom could further scold him, Little T curled up into a ball on the floor and began bawling. "The wolfies are gonna git me!"

His ploy worked. What was Wymbrom to do? Hit the child and make him cry? He was already crying and demonstrably frightened.

"By the dying light," Wymbrom began, determined to make at least a short, stern speech, "what have we told you!" He was flabbergasted— half angry with his son for having almost gotten himself killed, and half in disbelief at what he had survived. He had no other words for the boy. The stern lashing from his tongue would have to suffice.

"Well," Tarphoon offered, "whatever happened out there, the dead hounds accounted for every one that was involved in the hunt. That's according to the fire watchmen. So you need not worry about them tracking his scent."

"Whatever happened," Wymbrom said, "don't tell my father about this, or who knows what he'll make out of it. All we need is another eccentric Syyrilis in the family."

"Do not tell me what?" asked a cloaked figure standing in the doorway. The stiff body of an old man labored so slowly into the room that he seemed to struggle to keep up with his own walking stick.

Little T's mother intervened on Wymbrom's behalf as she eased the aged visitor into a chair by the center table. "We think your youngest grandson had a little scare with a wild animal in the woods," she said as she returned to helping Little T into his sleepwear. "But he's okay now, and we just didn't want to worry you."

"I appreciate your consideration and am thankful he is safe," Syyrilis said, eyeing the burn marks on the back of Little T's calf as Mother changed his clothes. The breath of a fire hound had left a nasty red mark on the back of Little T's leg in the shape of a backward six. "Shall I also take that to mean you do not believe a child escaping a fire hound attack significant enough to alert the academy?"

Wymbrom was silent. Maybe the reason he had never been a candidate for the Sayzr Academy had something to do with growing up with an absent father. It should have been enough that Wymbrom was an accomplished talent running composting systems for the village waste, and Syyrilis might even say as much, Wymbrom thought, but it didn't help sincerity for Syyrilis to show up once every few years expecting Wymbrom to raise his children the way Syyrilis wanted—the way Syyrilis had failed to raise him. If Wymbrom's work composting the village waste was good enough for Wymbrom, it most certainly was good enough for his children. Wymbrom's oldest son already accompanied him to work and was learning an important trade from his father, one that would not force his son to lose his connection with his own family to the ways of the sayzr.

"Here," Wymbrom said and placed an empty vial on the table before Syyrilis. "We just used up the last of the herbal paste you gave us the last time you visited." Wymbrom shook his head at how long ago that was. "That was so many years ago, it's amazing we did not run out sooner."

Wymbrom couldn't tell if his father failed to notice or was intentionally ignoring the jab. "It seems to have worked well to soothe the pain of his burns," said Syyrilis.

Wymbrom restrained himself to answer him dutifully. "Thank you."

Their father-son dynamic, or lack thereof, made for conversation that was awkwardly like the politeness between strangers.

Syyrilis lifted his wrinkled fingers from the table. "You're quite welcome. I only wish I had brought more with me this time around."

Mother wore a concerned look on her face. "He's going to need another application by the morrow."

"Yes, well, I do seem to recall leaving the Haanna household with a fresh vial during my last visit. Perhaps you should head over there first thing in the morning. The missus is bound to still have it on hand."

"Marla Haanna works at the dining commons," Wymbrom said to his wife. "You'll have to leave at first dawn to get to her house before she leaves to prepare the village breakfast."

"It's settled, then." Syyrilis turned to his son. "Well, now that he's doing well and is in good hands, have you a cup of tea for me?"

"What? Oh, sure."

While Wymbrom picked up the teakettle, Syyrilis, quick and nimble, picked up the burnt trousers that Little T had been wearing during his encounter with the fire hounds. The light reflecting off Syyrilis's quick and nimble movement was detected in the corner of Mother's eyes, and these wave patterns certainly entered her pupils, but by the time they made it to her brain, they could not pass through her filter of meaningful expectation and became translated as nothing more than a decrepit old man sitting motionless in his chair.

Little T was still wiping the sleep from his eyes when his mother led him through the wooded trails of the village to the Haanna residence.

The Haanna home was nestled among the evergreens, where the soft sound of a small brook told of its proximity to the house. Morning mist and tree pollen floated through the beams of light that shone a cone of yellow through the trees, illuminating the home from the shadows of pines. The mound of green grass and moss that made up the Haanna rooftop sparkled with dew. On one corner of the roof was a swirl of butterflies dancing in the spotlight above a patch of white daisies that had opened wide to face the sun.

Encircling the house was an area of ground that had been meticulously picked clean of such forest debris as twigs, stones, and pinecones. In their place, the dirt yard was decorated with long lines of small rocks and medium stones emanating outward from a common center—the home—like rays of the sun.

Mother placed her hand on Little T's shoulders. "Wait for me here, outside." She paused halfway up the porch stairs and looked back at Little T. "And don't even think about wandering off," she warned him with a stern finger.

Mrs. Haanna came to the door, and Mother disappeared inside the house.

Little T looked about, intrigued by the rows of peculiar rock formations. He didn't think wandering around the house was the same as wandering off. Besides, he was curious to see how many there were, and if they wrapped all the way around the entire home.

As he headed toward a fence along the side of the house, a young girl with dirty legs and a short, soil-stained dress passed directly in front of him. Though she was much smaller and scrawnier than he, she appeared to be about his same age. Little T watched as the little girl traced a course back and forth along the picket fence. She was staring rather intently at the fence and perhaps the interval of spaces that matched the width of each picket as she walked by, seemingly oblivious to Little T's presence.

"Hello," said Little T in his friendliest voice.

The girl didn't respond and continued taking exaggerated steps forward and back while simultaneously sweeping a look out the corners of her eyes at the pattern of pickets flashing past her peripheral view.

Little T tried again, this time in a louder voice. "Hello, little girl."

Nothing changed. The little girl continued eyeing the fence as she walked by it. Little T struggled to make sense of what she was doing. He could see that she was studying the pickets and watching the spaces in between flicker past her. He wondered, as well, about the unusual way she held her hands, stiffly. With both hands at either side of her head, she gripped her index fingers like a pencil between thumb and middle finger. He began to understand it as a symptom of her concentration, or perhaps it was an aid to it. What he began to think demonstrated the little girl in an even more intense state of focus was when she pressed her hands, in their finger-pencil configuration, firmly against her lips.

Little T pointed to the ground at the lineup of stones whose patterns circled the house. "Did you make these rocks like this?"

The girl went about her business, saying nothing.

"What's your name?" He tried tapping her on the shoulder. "My name's T'Ralo. What's yours?"

The little girl finally looked over with shiny, gray eyes of wonder, but then something else caught her attention and she walked around Little T and picked up a twig with a tiny sprout of pine needles that had fallen from above.

T'Ralo trailed this strange girl to the brook and witnessed her toss the twig into the running water and follow it as it floated downstream and out of sight. This he understood, since he also enjoyed watching things float down a stream. He looked around for other things to throw in the running water and watched as a curled-up leaf mimicking a tiny boat floated away. The little girl seemed receptive to this, and she looked on with delight. He then picked up a rock and was about to toss it in to watch it make a splash.

"No? No? No?" the little girl repeated in a question-like tone while reaching up for the stone in his hand.

When T'Ralo handed her the stone, she immediately turned back toward the house, clutching the rock in both hands. Curious to see what she was determined to do with it, he followed her back to the house and watched her place the stone at the end of one of the decorative configurations in her yard. She lay down, resting her belly in the dirt, and stared down the line of rocks while squinting intensely, sometimes with one eye closed.

"What are you looking at?"

The little girl did not answer him.

He broke the formation of one line by lining up three of its stones perpendicular to the rest.

As soon as the little girl took notice, she protested. "No? No? No?" she said as before. She picked up the three stones and replaced them to restore the continuous line.

"Are you making something?" he asked. "What are you making?"

The little girl seemed to be ignoring him and just stared down at the line of stones doing that finger-pencil grip, with her thumbs and middle fingers stroking her index fingers.

"How about adding this line?" T'Ralo placed a few twigs end to end to extend one of the lines of stones.

"No? No?" said the little girl.

T'Ralo picked them up before she could and then replaced them again, this time extending the line with six or seven sticks parallel to each other. He was pleased, if not intrigued, that the little girl didn't immediately jump to remove them.

Instead, she studied them from above while stroking her index fingers as if they were pencils in hand. She broke her deep concentration, only briefly, and relaxed her finger-pencils away from her mouth to smile at T'Ralo. She then lay on the ground and stared down the line of stones as she had done before, only this time with T'Ralo's run of sticks in parallel adding to the pattern.

Not far into the woods, Syyrilis ducked behind a tree when Little T's mother emerged from the Haannas' cottage with the restorative paste. She scooped up T'Ralo's hand and led him home.

CHAPTER 8

AND THEN

There was an epic battle in progress. From a distance, it was an acid war as the heavily armored armies deconstructed each other in corrosive rainstorms. Thousands of bodies and severed body parts littered the battlefield in layers of the dead. Each layer told an archeological tale of the violent events that had unfolded. So great were the casualties that it became impossible for remaining forces to know who or what they were targeting. Switching to close combat, the battling forces met face-to-face atop mountains of their fallen brethren, employing enormous pincers to snap their opponents in two.

At a pivotal moment, when the champion generals from each nation were fully engaged in a legendary clash, they were crushed beneath the filthy heel of a young elven girl skipping her way to school with her little friend in tow.

— Chapter 9 —

Time of the Red Bear: Encounter

"Gimme back my dolly! You're going the wrong way," Sissi complained. T'Ralo held Sissi's doll just out of her reach. It was a simple figurine, carved from bone and wraped with light blue ribbons for clothing.

"Just try it," T'Ralo said, tugging on the hand of his resistant friend. "If you don't like taking the back path, then we'll go to school the way you like to go."

"But this is the wrong way," Sissi insisted. "You're going to make us lost and miss school!"

"We can cut through the woods to get to the school from the path." Now that he had coaxed Sissi into following him, the tears in her eyes motivated him to try to calm and appease her. "This way leads up the hillside behind the back fields of the school, and we'll get a closer look at Nester Hill. We can go our usual way, but if you want to be a sayzr someday, you have to be open to trying new experiences. You do want to be a sayzr someday, don't you?"

"Yes," said Sissi. "But I want to be a sayzr that goes to school the right way and doesn't make us lost."

"Okay, Sissi. Do you want us to go your favorite way to get to school?"

"Yes," Sissi replied.

"All right, then, if you decide the back path is not your favorite, we don't have to take it again. We will only walk the path you say is your favorite."

"I want to take the regular path," said Sissi. "That's my favorite."

"Good, then that's all we'll do. You get to choose which path we take to school from now on, but you have to wait until we get to school before you make your choice." T'Ralo intentionally avoided certain phrases like "next time" and "tomorrow" when laying out choices to Sissi. He had learned in the past that these were trigger words that could send Sissi into a tizzy.

Before Sissi could complain any further about the unwelcome pattern change, a brawny, red-bearded man came sliding and stumbling down a particularly steep section of the woods above the trail.

"Red bear," Sissi announced as she pointed up the hill at the man.

"No, it's not a—"

A silver canister rolled ahead of the man and landed directly in front of them. One end of the cylindrical chamber popped off when it struck the path, and a roll of parchment slipped out of the chamber and partially unfurled itself. The empty case spun in place like a top before coming to rest.

"Bloody mother of hell hounds!" shouted the man from above as he tore through a terrain of thickets. In his rapid descent, the sturdy hulk took out a small tree before landing on his back in the middle of the path. "Ahhhrrr! Mother fu—Hi, kids!" the man said, concealing his pain behind gritted teeth as he met their faces staring down at him. "Eh, m' name's Grimby—"

"Red bear, red bear!" Sissi said, pointing at him.

"No, I'm Grimby. Look, we don't have much time—"

"Red bear!" repeated Sissi.

T'Ralo knew only from story tales what dwarves generally looked like, and he understood Sissi's struggle to make sense of Grimby's peculiar physique. He surreptitiously tilted the storybook he carried to steal a glance at the hand-drawn illustration of an adventuring party, and was overcome with excitement when he compared the depiction of a heavily armed dwarven character with the real-life stranger before him.

"Fine. I'm Red Bear, and Red Bear asks, where are your parents? Listen carefully now. These woods be dangerous, and you need to get to where there are a lot of grown-ups as soon as possible."

While T'Ralo fixated on the deadly gear worn by this furry hulk, he was aware that Sissi was no longer paying him any mind. Instead, Sissi, who since infancy had always been attracted to the comfortable reliability of numbers, letters, and other symbols, was immediately drawn to the scroll.

"We're on our way to school," T'Ralo said, hoping to be helpful to the intriguing stranger. "It has lots of grown-ups."

"Good," said Grimby as he rolled over to regain his feet. "Then you must run to it at once."

Two white cloaks stood in the path.

"Oh damn," Grimby muttered, then produced two hand axes and held them at the ready.

Something about the fearless dwarve fascinated T'Ralo. He wanted nothing more than to ingratiate himself to Grimby, and cringed when Sissi's verbigeration under the stress of the moment caused Grimby to visibly brush it off as an annoying distraction.

"It's flooding, it's flooding. Red bear, white wings. It's a flood. It's flooding."

T'Ralo pulled on Sissi's shoulders, urging her to go with him, but with Sissi on her knees, he had no leverage to move her.

"Is there something wrong with that girl?" Grimby glanced back at her quickly, not wanting to take his eyes off the Shanzi. "Why isn't she running away?" he growled. "And why aren't you?"

"She won't come!" cried T'Ralo. He didn't want his tears to show. He wanted to be like Grimby. But now he couldn't help it. Though Grimby might not have understood, T'Ralo knew, at a minimum, that Sissi was expressing her frustration over the confusing new personalities. "She's too upset. And she doesn't understand."

"Ohh, you kids really gonna tax me bones now, aren't ya?" Grimby complained with a sobering sincerity that filled T'Ralo with the shame of failing someone he admired as a hero. "Just taxin' me bones!"

Sissi knelt over the ancient scroll that lay unfurled behind Grimby, too focused to notice T'Ralo tugging at her shoulders. Even though she was only a first-year student at the academy, something familiar about the scroll caught her attention. She recognized the writings from what the prefects recently began teaching as the symbols and mappings of psychetropes. Her frenetic expression subsided.

Each symbol on the scroll represented a specific life experience. Each life experience determined a finite set of behaviors. Sissi took comfort in these reliable rules. Superimposed over the myriad symbols plotted on the page was a conglomeration of circular, oval, and figure-eight-like designs that connected the symbols together in various compositions. These designs were something new to Sissi, but they appeared as layers of overlapping snowflakes depicting every conceivable combination of the symbols. It was a map—an intricately labeled map of the elven and human psyche.

Sissi struggled to make sense of the illustrations and of all the congested scribblings that connected the various dots. But when the optical illusion of a three-dimensional drawing took shape, the complex webbing untangled before her eyes and she recognized the layers of snowflakes as various sized spheres within spheres.

Suddenly she was able to make more sense of the foreign people around her in the context of the psychetropic spheres. Sissi no longer saw the three strangers as a deluge of chaotic behaviors, but rather as rivers running the predictable course of their respective personalities. Each one of them now existed somewhere within the finite space of the psychetropic spheres.

She studied the map while observing the Red Bear, but managed to assign only a few ellipticals to his psychetropic profile. She simply could not conceive of the three-dimensional representation for him on the map. He was still leaky, she thought while staring up at his massive shoulders.

She had an easier time reading the two Shanzi. They were human in race. She ascribed to them as many psychetropes as she could from what little she observed of their behavior. As the lines and intersections of the spherical snowflakes, the psychetropic spheres within spheres, began to take shape, it was as if she was observing the stars in the sky and each man was represented by a signature constellation.

Grimby's standoff with the Shanzi earned T'Ralo the role of gathering up the scroll and returning it to the case for Grimby to bargain with. He felt the importance of his assigned task swell through his body. It was enough to overcome his fear of the Shanzi, and he proudly returned the empty scroll case to the plump girth of Grimby's hand.

"There's a good lad," Grimby said in a steady voice. "Now go 'n fetch the rest of it."

T'Ralo felt as if he was living inside one of his favorite hero stories and was determined to impress this story tale adventurer. Instead of wrestling the scroll away from Sissi, he first darted in front of Grimby to retrieve the cap to the scroll case.

Grimby shouted at him, but it was too late. By the time T'Ralo understood his tactical oversight, the Shanzi had him.

Sissi cried out and ran to his aid. "Leave him alone!"

T'Ralo wanted so badly to break loose and go to Sissi, but his captor's hold was firm and his blade sharp. The younger Shanzi grabbed Sissi and she, too, was held at knifepoint.

"Aw, come on!" Grimby said. "You kids really taxing me bones to the bone here."

"The scroll for their lives," demanded the older Shanzi, holding a knife to T'Ralo's neck.

"Whose lives? Oh, you mean those kids?" Grimby said. "Well, I suppose it's just like a Shanzi to murder helpless children. But, you know, they're no kin o' mine." Grimby shrugged.

T'Ralo witnessed, through the blurred vision of his tears, Grimby's confident stance despite his being outnumbered. He looked brave and strong, like a storybook hero. His beastly arms displayed prominent mounds of muscle on either side of his armor-clad chest, and his protective coat of hair was the thickest T'Ralo had ever seen on a person. But, for all of Grimby's impressiveness, it seemed it was too late for T'Ralo and Sissi to be saved. And from the way Grimby was talking, he knew it, too. T'Ralo's heart despaired, for himself and for Sissi.

Sissi would not stop talking to her captor, and T'Ralo wondered if she understood that they were about to be killed. She was speaking in a conversational tone to the younger Shanzi, who had his arm locked around her neck with his sword to her face. T'Ralo noticed her voice because of how out of sync it sounded with the heart-pounding rhythm of the moment.

"You know he's just trying to trick you to get rid of you," she said calmly.

T'Ralo had no idea what she was talking about, or who she thought she was talking to. He wasn't paying enough attention to hear everything she was saying, but it sounded to him like more babbling, like another odd way of coping with her confusion and distress.

"I can see that you both like the same nice lady," Sissi told the younger

Shanzi. "I think the nice lady prefers you, but your commander can have her all to himself if you are slain."

T'Ralo's Shanzi spoke loudly and authoritatively to Grimby. "We will do what is necessary to retrieve the artifact. It must be destroyed to stop the spread of evil."

"Then for the sake o' these younglings," Grimby said, brandishing the empty scroll case in the air, "this be yer last chance to set 'em free lest I shakes the cursed magic o' this thing out at you."

"Ha!" scoffed the Shanzi commander, still gripping T'Ralo. "You wool-headed dwarve, you're holding nothing but an empty cylinder. It's the scroll that has the magic."

"Oh yeah?" said Grimby. "Well, you're forgettin' this be artifact magic, and artifact magic is different. Everyone knows that."

T'Ralo noticed the long pause of uncertainty when the Shanzi commander did not answer right away. Personally, he didn't know what to believe, but hoped the magic Grimby threatened to have was real.

"He's bluffing," said the Shanzi commander, whose knife blade remained firm against T'Ralo's neck. "Go retrieve the scroll from him," he ordered the younger Shanzi. "If he gives you any trouble, I'll dispose of this little bugger and join you in bringing down the big heathen."

"See?" said Sissi. "He's trying to set you up to let the Red Bear kill you. And if that doesn't work, he'll just get you when your back is turned."

"Well," Grimby said to the commander, "if y' doubts the magic o' dis here artifact, then surely there's no harm in me saying, I command you to feel the wrath o' dis . . . metal . . . silver . . . ting."

To T'Ralo's surprise, as soon as Grimby gave the commandment, the younger Shanzi warden relaxed his sword away from Sissi's face. This allowed Sissi to run back behind Grimby. T'Ralo wished he could have done the same.

"What are you waiting for?" T'Ralo's captor asked his fellow Shanzi brother. "Hey! What are you doing?"

The younger Shanzi had turned his attention and his sword on his commander, forcing him to release T'Ralo in order to defend himself.

"Don't be a fool! Can't you see that he's using the magic of the artifact on us?"

The younger Shanzi stabbed his sword into the belly of the Shanzi commander and released a stream of blood. "That's for Lucy and me," he said as he watched his commander collapse onto the trail.

T'Ralo backed away in an arc until he could safely join Sissi behind the Red Bear.

"One on one," Grimby remarked wryly. "I sure does like dem odds." Grimby wasted no time advancing on the young Shanzi warden. "And this is for my Terminator brothers!"

— Chapter 10 —

The Challenge Challenge

After they were seated, Ghostas prompted Prefect Mazer to take over.

"I begin with the ancient maxim: Moranim Divinijin Hom, Velan Alam. Our concept of Nature and our relationship to it defines us all." Prefect Mazer picked up a mint leaf, sniffed at it, and then took a sip of tea.

"Recall, Governor," Mazer said after taking another sip, "that in order to graduate from Sayzr Academy and be deemed a sayzr by members of the Sayzr Order, students must demonstrate effective use of what we refer to, generally, as sayzr magic. In order to accomplish this, students must learn to be in tune with the Song of Nature—the Djin. Our understanding of Nature's code reveals the infinite patterns of cyclical systems within systems that make up the whole of existence." He returned his teacup to the table. "A sayzr's visceral familiarity with Nature's code, the laws of Nature, and sensing the Djin represent three of the four keys to unlocking mastery, not only of sayzr magic, but of that all-important subset known as chambers magic. The fourth, and most difficult key to obtain, is overcoming and conquering the self. Part of Nature necessarily includes the self, and how we perceive the world inter-determines everything. It may be said that the degree of true seeing a given person has correlates with their ability to access sayzr magic, and to use chambers magic to tap in to other dimensions. This holds true for ordinary people as well, though they may not possess the understanding to repeat their successes or to apply them in other scenarios. But when an intelligent being sees things that others do not—sees the real world, especially as seen by a sayzr—anything is possible.

"When sayzrs use magic to manipulate the laws of Nature within our native dimension, we call that 'pure magic.' From there, we all know about that great moment of enlightenment for our people. Armed with a sayzr's knowledge of reality, the ancient elvenmen, inspired by what they experienced inside the sacred caves, first learned to transdimension."

"For a graduate to have any hope of developing into a true seer—a *sayzr*," Ghostas emphasized, "and not just any sayzr, but a master sayzr, the ability to transdimension, unaided by enchanted items, must be attained."

"In this way," Mazer continued, "a master sayzr can cause aspects of one dimension to cross into another. Thus, what appears as supernatural, in fact, remains subject to the laws of Nature in the dimension of origin. Transdimensioning allows a sayzr to rewrite portions of Nature's code by weaving a new pattern into the fabric of the Djin.

"Thus, the primary goal of the Sayzr Academy is not just to graduate sayzrs but to prepare them for the Chambers Challenge, when they will be brought to the chambers of enlightenment. Our hope is always that, upon entering the sacred caves, at least one of them will demonstrate the ability to transdimension."

Governor Multhrobe raised his finger to ask a question. "In a given twenty-year graduation cycle, how many students end up attaining this ability?"

"Anywhere from one to three," Mazer answered, "if we are fortunate. And that has been with graduating class sizes of sixty or more."

"Is there any reason why students who fail to transdimension prior to graduation cannot learn to do so at some later date?" asked Governor Multhrobe.

"No," answered Mazer. "However, the likelihood of successfully doing so is very poor—and worsens over time. Mental pathways in the mind become more set and made rigid by the imprint of daily experience."

"It is far too rare an occurrence to be relied upon," Ghostas added. "That said, there were master sayzrs long before there was ever a school teaching chambers magic, so it is within Nature's design that among the diversification of our people exists the ability to figure it out, unguided and unassisted."

"That can't be," said Governor Multhrobe. "We know plenty of students who have gone on to become accomplished wizards well after the time of graduation."

"True enough," said Ghostas, "yet every one of them manage with a wand, or a crystal, or some other crutch, and they remain dependent on that crutch. They are not innately masters." He leaned in toward Governor Multhrobe. "Mind you, for purposes of this meeting, we are not concerned with producing good or even great sayzrs, we are only concerned with producing *master* sayzrs. Master sayzrs built this institution. They are the teachers and the last line of defense to preserve our sacred culture and our ways."

"I understand," Governor Multhrobe said. "What I don't quite grasp is why transdimensioning is so difficult, even for a sayzr."

"Allow me to explain, Governor." Mazer picked up a mint leaf and began twirling it by the stem, studying it. "Transdimensioning requires a wizard to divorce his mind of the conditionings of perception, such as perceptions of time, perceptions of space, perceptions of one's own bodily form, and so forth. It is a tremendous skill to remain open, to have flexible and unattached concepts of oneself, of ordinary meanings, and of normalcy. This is why Miss Haanna will never be able to transdimension. While she is adept at identifying patterns, she is the antithesis of one who can accept when patterns may need to change. Simply put, she lacks the ability to 'see' as a sayzr sees. Fortunately for her, the ability to control others is so powerful that her mastery of psychetropes warrants her being classified a master sayzr, despite the source being exclusively of the pure magic variety. But, absent use of an enchanted item, if a person cannot personally cross over into other dimensions, they will be unable to bring forth manipulative forces into our own."

Prefect Serren raised his finger to speak. "And that is really the whole key to successful wizardry. Otherwise, we could teach most of our academics in just a few years. It takes time to develop a habit of not developing habits and being conscious of which habits you will permit yourself."

Prefect Frendle, silent so far, chimed in. "Our class on sensory diffusion is designed to promote just that. Assignments like not using your right hand for the week, deaf days, blind days, and so forth. If you have ever hurt yourself and find you continue to make the same movements out of habit, even though those movements cause you pain, this is the result of a conditioning that could prevent transdimensioning and the use of magic drawn from it."

"It is a hell of a thing to detach yourself from the form in which you were born," Moshe-djin croaked through his beard.

"That is the reason so many exceptional students fail," Mazer explained. "When faced with new situations and interacting with laws of Nature whose results are alien to their dimension of origin, people are inherently inclined to make sense of things based on their own conditioning of what is normal and to prejudice themselves with misplaced expectations. Fear, doubt, and the love of self are among the many hurdles to such mastery."

"Yes, and words are also very powerful things," Mazer added, "and the use of words like 'normal' or 'weird' can be a death knell for transdimensioning."

CHAPTER II

TIME OF THE RED BEAR: FRIEND AND HONOR

"You call that running?" Grimby complained as he caught up to the two little elven children. "So, eh, you kids got names?"

"T'Ralo," whimpered the little boy.

The little girl did not respond. Her thoughts seemed elsewhere.

"And this one?"

"Her name's Sissi," said T'Ralo.

"Well, you know, you kids were brave back there. So, in reward, I'd like to make you both junior members of the Terminators—that's my group. Now, understand, this is a very special, very elite group." He seemed to have especially captured the little boy's interest. "But to earn that title, you have to lead the way correctly to that school o' yours. Do you think you can do that?"

T'Ralo nodded.

Grimby had little choice but to put his faith in the tearful babes. And so here he was, the hardened brute, using children to lead him safely through the woods. Should anyone see him this way, he was sure he'd never live it down. But the little elves, T'Ralo and Sissi, did seem to know where they were going. Plus, they were keeping themselves together remarkably well for having just gone through such a traumatic ordeal. Their remarkable resilience wasn't the sort of toughness he expected to see from elven children, and he was proud of them for showing such grit.

By the time they had abandoned the trail for the woods, Grimby found it was he who was struggling to keep up. All the running, the dirt that dried his mouth, and recent fighting had taken their toll and left him breathless. They eventually came through to a partial clearing where they spotted a shirtless man in black leather pants with sword in hand, balancing on one foot atop an eight-foot tree stump.

"Ho there!" Grimby called out to him.

The man practicing with his sword dropped his foot and relaxed his stance. He stared down as Grimby approached. Grimby knew the peculiar spectacle of a weapon-clad dwarve huffing and puffing behind two little elven children was bound to look suspicious.

"Hey thar, mister," he said between intervals of rapid panting. He slowed to a walk and then, leaning one hand against a large boulder by the tree stump, tried desperately to catch his breath. "Thar be trouble coming and—" He paused again to refill his lungs. "—and we sure could use some help."

"What trouble?" The swordsman's voice was low and measured.

"It's too long a telling, but they call themselves . . . the Shanzi, and they're . . . they're after this here scroll." He held it up for the man to see while gulping for enough air to release more words. "They aim to destroy it, and everyone connected with it."

The man sheathed his sword and stepped off the stump. Grimby was impressed with the way the man bent his knees, one forward, one rearward, and absorbed his landing as graceful as a whooping crane. But when the man went to examine the scroll, Grimby was quick to pull it from his reach, thrust an axe blade between them, and shoot the man a suspicious scowl.

"Look with y'er eyes, not with y'er hands!"

The swordsman relaxed his shoulders and just gazed back at Grimby with a poker face. Grimby tried showing the scroll to him again, this time a little more slowly. "Do y'know what it be?"

"I believe I do. I believe it may be something that could be priceless in the hands of the right person . . . and dangerous."

"Well, it's brought me nuttin' but troubles, and I've lost half me brothers over it."

"How did you come by it?"

Grimby didn't know where to begin. Instead, he watched the bare-chested swordsman stare into the eyes of the little elven children.

"And what business do you have with these children?" he asked Grimby while examining the little boy further by tilting up his chin, no doubt taking notice of the red mark across his neck where the Shanzi commander's blade had been pressed.

"Uh, that's also a bit of a telling," Grimby stammered. "More than we have time for, I'm afraid. But I was hoping you might know them."

"Not specifically," said the swordsman. "But my village is a village of wood elves."

The little boy looked nervous and ashamed. "I'm T'Ralo, and this is Sissi. We didn't mean to do anything wrong. We were just trying to get to school."

"I know that, little ones, but can you tell me if you've reason to fear this man?"

Grimby clenched his teeth and squinted his eyes at the question. He knew he was a stranger in a strange land and there was no telling what the little one's might say about him. The one called Sissi had been staring at her toes, seemingly ignoring the situation.

"The Red Bear is a nice bear," Sissi said without looking up.

In spite of his serious mood, the corner of the swordsman's mouth revealed the hint of a grin.

"He saved us." Added T'Ralo.

Grimby felt it was his turn for caution. "You don't look much like a wood elve to me," he said.

"I didn't say I was a wood elve. I just live among them."

Grimby turned the corner of his mouth frownward. "Hmmm."

"That's also a long telling," the swordsman explained.

"Well," Grimby said, still struggling to catch his breath. "Would y' know anything about a school where they can get to for safety?"

The swordsman nodded as he pointed over his shoulder. "Ten minutes in that direction. It's through the woods then over a rope bridge to the second clearing. What sort of danger hunts you?"

Grimby grabbed T'Ralo and Sissi by their arms and gently thrust them in the direction indicated by the swordsman. "You younglings better run ahead now and get yourselves safely t' dat school o' yers."

He watched until they were safely on their way, then turned back to the swordsman. But before he could speak, a flash of white at the edge of the dense tree growth caught his notice.

"Right there!" Grimby pointed his finger. "Did you see that?"

"No. See what?"

"They're here. They're here. I tells ya they're here!"

"Who's here?"

In an instant, the brightness of a white cloak appeared next to the dark tree bark of a wide pine. It was a Shanzi warden concealing his face behind a white mask. In a flutter of white, two more Shanzi fanned out from behind the first. A moment later, the white harbingers of doom numbered five.

The two men stood fixated on the white cloaks and spoke without taking their eyes off them. Grimby tensed his muscles and squeezed his axe handle. "M'name's Grimby."

"Karmin," replied the swordsman.

The five Shanzi drew their weapons.

"I reside with my master only five minutes from here," said Karmin. "Do you think you can make it?"

"I'm afraid I've run me last step," said Grimby, with his chest still heaving. "You go on, and let this be my final stand. Just swear to me you'll look after them remarkable kids."

Karmin nodded. He looked much younger than Grimby had originally thought. He was still a man, but young, like a teenager.

"I'll hold off these Shanzi for as long as I can," Grimby said. "Oh, and, uh . . . I suppose you'd better take the scroll, after all. Do keep it outta their slippery Shanzi hands. And y' can be sure me blade tastes Shanzi blood before I go down."

Karmin glanced over and gave him a long, deep stare. "No," he said. "I can see that you've already done your piece and performed it admirably. As friend to our village, the plan will be for you to start walking, quickly as you are able. Head for the school and leave these Shanzi to me."

Grimby cocked his head and stared back at him. The young man had turned away the artifact and was now offering him, a complete stranger, the chance to die another day. "You really believing you can handle all five?"

"I'm prepared to find out," said Karmin. "Just go now, and find the school. Give your scroll to one of the prefects there. They'll know what to do."

Grimby would rather die fighting than die running. His choices burned in his gut. It wasn't right. It wasn't fair. But they couldn't risk losing the artifact to the Shanzi. Doing it Karmin's way meant he could track behind T'Ralo and Sissi to ensure his youngest party members made it safe. And he would live another day to avenge his party members against the Shanzi.

"Ooh . . . ooh . . ." Grimby moaned as if punched in the gut. There was no time to argue. "All right, all right! I don't likes it one bit, but I'll do as you ask—for the security of the scroll." He placed a hand on Karmin's shoulder and said goodbye. "I never missed out on a fight before, but not staying to fight by your side will be me greatest regret."

When he turned to leave, Karmin stopped him. He looked at Karmin, but Karmin wasn't looking back at him.

"Mr. Grimby," Karmin said in a soft but resolute voice. "You will have no such regrets. I'm afraid there's been a change of plan."

Grimby traced Karmin's line of sight to the dire scene of triple the number of Shanzi now whiting out the wooded scene before them.

"Oh damn," he said under his breath. "All right, y' Shanzi bastards," shouted Grimby while shaking the encased scroll at their regiment. "I commands y' all to drop dead!"

Karmin shot him a puzzled look. "What are you doing?"

"I don't know how I did it, Mr. Karmin, but I'm sure I got magic to come outta dis ting. If you knows anything about the magic o' dis here scroll, now would be the time for you to use it." Grimby held it out expectantly, but Karmin declined to take it.

"There are no enchantments on that scroll of yours, my friend. It holds only information. Powerful information, to be sure, but I have no proficiency for it. Few do."

Grimby released a heavy sigh as the fifteen Shanzi marched toward them. "Well then, Mr. Karmin, it looks like we're in for a heap o' trouble."

"Not necessarily," Karmin said, drawing a long, sleek sword. "I have other proficiencies."

Grimby raised a bushy eyebrow and looked Karmin over. His sword fit his bearing naturally, as if it was part of his body. Karmin didn't sound like he was boasting; he sounded deadly serious.

"All right, Mr. Karmin. How'd you like to handle this?"

Karmin gestured with his chin to the boulder beside the eight-foot stump. "Put your back to that rock. I'll do the same against this tree. It will narrow their field of attack."

Grimby did as instructed, and only the narrow space between the boulder and tree stump separated them.

Karmin stood ready. "Your special target is anyone appearing as their leader or champion. If you can take out the right person, the others may fall back."

"And if they have arrows?"

"Take cover behind the rock. We'll draw them in as best as we can."

A cluster of white cloaks closed around them like curtains. Almost immediately, the tallest in a trio of Shanzi signaled for the other two to attack. They raised their swords against Grimby, but one of them dropped his when a rock struck him in the face. The other Shanzi managed to hold onto his weapon, but he, too, was temporarily incapacitated after another stone that Karmin had thrown cracked the Shanzi's cheekbone.

The tall man in the middle revealed himself as their commander when he gave another hand signal, and six more men stepped forward, three on each side of him.

"There, you have your target!" Karmin shouted.

Grimby let fly a hand axe that went spinning through the air. It missed every vital part of the commander but wedged itself below the shoulder of his weapon hand. Grimby had failed to make the kill. There would be no Shanzi retreat. A swarm of white cloaks engulfed them.

Beaded sweat sprayed off Grimby's forehead with every swing of his axe blade. His broad sweeps, full force across his body, had earned him two kills. But more Shanzi filled their place by stepping over their fallen, and they kept a constant pressure on Grimby. He could feel himself tiring out. He continued to battle back the onslaught with grand gestures of brute strength, but occasionally had to give up ground until the boulder was shielding his left flank instead of his back. Luckily, with Karmin to his right, none of the other attackers had broken through. This allowed Grimby to focus his defenses on only the Shanzi directly in front of him.

From what Grimby managed to observe, Karmin's fighting style could not have been more different. His body barely moved at all, and he had yet to give up any ground. Strangely enough, Karmin had made zero kills. With what appeared to be a mere flick of his wrist, he would slap away his opponent's blade and, in the same swift gesture, puncture him in the crook of his arm.

Disabled but alive, the front line of Shanzi stood stunned and disoriented about what to do. Their training had no answer for this unique pattern of events. When they attempted to retreat in a panic, they ended up bumping backward into the next line of attackers, even knocking some over. The Shanzi could not reinforce the line against Karmin by simply stepping over the dead, as they had been accustomed. Karmin's tactics exploited their greater numbers. He clogged up the flood of attacks with their own men, ultimately curtailing their greatest advantage.

CHAPTER 12

THE MISSING CHAPTER

"Damn you, wretched heathens!" a retreating Shanzi cried out.

Karmin kept a watchful guard as they dragged their injured comrades into the woods. "Wretched? If I adhered to your beliefs, you wouldn't be allowed to live." He shook his head.

The Shanzi blended into the understory and were gone. Karmin turned to find his friend lying sprawled on his back, motionless. Hollowness filled his stomach when he realized how quiet Grimby had been. It mattered not that a visitor had arrived already in weakened condition. Having dubbed Grimby a friend to the village, Karmin was obligated by the swordmaster's code to protect his life. Dwarves were said to possess remarkable resilience, but even a sturdy dwarve, he knew, had his limits.

With measured footsteps, Karmin approached the Red Bear's body, stalling to confirm the fate of a village friend, lest he learn of the failure of his first charge. He peered down at Grimby's ashen face, and then picked up a stick and prodded him with it.

Karmin sighed. "You look pretty good for a dead man."

Grimby popped open one eye and raised his bushy brow. "How 'bout a man alive?"

"Eh . . . you have my condolences." Karmin lent his hand to hoist him to his feet.

Grimby grabbed Karmin's shoulder to stabilize himself. "That's 'cuz y' be lookin' at me through the tainted eyes of a human. I'll have y' know that I be considered quite a fetch among my kind."

"Surely you jest," Karmin said.

"No, sir. Many a dwarven lady would offer half her family's fortune for me hand in union."

"I see," said Karmin. "Are all dwarven women born blind, then?"

"Ho ho, Mr. Karmin!" Grimby bent over, bracing his hands against his knees. "If I gets me through this day and has a chance to rest up and then one day comes to outlive you—as I surely will, given your fleeting lifespan—then I'm gonna drink meself drunk and piss all over your grave!" He caught his breath, stood upright, and stroked his beard. "And that's my solemn promise to ya."

Karmin slowed his pace to keep a watchful eye out for trouble as Grimby labored ahead. Rather than detour to alert his camp about the Shanzi and the scroll, he deferred to friend Grimby, who had been adamant about immediately tracking the children and seeing them and the scroll delivered safely to the school.

Grimby paused and rested his hand against the trunk of a maple. "Maybe you should . . . run ahead. We're more likely to find those precious younglings without me slowing us down."

"What younglings?" Karmin asked.

"What younglings!" Grimby frowned. "Have you gone daft? The two elven children, Sissi and T'Ralo—"

"Oh, *those* elven children." Karmin was still amazed at how such an intimidating, hardened brute like Grimby could appeal to a little girl like Sissi—or, the Red Bear, as she called him. "Thank you for reminding me. And here I thought all we cared about was the scroll."

Grimby deepened his scowl. "Don't ya be mixing things up, Mr. Karmin. I'm just tryin' to get this scroll to the school for me proper reward. Once I gets me reward from your prefects, I'm gettin' outta dis place."

"I guess I shouldn't bother trying to track them then, right?"

"Wha—no. I mean, not that it's any of my concern, but those were some great kids, y' gotta admit. So we should do what we can to lend them some help."

Karmin smiled to himself, amused by Grimby's use of the scroll to conceal his concern for the children.

The path to the school was obvious. Karmin already knew that anyone headed for the school had to come through this area and that they would likely cross the nearest rope bridge when they reached the edge of the river valley.

With little effort, he found a bounty of overturned leaves lying damp-side-up among the litter layer—no doubt stirred up by the children not too long ago. "There's a bridge ahead that will get us to the field behind the school. Once we get to the bridge, we'll have a straight line of sight to the school."

Grimby glanced back at Karmin and held him in his gaze.

"And . . . we should be able to spot the kids, as well," Karmin added. Grimby seemed satisfied by his reassurance.

Where the trees began to thin out and a crevasse came into view, Karmin and Grimby scrambled down the face of a sun-exposed boulder and onto an area of packed dirt that led up to an embankment, where they found a rope bridge that wasn't there.

Grimby ran up to the two posts in the ground and placed his hand atop one of them. "What is this?"

Karmin ceased his examination of the ground to answer Grimby. "Somebody cut the bridge."

Grimby's expression froze. "Can you tell who? Was it the kids?"

"I don't think so," Karmin said. "It would have taken a good deal of leverage and someone with a hearty blade to cut through those thick support rails." He knelt over the edge to reel in one of the lower support ropes and held up the frayed end. "Aside from that, it was cut from this side of the ravine. If it had been the children's doing, they'd have cut it from the far side to prevent . . . from being . . . followed." He backed away from Grimby when he realized Grimby's face had been turning increasingly red as he spoke.

Grimby surveyed the bottom of the valley that ran north and out of sight to the south, where it took a sharp turn around a lone pine tree that seemed to mark the curvature along the top ridge of the ravine. "You tellin' me thems Shanzi got our kids?" His grave voice sent shivers down Karmin's neck.

Karmin tried to calm the Red Bear. "We don't know that for certain."

"But, you said we'd be able to see them. We gots a clear line o' sight to da' school." Grimby pointed at the curtain walls in the distance. "If the kids made it across, we should be seeing them running over there right now."

"I thought we might be able to catch them running toward the school if we got here in time," Karmin said. "It's also possible that the children already made it across and we just didn't get here in time to see it."

"By the mighty Gedtor, which is it, man?" Grimby started pacing the area and waving his hands in the air. "You said you could track them. Can't you tell what happened to them?"

"Tracking is just picking up clues and trying to fit pieces of a puzzle together," Karmin explained. "Look around us. The ground is dry and unforgiving. And this happens to be a frequently traveled location. Can you see any discernable footprints? Can you distinguish any markings from others and tell how old they are?"

"No," Grimby grumbled. "But I expected you to be able to find . . . *something*."

"Like what?"

"Like—I don't know. *You're* the tracker. Can't you find a piece o' fabric from a Shanzi cloak, or somethin'?"

Karmin relaxed his shoulders. "I don't care if they left an entire robe behind. Would it aid us to know there's a naked Shanzi running around?" He could feel time nipping at their heels. "It's the scroll they're after, not the children. I can't make sense of how they got ahead of us, but it's starting to feel like a setup."

Grimby clenched his fists and gritted his teeth. "Dis 'da kinda 'ting me hates most."

"Who are these guys?"

Grimby shook his head side to side. "The Shanzi be one freaky bunch. And I'm not sure what to think."

"If the bridge was disabled before the children got here, they'd know to run to the next bridge, which lies in either direction." Karmin waved a finger at the crevasse and then pointed southward. "The nearest bridge is just around that bend and several hundred yards to the south."

"Several hundred!" Grimby huffed as if catching his breath just to say the words. "Can you not see me so tuckered?" He thrust the scroll into Karmin's hands. "That's it. No more runnin' for me. No more slowin' us down." He found a seat against a sun-bleached boulder. "One of us should remain here anyway, in case the children circle back. Be they ran north and discover that bridge out, too, or run into any more Shanzi, they may be forced to return."

"Not a bad idea," Karmin said, unable to think of a better option. He spun around and ran south. "I'll return as soon as I'm able," he called back.

— CHAPTER 13 —
MEETING ADJOURNED

Mazer put down his teacup and picked up a folder. "Without further ado . . . Glimmer Trezpin."

Ghostas noticed the mood in the room brighten at the mere mention of Glimmer. With a hint of festivity, the governor and other prefects began to indulge in the teas set before them.

"Glimmer comes from a long line of sayzrs," Mazer continued, "and we would expect nothing less from the Trezpin household."

Just then, a blackbird flew between the thick door vents and landed on the table beside a silver platter. Moshe-djin raised a bushy eyebrow and grunted at the winged intruder. All in attendance fell silent for a brief moment of caution.

"One of yours, Frendle?" Ghostas asked.

Frendle disclaimed with the shake of his head. "I sense this one as a free bird."

The prefects sitting around the table exchanged looks with one another, confirming their mutual assessments.

The bird hopped three times along the stone table and located a stranded bread crumb before taking off.

Ghostas studied the face of his old schoolmate observing the prefects' reactions to the bird. It was plain to him that the governor's years away from the academy immersed in a life of politics had dimmed his awareness of a sayzr's concerns.

Mazer regained the attention of Ghostas and the governor with his closing words. "The only trace of any possible concern for Glimmer is that his abilities come to him too easily. He is a true natural. Being born with such natural talents could cloud his understanding of his own successes. As Mr. Trezpin continues to take on the increasing challenges of a sayzr, it is possible that he may face difficulty learning from his mistakes."

Ghostas could see that the governor would require a more concrete example, which Mazer was quick to provide.

"By way of analogy," Mazer explained, "as you all sit and sip your teas, none of you are consciously aware of the force, direction, and specific calculations required to bring your cups to your mouths, and you could all perform just as well if you were blindfolded. What about feeding the person seated next to you? Now consider the calculations and strategies you would employ if you were blindfolded and seated back-to-back while trying to feed each other a cup of hot tea. You have to imagine yourself in both roles: an entity with arms and an entity with only a mouth."

Moshe-djin smiled when someone suggested that blind or not, it would make no difference if they had to feed his mouth. The black patch on his gray-and-white beard was not much help with a smile, but his shoulder movement told a keen observer that he took it in good humor.

Prefect Mazer waited for the room to quiet. "This is an area where Mr. Trezpin might actually display weakness. To date, Glimmer Trezpin has not had much experience with failure. Experiences that will not come naturally, but rather present as entirely foreign in the practice of wizardry, are inevitable."

Ghostas knew the governor was a close personal friend of the Trezpins. He watched him place his fingers over his mouth and rest his elbows on the table.

"The good news about this," Mazer continued, "is that, even assuming this to be a real weak point for Mr. Trezpin, if anyone can overcome it, and particularly with our assistance, Glimmer can. Thank you."

"Thank you, Prefect Mazer," said Ghostas.

Prefect Mazer bade the room a farewell, bowed outside the doorway to the conference room, and returned to his class.

They went through eleven other students, mostly agreeing that Rasilla was ahead of the pack in spite of her vanity and ego.

"I wonder what might become of her if her appearance should be dramatically altered, or if she were isolated from the encouragement and adulation of others," offered Prefect Frendle.

The remaining students, such as Salyndra, Matyr, Bendton, and, to a lesser extent, Phylo, the prefects decided, were developing on a comfortably average track for their typical student body.

"I understand that the numbers are low," the governor said, "and that the chances for mastery are thus substantially reduced, but is there any concern that we may lose any further enrollees?"

"The boys especially like to learn to fight," Ghostas answered. "Some leave to train or enlist with the military of other communities or kingdoms. Assuming they do not die in battle, some return to the village and some do not. We have already winnowed out most that were underperforming or simply could not take the pressure. I would say there are maybe five or six students remaining who might fit into that category." He looked around the room for a consensus.

The others nodded in agreement.

Such an accord wasn't always easy to establish at these types of meetings, but all in all, Ghostas was pleased with the spirit of the gathering. The trick would be maintaining that unity moving forward. And that, he knew, depended more on the governor than on anyone else. Inside these walls, his faculty worked more or less as a team. Outside, in the world of commerce and politics, discord was difficult to predict—and just as hard to control.

CHAPTER 14

TIME OF THE RED BEAR: THE DOUBLE CROSSING, SOUTHERN BRIDGE

Karmin's hopes faded as a rope bridge failed to come into view. What had once been the southern rope bridge now hung like a desperate centipede from the cliff on the opposite side of the gorge. Karmin felt the centipede begging for a leg up. He pivoted toward the exposed area, expecting an ambush of white cloaks, but instead was met with the east winds whispering gently through the swaying pines just up the hill ahead of him. The pines first in line stood like sentries outside the western gates of the forest. He tried to think it through. First, the Shanzi had invaded his village. Then the bridges had been cut. And now? Nothing. Not being able to sort things out was like having someone else in control of drawing and sheathing his sword. He was out of measure and unable to move forward.

He put a fist to his mouth and bit down, trying to calm himself. If the children had already reached the school, then the saboteurs must have intended to trap him and Grimby to capture the scroll. *So why hasn't the trap been sprung?* He didn't want to believe he was being outmatched by smarter people than him, but in a village full of sayzrs, it wasn't unthinkable. If the children hadn't made it across the bridge—he didn't even want to think about that. Had he already failed them? Could they be used as leverage to obtain the scroll? He hoped they were safe at school. He certainly didn't need more people to worry about or to protect.

Sweat poured from Karmin's pores and gathered along the back of his neck as the sun warmed his shoulders. The desire to cool down reminded him to slow his heartrate, control his breathing, and remain loose and relaxed in case he was forced into another melee. That, in turn, reminded him about the art of seeing. What did the sayzr prefects like to say? *If you can't see the answer, chances are the answer is staring you in the face.*

Nothing presented itself. If there was really nothing here but they were still after the scroll . . . "Grimby is the target," he said to himself.

Just as he pivoted to leave, Karmin spotted something colorful. The breeze swept a blue ribbon against the base of a boulder. He picked it up, wishing Grimby was there to witness him finding such a clue. The ribbon had been sewn together to form a small circlet about an inch and a half in diameter. His heart sank when he remembered the little girl had carried a doll with light blue ribbon dressing.

"... *staring you in the face,*" he whispered.

"Children!" Karmin called. "Are you here? Please come out to let me know that you're all right."

To his surprise, the two little elves, T'Ralo and Sissi, emerged from a tight cluster of boulders.

Karmin shook his head. "Remarkable."

The children ran to him and complained about the bridges being out.

"I know, little ones," he said, trying to reassure them.

Sissi was still clinging to her doll. A groove encircling the doll's head had been carved the perfect width to accept the missing ribbon.

Karmin slid the ribbon over the doll's forehead, and Sissi rewarded him with a smile.

"Come," he said, surveying the immediate area. "We're not completely out of danger just yet. I want you to follow me to the northern bridge, where we'll regroup with your friend, Grimby—the Red Bear. If we get into serious trouble, you should run back here—if you can make it—and hide in that same spot. Otherwise, just find another clever hiding place."

"What's going on?" T'Ralo asked.

The little boy's question stopped Karmin in his tracks. That was precisely the question. "I can't say for sure," he answered. "But we have no other choice than to try. If the northern bridge is down, as well, then we'll continue north until the land reunites itself."

No other choice? He wondered if he was falling further into someone's trap by being predictable. If they were being played and the Shanzi knew his moves, then why hadn't they already shown themselves? Here were the children. Here he was with the scroll. Where was the attack? Something didn't make sense. Karmin strained himself to fully understand what he had been missing. *If you can't see the answer, chances are the answer is staring you in the face.*

"Karmin, old buddy. There you are!"

Karmin was surprised to look up and find Grimby staring him in the face.

"I grew impatient with concern," Grimby explained. "It's good to see you all well."

T'Ralo ran up and hugged Grimby's leg. Sissi, staring down at her feet, remained by Karmin's side.

"How did you get here?" Karmin asked.

"I ran," Grimby said.

"But you've been running and fighting all day," Karmin said. "Can you press on, or do you need to rest a bit more?"

"We dwarves are hearty folk and are more than accustomed to hard work," Grimby said. "I happen to be blessed with a strong constitution. We should head to the north bridge right away."

"That's not right!" Sissi shouted. "It's a flood! It's flooding! It's a flood! It's a flood! Flooding! It's flooding!"

The men tried to ignore her and let T'Ralo handle her outburst.

"Now that we're all together," Karmin said, "we could go south until the land reunites there. Then we could place ourselves well into the village before we even reach the school."

"But the third bridge is closer," Grimby said, "and we've already traveled half that way and found it free of Shanzi. There's no telling who we might run into if we go south. I say we go north."

"It's not shorter if the northern bridge is out," Karmin said.

"The northern bridge is fine," Grimby said. "Nobody cut it."

"How can you know that?" Karmin asked.

Grimby shrugged. "It's just a feeling. But it's a strong feeling. Trust me. I'm never wrong about these things."

Karmin didn't know what to make of Grimby's idea, but having just survived a life-threatening battle with him, he owed him his trust.

Sissi was now lying on the ground, kicking and screaming.

Karmin had to pick her up so they could follow Grimby to the bridge. "What is she doing?" he asked.

"I don't know," T'Ralo answered. "She usually only does this with strangers."

"Well, see if you can get her to quiet down. That would be a big help."

"It's all right, Sissi," T'Ralo told her. "Grimby is our friend. Remember?"

"No. That's not right," Sissi protested. "It's a flood. It's flooding. It's flooding."

"Do you want me to take her?" Grimby asked. "I'll keep her safe. I'll keep us all safe."

Sissi clung tightly to Karmin. It was clear there would be no exchange.

Grimby shrugged. "Well, at least we know the children are safe," he offered. "And the scroll is safe. You still have the scroll, right?"

Karmin nodded as he tried to coax Sissi, who had been burying her head in his chest, to at least look up. "I thought you said the Red Bear was a nice bear."

"Not red!" Sissi cried. "Not bear! It's a flood! It's flooding!"

"Here," Grimby extended a hand to Karmin. "You have your hands full. I will protect the scroll."

Karmin handed the scroll back to Grimby while juggling Sissi's weight.

"No!" Sissi protested. "No. No. No. That's not right. Not red. Not bear."

Karmin stepped carefully along the rocky terrain to keep pace with T'Ralo and Grimby while carrying Sissi. She was a waif, all skin and bone, but holding her to his chest was not the ideal position for the length of their journey and made balance and visibility of the rocky terrain more challenging. At the risk of disturbing her and causing her to blow up again, he shifted her to his back. He was grateful when she wrapped her arms around his neck and reoriented herself behind his shoulders. Karmin felt Sissi clinging tightly with her face pressed against the side of his neck. She continued complaining about Grimby into his left ear.

"Mr. Grimby!" Karmin shouted ahead. "Perhaps we should move into the woods a bit to get away from the edge. If a band of Shanzi come out of the woods, we will be an easier target with our backs to the ravine."

"There's no time," Grimby said. "I just want to get you all safely across the northern bridge before we have to deal with any more Shanzi. Besides, I think their plan already failed. Otherwise, they would have caught up to us by now. And if any more of them are out there, we sure don't want to go looking for them."

Karmin had to admit that his friend's plan carried some logic, even if Grimby was far more confident than he was about the Shanzi threat having been quelled or the northern bridge still being intact. But, as long as he was correct about the Shanzi, it wouldn't really matter whether the bridge was crossable, because their trip, even if extended, would remain uneventful.

Upon reaching the original spot where they had first discovered the central bridge had been cut, Karmin caught himself double-checking the boulder where he had left Grimby to rest, half expecting to see him still lying there. Instead, with Grimby leading the way and the little boy, T'Ralo, having to double-step just to keep up with him, Karmin marveled at how quickly his dwarven friend had recovered his strength and vigor. Along the middle of the river valley, a hawk flew past them carrying something in its talons. At the opposite side of the gorge hung the central bridge like another centipede caught in a climbing tribulation.

Grimby's eyes darted back toward them. "Keep it up now. There's only a few hundred yards left to go."

T'Ralo seemed desperate to keep up with Grimby and to prove his worthiness. The boy, Karmin thought, was yearning for some praise, but Grimby appeared too focused on reaching the northern bridge to notice him.

Sissi's whining about floods had evolved into additional pleas. "I want the Red Bear," Sissi blubbered into Karmin's ear.

"Would you like him to carry you for a while?" Karmin asked her.

"Not that!" Sissi's protests became louder. "It's a flood! Not red! Not bear! It's flooding!"

Karmin had no idea what she was talking about, but when T'Ralo looked back at her, Karmin asked the little boy if he knew how to help.

"I don't know," T'Ralo said. "Tell her the flooding will stop when we get to school."

Karmin tried reassuring Sissi that the flooding would soon be over and that she would be arriving at her school. He didn't know what "flooding" meant to her or if what he was saying made her feel any better, but at least the volume of her complaints grew quieter. *Only a few hundred yards,* he thought. He wondered if Sissi was picking up on Grimby's improved physical condition and perhaps had gotten confused by the subtle changes in his voice and movement, now that he had found his second wind.

Despite Sissi's near weightlessness, Karmin began to feel the burden on his back. He was sweating even more now with the heat of Sissi's body insulating him. Fatigue rose up his thighs like a blanket being pulled up from the foot of the bed. He leaned forward to redistribute her weight and offer some relief to his muscles, and didn't look up again until he heard Grimby cry out.

"There it is! Behold, the northern bridge! Just as I promised."

CHAPTER 15

TIME OF THE RED BEAR: THE DOUBLE CROSSING, NORTHERN BRIDGE

Where the ridgeline straightened, Karmin was encouraged to be able to see for himself the northern bridge, proud and defiant, spanning the ravine. He was learning impressive things about his dwarven friend and couldn't have been more grateful for Grimby's instincts. He decided not to say anything when Grimby's exuberance caused him to race too far ahead. Grimby even outpaced T'Ralo by an imprudent distance and was the first to reach the northern bridge.

Grimby leaned against the second pylon as if he were a gatekeeper welcoming them to cross. Karmin searched the western flank for any sign of the Shanzi, a saboteur, or a final ambush. But he saw no signs of trouble.

He slid Sissi down off his back when they reached the bridge and met Grimby with a big smile, grasping Grimby's shoulder firmly as a congratulatory gesture. He might have been too cautious to accept it easily, but it seemed Grimby had been right about that, too: they had not only defeated the Shanzi but had crippled their mission and thwarted their plans. But with two downed bridges, what *was* their plan? A refreshing breeze from the roaring river at the bottom of the ravine cooled his face.

"Go ahead, my friend," Grimby said, gesturing for Karmin to cross the bridge. "You earned it."

Karmin patted the children on their heads and instructed T'Ralo to go first, followed by Sissi. "You're going to go directly to school now, kids," he

97

reassured them. "Everything will soon be back to normal." He took about eight steps before he realized Grimby wasn't following them. He turned. "Aren't you coming?" he asked Grimby.

"I'll be along shortly," Grimby said. "Just to be safe, you go on ahead. I'll feel better if I stand guard until I know you're all safely across."

Karmin nodded to his friend and then turned to coax along Sissi, who appeared to be counting each rung as she crossed it. "Come," he told her. "Now's not the time for that."

Sissi either wasn't listening or didn't want to listen to him. "Seventy-four, seventy-five, seventy-six . . ."

"Please," Karmin said, "there's no time for counting."

"Just to eight hundred thirty-three," Sissi insisted. "Just to eight thirty-three. Halfway."

"No, we can't. What do you mean—eight hundred thirty-three, halfway?"

"There's one thousand, six hundred and sixty-six wooden steps," Sissi said.

"How could you know that?" Karmin asked.

"There's one thousand, six hundred and sixty-six wooden steps," Sissi repeated.

"The faster you move, the sooner you'll get to school," he encouraged her. "Let's not keep Grimby waiting."

"Yeah, Sissi," T'Ralo said. "Mr. Karmin is right. We still have to hurry to get to school on time. Come on, Sissi. Show us how fast you can go."

Karmin didn't know if it was something T'Ralo had said or how the boy had said it, but Sissi at least started counting faster.

"Two hundred ninety-seven, two hundred ninety-eight, two hundred ninety-nine."

She wasn't moving at full speed, but it would have to do.

As they traveled across the bridge, Karmin looked back to give Grimby a thumbs-up, and Grimby returned the sign. When Karmin turned to face forward, he almost stepped on Sissi, who had been lying down studying the stretch of slatted decking.

"Hey, hey, what are you doing?" Karmin asked as he bent down to grab her arm. "You've got to stand up."

Sissi resisted by pulling away. "Eight hundred thirty-three," she said. "This is eight hundred thirty-three."

Karmin deferred to T'Ralo. "Do you think you could convince her to get up? It's not right to keep Grimby waiting this way."

T'Ralo's face lit up. He appeared eager to be helpful again, but a question hung over his brow. "Why isn't he coming with us? What's he doing?"

"Your friend, the Red Bear, is keeping guard until we're safely across," Karmin said. "If anyone tries to cut the bridge, he will stop them."

"Not friend!" Sissi shouted. "Not red, not bear!"

"Sissi," Karmin began, "you shouldn't say such a—"

"Someone's going to cut the bridge down on us?" T'Ralo cried.

"What? No." Karmin wasn't accustomed to managing children, and they were making him regret his words.

Sissi screamed in protest.

"No, no. It's just a precaution," Karmin explained, mostly to T'Ralo. "They're objective was never to hurt us. They only wanted the scroll."

"Not Grimby! Not red! Not bear!"

"Listen, as long as we have the scroll," Karmin said, pressing his hand to his chest, "it wouldn't make any sense for them to want to cut the bridge down now. But it would only be polite to hurry to get across so our friend Grimby can join us."

Sissi sat defiantly, refusing to get up. "That's not right! It's a flood, it's all a flood. It's flooding!"

Karmin continued frisking his chest, his hand dancing in denial of the realization that he no longer possessed the scroll. A cold sweat formed on the back of his neck when he remembered that he had handed the scroll back to Grimby. But he hadn't judged Grimby the type to betray them. After surviving such an ordeal together, Grimby wouldn't suddenly succumb to greed by keeping the scroll for himself, would he? He wondered if it was possible that the odd little girl had detected such a change in heart. Sissi's ramblings about names and identities might have been her way of communicating Grimby's motives.

Karmin cursed himself for thinking ill of a friend. He stole a glance at

Grimby, and then knelt before Sissi and took her by the shoulders. "Please, I beg of you. Answer me this: Is that Grimby?" He pointed at the dwarve.

Sissi clenched her eyes shut and violently shook her head.

"Please help me," he said, desperate to get through to Sissi. "I promise I will try to bring back the Red Bear if you promise to get across as quickly as possible." Karmin stood up and wasted no time giving orders. "T'Ralo, I need you to keep Sissi in front of you and do whatever it takes to get you both across. Be prepared to keep a hold on the bridge at all times, even while you're moving."

T'Ralo leapt to Sissi's aid.

Karmin then turned and began casually walking back in the direction they had come, beckoning Grimby from a distance. "Come on!" he shouted to Grimby. "You can join us now."

Grimby waved him off. "What are you doing?" His voice echoed off the cliff walls. "Keep going."

The chilly river spray that rose from the chasm cooled the sweat on Karmin's neck. He kept his upper body stiff to maintain a walking posture while stepping as quickly as he could, hoping to conceal his advance. "It's okay now!" he called back, again motioning Grimby forward. "Join us!" The more Grimby continued to wave Karmin away, the more Karmin's uncertainty began to grow. He motioned Grimby to wait, as if he had something to say or do as he picked up his pace to a casual jog.

"What are you doing?" Grimby began waving Karmin away more frantically and shouted for him to get back to the children. "Stick to the plan. I will protect you!" He brandished a dark-bladed dagger over his head. "Get back! I'll protect you!"

Karmin puzzled over what he would do when he reached Grimby. How would he temper his enormous embarrassment? Plagued by doubts and determined to remain loyal, he questioned his every step. Grimby was risking his life to save theirs with every moment that passed.

Karmin decided he had gone too far. His heart told him to stop and turn back, but at the risk of dishonoring a friend and playing the fool, his feet continued moving. As an updraft of high-pressure vapor coiled around the northern bridge like a nimbus snake, Karmin began to feel uncomfortable in his own body. His cushioned footfalls on the deck of the undulating bridge added to the alien sensation. He thought his mind and heart were in agreement, and yet, his feet pressed onward.

Karmin couldn't believe his eyes when the fog lifted like theatre curtains, revealing a scene of Grimby cutting away at one of the bridge supports with his black dagger. The only thing that registered was that he had made a fatal mistake and was about to die. Karmin broke into a sprint as best he could manage on the back of this giant centipede. Now *he* was the one begging for a leg up to reach the embankment. His thoughts flashed to the children, and he shouted over his shoulder at T'Ralo to hold onto the rail. He had to hope T'Ralo and Sissi could see enough of what was happening to figure out which rail to grasp.

Just as he whipped his face forward again, the centipede twisted its body away from Karmin's feet. Grimby had cut the rail.

Karmin's feet ran him clear off the slatted decking. He continued kicking into the air as he plummeted, flailing through patches of fog in search of solid ground that wasn't there. With one final swipe of his right hand, he caught hold of the dangling handrail and grunted as his shoulder and arm bore the full weight of his body. Seconds later, he managed a firmer grip with both hands and hung beneath the bridge. Peering up through the slats, he could make out Grimby's expression and see that he seemed to be scanning for his falling body. The wind held Karmin at an angle beneath the decking where he hoped to remain concealed from Grimby. He studied Grimby's face through the spaces between the wooden slats. An eerie feeling overcame him as he spied on Grimby like a helpless prey, waiting for him to look away. But, just when it seemed things couldn't get any creepier, Grimby's eyes suddenly met his between two of the decking boards.

"I thought I sensed something wasn't . . ." Grimby stepped to one side to get a better look and then placed both hands on his hips and laughed. "Literally clinging to life, are you? What do you think you're going to do? Run hand over hand before I cut another line?"

Karmin was still kicking his feet and dangling from the bridge while wrestling with the thick rope to maintain a stable grip. His sword and his slender scabbard swung stiffly beside his thrashing legs. He managed to leverage his hands around one of the slender suspension spindles that was tied perpendicular to the former handrail. He didn't imagine he'd have the strength to carry himself hand over hand the last twenty yards, let alone the time, considering it had only taken Grimby a minute to cut through the dense threads of the support rail.

Karmin thought about dying, about how he'd be remembered, and about who might come to know his deeds this day. In the midst of despair, he summoned the courage to glimpse what might have become of the children on the other side of the gorge, but a massive cloud had rolled in to devour his view of the other half of the northern bridge.

"Why are you doing this?" Karmin called out to Grimby.

Grimby did not answer. Instead, he flipped his black dagger over to apply the serrated spine against the lower support rope.

"But we fought together," Karmin said as he gave all he had to walk his hands over to the next spindle. "I trusted you. Where's your honor?"

"Dwarves lie. We have no honor, and I never liked you." Grimby scowled at Karmin's feeble efforts. "Well, look at you. You've made it an entire three inches already. Keep at it. You've only another twenty yards to go."

Grimby's sarcasm was warranted. Karmin knew he couldn't hang on for long. And when the next support rope went, the drop was liable to shake him loose. He began swinging his legs in parallel with the bridge to get them to wrap around the disabled handrail and weave them between the spindle lines. He then arched his neck and held Grimby in an upside-down gaze.

Grimby had been kneeling before the anchor post, vigorously sawing through one of the lower support lines. When he paused for a moment to wipe his forehead, he found Karmin's eyes and waved him goodbye. He then flipped the dagger, spine side up, and swatted the blade at whatever remained of the deck line. Karmin plummeted in the same direction as Grimby's swing, as if following his orchestration.

The centipede twisted again. It had anchored itself across the gorge using only one side of its body while the other half of its legs freely swayed. Hugging the centipede's feet, Karmin went along for the ride. It was not as violent and abrupt as the first. This time, he swung smoothly and rocked like a baby above the cradle of his demise. He stretched a leg through the rope spindles up to his groin and then slid his head through. With his weight centered over the support line that had once been a handrail, he managed to walk his hands backward until he was sitting upright and straddling the rail. Wind currents carried him backward as if the centipede were stretching its legs, making it easier for him to climb over the several spindles and to get a footing on the cut handrail. He ran his fingers up the spindles until he reached the severed deck line and then stood with his head against the planks. He got a clear view of Grimby flipping his blade to make that final chop through the remains of the third support cable.

Karmin gasped as he and the planks dropped to an abrupt stop. He braced his legs against the impact and managed to remain with the rope bridge, but it wouldn't be enough. He was still the same twenty yards away from Grimby, and Grimby had already started sawing through the last support rail. *Power runs in both directions. The solution is usually staring you in the face.* Sayzr teachings raced through his mind. *Nature is contradiction.* Whatever simple solution a sayzr might have had for this predicament, Karmin was no sayzr. Under the stress of the moment, he could conceive of no other counterintuitive action than to jump off the bridge—or let go. He had the fleeting thought of climbing to the last handrail and trying to run along the tightrope despite the swaying bridge and shifting winds. But even if he could manage such a feat, he told himself, there wasn't enough time.

Time, meanwhile, seemed to stand still as he watched Grimby in his final move. Grimby flipped the serrated spine of his dagger upright and raised it over his head. Karmin turned away and closed his eyes.

"Hey! You face-swerving gobermouch! Thy vile canker-blossom'd witchery curdles milk and sours beer!"

Karmin opened his eyes to catch Grimby, still at the foot of the bridge, drop his dagger on the ground and double over with a hand axe lodged in his knee. Charging up the way—from where the familiar voice had come—another Grimby was wielding a hand axe and had strands of twine dangling from his wrists.

Before Karmin could process the effect that imminent death had had on his senses, the two Grimbys began to engage in hand-to-hand combat. Just then, a gust of wind from the gorge caught Karmin, causing him to swing. The stretching fibers of the braided cable responded to his every move with a creaking, squeaking, and staccato snapping that was indistinguishable from the friction of fibers or the tearing of tatters. He clenched his eyes and fists as he pictured the frayed, thin remnants of the line unraveling.

As Karmin clung to the northern bridge, the chilled air sharpened his mind. Questions still lingered about what was happening on land with the Grimbys, but he was still alive and had been given a second chance to act. He held the vision in his head of the remnant fibers of the handrail. Their lack of girth and stoutness remained vulnerable to a single chop from Grimby's black dagger. A white mist continued to shroud the fate of the children, but Karmin suddenly realized that whatever the condition of the frayed line, it was holding up the weight of the entire bridge across the span, including him and possibly the children.

It suddenly came to him—the sayzr-like solution that had escaped him moments earlier, the dictates of Nature's patterns of harmony and contradiction that led to counterintuitive solutions. He knocked his forehead against the disabled bridge in disbelief at how blind a person—*he*—could be to the simple and obvious.

He squeezed his body through the spindle strands and then froze like a statue when he heard the snapping and tearing noises. Gradually, he shifted to the opposite side of the planks—the underbelly of his centipede—where the first support rail beneath the decking could be accessed for a handhold. His biceps rippled as he executed a stationary pull-up behind the wooden planks to counteract his weight. He then shimmied up the underside of the decking to get a foothold atop the first decking cable.

After his weight shifted back toward the center of gravity, he felt a rapid succession of knocking and snapping as it vibrated through the handrail to his hands and feet. He had to raise one leg the width of the deck to get it over the second deck rail by bending his left knee and sliding his foot through the fiber spindles. He performed this feat and straddled the deck line such that he was facing the Grimbys on land.

Like a cruel audience, the muffled claps of the tenuous suspension rail taunted Karmin for his accomplishments in unison with the racing of his heart. He held his position until his unseen audience quieted. It was an easier task to stand up with his feet on the deck's severed rail, but mounting the tenuously fastened handrail seemed to cause a more direct impact. The applause grew louder. One snap, in particular, turned his stomach. He was certain it was the fraying line busting apart.

Karmin had been vaguely aware that the second Grimby on the scene— the Red Bear—had wrestled adversarial Grimby to the ground and was likely preparing to finish him off. He was aghast to discover the Red Bear with a hand axe raised over his head, poised to split Sissi's head in two.

"Please don't kill me!" Sissi cried.

Unable to bring himself to do it, the Red Bear hesitated, which earned him a black dagger in the hip when Sissi sat up to meet him.

"Argh! You vile, canker ridden—"

In the blink of an eye, Sissi was gone and the tables had turned. Now, in place of Sissi, adversarial Grimby held the Red Bear partway over the ledge. The freshly stabbed Grimby—the Red Bear—hung over the embankment upside down with his legs anchored around the other Grimby's waist. But adversarial Grimby, who had a wounded knee, was now on top of things and trying to strangle the Red Bear with his bare hands.

Upside down and in mid-strangle, the Red Bear noticed Karmin hacking away at the last remaining support cable upon which he was seated. "In the name of Gedtor!" He choked out. "What are you doing?"

"What I should have done sooner," Karmin replied. He allowed the swinging action of his sword arm to guide his blade to a consistent point behind him where it peeled away at the fibers of the cable as if he were whittling a stick.

Red Bear tried to fight his way back, but the other Grimby out-leveraged him by throttling his neck while pushing against a bridge post with his good leg. The Red Bear's back scraped against the gravel as he was being forced over the ledge.

Karmin's sword sliced through the final support line. As if swinging from a vine, he flew along a sixty-foot arc and felt a rush of adrenaline as the cool mist blasted him in the face. The planks and opposite handrail directly in front of him twisted against the wind and ended up behind him. Karmin had to spin himself around and adjust his grip on the handrail to land feet first, into the side of the cliff. He bent one knee forward to absorb the impact with the elegance of a whooping crane, but it was a bit more than he could handle, causing him to slam his shoulder against the rock. In a single motion, he leveraged the rock sheer to twist out of harms way of the wooden planks that immediately smacked into the rocks instead of his skull. Once again, Karmin had survived the bridge. He still faced a twenty-yard climb before he would be able to reach the Grimbys, but at least he was in his element.

Purposely peaking ten yards away from the rope bridge and the wrestling

Grimbys, Karmin stood over his last foothold, pulled himself over the ledge and rolled away from the sheer embankment. The Red Bear had managed to prevent himself from being pushed over the cliff by keeping his legs wrapped around adversarial Grimby. "If I goes, I be takin' you with me!"

It looked to Karmin as though adversarial Grimby was preparing to *unanchor* the Red Bear by stabbing him in the leg. It would surely send him freefalling to his death.

The shadow of adversarial Grimby wielding a black dagger had darkened the Red Bear's face, but then Karmin leaped in and surprised everyone with the tip of his sword to Grimby's neck.

"Stand and deliver," he said. He lifted Grimby to his toes, keeping his blade pressed firmly under his neck. "Who are you?"

Grimby stared back at him, wide-eyed.

Before he could answer, the Red Bear tackled adversarial Grimby and began pounding him in the face. "Of all the vile, cankerous, mud-suckin', fish-cuttin'—turn, you abomination! Get outta my face, you face-swerving boil!"

Grimby transformed to Sissi. The Red Bear winced and then closed his eyes while pressing his thumbs into Sissi's windpipe. "Change into yourself, you orphan-of-an-orc, fish-cuttin' face-swerver!"

Karmin wrestled the Red Bear off of Grimby and reasserted his blade. "He's right. Show yourself or die."

The likeness of Sissi stared up at Karmin with its teeth clenched.

Karmin applied more pressure to his blade. "Do it!"

The creature revealed itself as having amphibious-like features, including shimmering scales and spiny fins in place of ears. Its bright yellow saucer eyes showed cross-slit pupils, while its feet appeared humanoid.

Grimby was quick to snatch the scroll and then looked away. "Great Gedtor, give me strength! It curdles the milk to even look at it. Put it out of its misery. I can't stands a hippogriffin!"

The creature spat at Grimby, who then kicked it in its side.

"It's not a hippogriff," Karmin said. "It's a doppelganger."

"Then I hates that, too!" Grimby snapped. "Just kill 'em, I say. Kill 'em all before the world fills up with more."

"Do you have anything to tie it up with?"

"Tie? Oh right. Lash the filthy animal like it did to me. It doesn't deserve a quick death." Grimby brought the black dagger to the precipice and returned with cut spindle strands from a segment of the rope bridge.

Karmin watched over the doppelganger while Grimby fastened its wrists behind its back. From Grimby's wrists, frayed rope strands still dangled where he apparently had snapped them apart. Karmin could see deep, irritation marks where the rope had cut into his skin.

"Wretched hippogriffin," Grimby complained. "I hates to even touch the vile creature."

"Doppelganger," Karmin said, correcting him once more.

"So you know about these things, then?"

Karmin shook his head. "Only the name. Before today, I never would have imagined such a thing actually existed."

The two men stared at each other. It was their first moment of peace since the recent ordeal.

Karmin relaxed his shoulders, relieved to see that his friend Grimby, the Red Bear, was still his friend Grimby. All his feelings of self-doubt and shame had been washed away.

Their chuckles grew to a knowing laughter and they locked arms by gripping each other's biceps.

"The children," Grimby inquired.

Karmin gazed out across the chasm. The curtain of mist had opened to a clear view to the other side. The northern rope bridge hung from the opposite edge like a centipede in search of a footing, but there was no sign of T'Ralo or Sissi.

"If there's any justice in this world."

CHAPTER 16

TIME OF THE RED BEAR: A CROSS CROSSING

Having captured a rare and fantastical creature as his prisoner, Karmin wasn't taking any chances. They had bound its hands and fastened a rope around its neck. Grimby trudged along with a firm grip of the other end of the leash, doppelganger in tow. Karmin had been leading them north along the edge of the cliff. He planned to bring them to where the river went subterranean, the fissure narrowed, and the land formed together. He knew well the worn path they could hike to circumvent the great gorge. There, they would return south along the patches of thorn bushes lining the trail and head directly to the school. The prefects at the school would know what to do about the Shanzi and the scroll, and as long as the children were still alive, perhaps they could aid them as needed.

Karmin sighed, astounded at how frequently their fortunes had changed in but a single day. He couldn't escape his concern for the children, yet, a part of him beamed wondering what the sayzr prefects would make of his unique prize: the doppelganger.

Behind him, he heard Grimby's perturbed footsteps. Each time he checked over his shoulder, Grimby wore an increasingly annoyed expression.

Grimby held the leash taut, and his arm jerked back with every alternating step. Eventually, his patience lapsed. He tugged firmly on the leash, pulling the doppelganger by her neck and causing her to stumble forward and nearly lose her footing. "Quit your lagging, you face-swerving gobermouch!"

"My hands are tied," the shapeshifter snapped, "and I have a gash in my knee. Anyone but a flosh-brained troglodyte could see that."

"Ask her where she comes from and who she works for," Karmin said.

"Flosh-brained?" Grimby pumped his fist. "No orphan-of-an-orc abomination should be vomiting insults at me."

"You're no bellibone, you delusional, bugle-bearded acersecomic," the shapeshifter shot back.

"Ask for her name," Karmin suggested.

"Don't bore at me with thy back-slang, ya scaly scupwitch!" Grimby countered.

"Tis no back-slang, you tender-peaked tumbleweed," the shapeshifter said with a laugh. "Thou hast mongered his portion of outwit for gluttonously stuffing thy aletude with bellytimber."

Beads of sweat popped out on Grimby's ruddy complexion. "Listen 'ere, ya chitty-faced wind-sucker. You're the one sponging her appearance off others. Body mumper!"

"Of all the putrid grubs and insects in this cursed world, the dwarven form is the most vile I've ever suffered."

"Hu-hoa! Now who's the dimwit? We dwarves are the descendants of original creation. We are the chosen ones to inhabit Gedtor's world, and we wouldn't perfle ourselves with your likeness if our lives depended on it. Dwarven children suffer nightmares at your very mention. Your face is ribbled and scaly, and deaf, mute sirens flee your rooped song."

"You misgloze the humor of the gods, you dimwitted dwarve. You're nothing but a farce. Your whole race is a farce—and a bad one at that. Some god's kitten must have coughed you up into some half-a-man hairball."

"Oh yeah? Well, you're nuthin' but the scrogglings of an orc's orchard, an utter cumberground."

"Cumberground?"

"Cumberworld!" Grimby added.

"Cumberworld? You're a cumbersperm! And your half-a-man sex is but a spit-frog."

"Don't blutter to me about sex when you've got to face-swerve just to find one. Other than a bumpy chest, you stand naked with nothin' between your legs. Have you ever even been plugged before?"

Her cross-slit pupils narrowed to thread lines as she spat back through gritted teeth, "Not by a dwarve!"

Grimby yanked hard on the leash and sent the doppelganger sailing off her feet. She landed in his arms, and he lifted her above his head so that their faces met. He stared directly into her yellow eyes. "Well, you're plugged now!" he shouted and tossed her over the precipice and into the great chasm.

"No!" Karmin raised his hand but spoke too late. He watched the shapeshifter plummet into the depths of the canyon and disappear into the clouds below.

Grimby faced Karmin with open palms and chuckled with a devious smile. "What?"

"We could have learned something from her," Karmin said.

"I thought we already had."

—— CHAPTER 17 ——

TIME OF THE RED BEAR: DEDICATION

In the tallest tower overlooking the school's campus, Grimby stood before an enormous conference table with his arms crossed, waiting impatiently for the elven prefects to assess his find. He cared very little about the actual content of the scroll—a map of some kind that had no meaning to him. What he did care about was that the artifact might be priceless to this elven community, and that he had lost eight of his fellow Terminator party members chasing after it.

The impatience was beginning to make Grimby feel claustrophobic in the sealed room. When he had first walked into the conference room, it had been exposed to the outside through an open-air observation deck. Then one of the prefects sealed off the pleasing natural light by closing a series of heavy door panels that collapsed against each other like the fins of a giant vent. Candelabras on the table and torches set in wall sconces had been lit to offer sufficient lighting to examine the scroll from within the secured room.

Grimby had no idea who or what the prefects were hiding from. In truth, he hadn't yet made up his mind as to whether or not he should trust them. Having nearly died today running breathless with a mouth full of mud, he had felt extremely grateful for how the prefects at the school first received him and Karmin with plentiful water to not only drink, but to rinse clean with. Thus his first impression was positive.

On the other hand, said a voice inside him, *be these elves the devious sort, maybe they did that to lure me trust so they could swindle me out of a proper deal on the artifact.*

Having Karmin standing beside him helped somewhat to alleviate his distrust of these alchemistic village seers. Surely, as members of Karmin's community, he could expect fair treatment from them and fair value for all that he'd sacrificed to bring them this scroll.

On the other hand, he couldn't help but think that although Karmin lived among them, he was not one of them. What possible reason would the prefects have to be honest with him about the true worth of the artifact?

Grimby had never expected it to be an easy negotiation, but . . .

He clenched his teeth and looked around the conference room, sizing up the table, chairs, framed murals, and anything else he might smash up. It was an impulse he often felt whenever he became frustrated or confused. Much like he was feeling now at how difficult the negotiations seemed to be going, when, in fact, they had yet to even begin. The only thing that was making any sense to him at the moment was the thought of the wooden chairs splintering to pieces if he slammed them with enough force against that sturdy conference table.

The prefects all glanced at him at that very moment, then returned to what they were doing, only more speedily.

Based on their initial greeting, he had expected the headmaster to take the lead, but instead, they had deferred to the one they called Sparzd to evaluate the scroll. Prefect Sparzd kept his nose down, voraciously studying the arcane scribblings. Grimby couldn't understand what was taking Sparzd so long just to verify that there were a bunch of lines on a rolled-up piece of parchment. He was far more intrigued by the multicolored metals that made up the skullcap Sparzd wore.

Finally, after what seemed like hours, Prefect Sparzd looked up from the map, signaling that he had completed his assessment. He acknowledged Grimby and then addressed the headmaster and the other two prefects, Frendle and Serren.

"The potential for the existence of such maps as this has long been the subject of conjecture among the Sayzr Order. It makes sense, when you think of it, that when threatened with the Wars of the Third Cycle, our ancestors would secrete away this knowledge in order to preserve it for future generations, lest the ravages of war extend its hand to these sacred writings." Sparzd directed his attention specifically at Grimby. "Your discovery, Mr. B'Dalard, most importantly proves out that theory, marking this day an important event in our history. You see, embodied within these maps of the psychetropic spheres is the cradle of an ancient and precious civilization."

It all sounded good to Grimby, but still, he couldn't help but notice that Prefect Sparzd had yet to say anything about how much gold they were going to pay him for the scroll. Was it a good or bad thing to have it appraised as a cultural symbol rather than as a magic weapon?

As if reading his mind, one of the other prefects—the one who had introduced himself as Serren—spoke up.

"What of the specific psychetropes plotted out on the map? Did you happen to notice any that would add to our present compendium?"

"Indeed I have," answered Sparzd. "Amazingly, I must be looking at . . . thousands that were heretofore unknown to us."

"Thousands?" asked Serren.

"This map before us constitutes an entirely separate revision of the psychetropic spheres," Sparzd explained. "The addition of so many new psychetropes will greatly advance our work in this field, and provide a substantial advantage to our current read skills."

"The path to restoring this lost art within our lifetime has just become a reality," said Prefect Serren, still shaking his head. "It's no wonder those Shanzi were so aggressive to seize it. But what's troubling is how they would come to know these maps even existed, let alone their significance. We are incredibly fortunate they did not succeed in destroying this one."

"Now that it's been proven out," said Sparzd, "it stands to reason that other maps may have been hidden away with the same precautions in mind."

"Yes," Serren agreed. "And we should make an effort to locate them before someone else does."

"Well," said Grimby, feeling he'd waited long enough. "If it helps any of you to gain an advantage over others like yourselves, then it should be worth paying my weight in gold for." Grimby smiled and rubbed his hands together.

"Grimby B'Dalard!" said Sparzd as if he were a chastising mother. "This is not a barter exchange, and you are no monger. This is a moment in history that shines a light on you. This item has always belonged to our village and was hidden away for safekeeping. And because it was never sold, it would be robbery to ransom it back to us. You would not have your noble role in this historical moment debased by a peddler's dickering, would you?"

The smile melted from Grimby's face. He squeezed his hands together to stop them from moving. "Uh . . . No?"

"No. You most certainly would not. This moment in history records you as the great and selfless hero who protected our children and returned the sacred scroll to its rightful owners."

The story had a nice ring to it, but that didn't stop Grimby from wanting a bucket full o' gold. "No, no I didn't mean that—I meant, I mean, I'm happy to have performed such deeds. But I also made sacrifices and suffered losses in order to accomplish these feats."

"I assure you, Mr. B'Dalard, we would not stand for you to be penalized for being a hero. But the manner in which we express our gratitude is not something to be bargained for. Rather, it is something we extend to you as a courtesy," said Sparzd as he ushered him out of the conference room and into the tower stairwell.

Karmin placed a reassuring hand on Grimby's shoulder and urged him down the stairway. "Have faith, my friend."

When they stepped out into the courtyard, Prefect Serren was waiting for him beside a horse-drawn cart. The little girl, Sissi, was there to see him off as well. It pleased Grimby to see her again, and to see her safe.

"Our boundarymen are anxious to investigate this incident," said Prefect Serren. "They will escort you back to your campsite to ensure your safety, and ask that you be patient with them until their investigation is completed before disturbing the grounds. Following their investigation, they will assist you to retrieve and bury your dead if you desire."

With most of his attention now on Sissi, he nodded to Serren and knelt to greet her. Grimby glanced up at the prefects. "And what of her friend, the little lad?"

"I'm afraid his parents weren't keen on the idea of him getting too mixed up with . . . someone of your lifestyle," Serren explained. "The boy is very impressionable, and enjoys tales of battles and adventures as glorified in storybooks." Sparzd pointed to the small horse and cart. In the cart were a few picks and several shovels. "Please accept these offerings as a token of our gratitude. They are yours to keep. We hope they will ease your return trip to the city of Pto."

When prompted, Sissi was given a bloodstone on a leather strap to place over Grimby's head so he could wear it around his neck. The prodigious stone appeared delicate and diminutive in the palm of Grimby's massive hand when he pulled it away from his chest to examine it more closely. The bloodstone had been carved into the crude likeness of a bear. With its abundance of legs, it reminded him of something a child might have drawn.

Grimby knelt before Sissi, held one of her shoulders, and smiled sweetly at her. "Will ya' look at that," he said, gesturing to the stone. "It's a big red bear just like me, isn't it?" He tried not to let the prefects see how Sissi's heart-melting smile brightened his spirits.

Then it dawned on him that she was also shaking her head at him.

Grimby held his hands apart with his fingers spread menacingly to symbolize size and ferocity. "You mean it's not a giant, scary bear?"

The sweet innocence of her smile washed over him again. He thought she might burst into a giggle this time, but she managed to remain silent behind her beaming pearls.

"Well, if it's not a big red bear, then what kind of animal is it?"

Sissi scrunched her fists together and held them up to her face, staring at the small space between them through a squinted eye.

Grimby laughed and ruffled her hair before he stood up to face the prefects.

"We owe you a debt of gratitude for recovering this elven artifact and more importantly, for protecting our precious children," said Serren. "With this gift and commemoration, you shall forever bear the friend name, Red Bear, to this village."

Grimby looked down and winked at Sissi.

"Grimby B'Dalard, it is therefore our great honor to award you this enchanted Bloodstone of the Red Bear. May it serve you well by increasing your stamina in times of need, and by temporary transformation, restore your vitality and bestow partial healing to your wounds."

"And I have this for you," said Prefect Frendle. He placed a small wooden keg into the back of Grimby's horse-drawn cart.

"And what might that be?" asked Grimby, silently wishing for gold.

"Ale." Frendle shot him a warm, knowing smile. "I believe you have some urinating to do?"

"Hey! How would y' know about that?"

"We all possess certain heightened perceptions," said Frendle.

Grimby tugged on his thick red beard and shifted his eyes from one prefect to the other. "Well, that be the most insightful trick I ever did see a seer pull."

"Forgive me, Mr. B'Dalard. I did not intend to make you feel uneasy. You are, after all, among friends here. We just wanted to be respectful of your death ritual."

Karmin stepped forward to address his friend. "And I shall bid you farewell," he said, offering his hand, "as I must return to my master's keep to continue with my training and explain how the day's events took me away from my daily chores."

"Your master?" asked Grimby. "You have a master? After the way you fought today?"

"I thank you for your generous praises, but I have years of training yet ahead of me before I could hope to be worthy of that rank."

"Years of training . . . you? Surely you must be joking. How old are you?"

"I am fourteen years of age," said Karmin.

"Fourteen? Ha!" Grimby couldn't contain himself. "Do you know that if you was a dwarve you'd still be suckin' on your mammy's teat?" He allowed himself a hearty chuckle, then shook his head in disbelief. "I can't even imagine what it be like to be human when you look at a baby thing like that . . ." He gestured toward Sissi . . . and realize she's actually older than you are."

Karmin resigned himself to the comment with a smile.

"Just the same," Grimby said while placing his hand on Karmin's shoulder, "after what I saw you accomplish against that small army of Shanzi, and you don't yet consider yourself a master?" He scanned the faces of the prefects standing around him and shook his head from side to side. "In all me travels—and drinking—I have heard tales told about a special class of fighters known as blade dancers, but I always just figured it for tavern talk, until now. I don't know what goes on in this village of yours, but if ever you'd like to be part of an elite adventuring group, the Terminators will have a place for you."

"You honor me. But I should not like to disappoint you when I know I've much yet to learn."

"Disappoint me?" Grimby shook his head again. "Well, my friend, if you insist that your destiny calls upon you to remain here, then so be it." He leaned in closer and whispered against the back of his hand to Karmin.

"What do you think o' this here?" He gripped the bloodstone given to him by the prefects. "Do you think it might be worth a pile o' gold?"

"If it enhances your abilities," answered Karmin, "then I believe it's priceless."

CHAPTER 18

TIME OF THE RED BEAR: MYSTERY

Prefect Quarternine did not turn around from the stacks even though Harken had entered the library with his weapons clanking against his armor like an imbalanced wind chime. His feet scuffed to a halt when he stood at attention to deliver his report on their investigation.

Quarternine, who appeared to be busily sorting through some books, showed no sign of acknowledgement. As a boundaryman, Harken was well-accustomed to serving in an organized security force with clearly defined protocols. But all of that changed now that he found himself dealing directly with one of the sayzr prefects. To reannounce his presence, he shifted his body, allowing the chains of his triple-balled flail to rattle by his side. He stopped short of clearing his throat.

Still, the prefect failed to regard him and offered no indication as to how Harken should proceed. After two more minutes of silence, Harken decided that the longer he waited before speaking, the more awkward it would appear. He drew a silent breath and spoke.

"The Red Bear fulfilled his death ceremony and began his journey to return to the city-state of Pto."

Prefect Quarternine neither slowed his movements nor paused from his task of stacking books. "And yet you are still standing there," he said with his back still turned.

Among the boundarymen, there was almost always a story to tell about the peculiarity of their exchanges any time one of them occasioned to interact with a village sayzr. Harken drew another steadying breath.

"Right. I ... um ... We found evidence of spellcrafting, but not from the Terminators' caster."

Though he kept his back to Harken, this time Quarternine stopped what he was doing. "The enemy of magic used magic?"

Despite being a hardened boundaryman with years of service under his belt, Harken found himself squirming in his own boots. It was a sensation he hadn't felt since he was a child. He was further disquieted when he caught himself nervously fondling the burnt end of a short stick. "Er, um, I know it doesn't stand to reason, but that's why we reviewed our findings several times. As strange as it sounds, in this instance, magic use came from the Shanzi." When he looked up from his fidgeting hands, he was shocked to see that Prefect Quarternine was standing directly in front of him.

"Well then, we have something of a mystery on our hands."

"There's more."

"Of course there is," Quarternine said reassuringly. With a single hand gesture, he invited Harken to join him in sitting down on a cushioned bench. "That's what a mystery means." Quarternine sat close to Harken with one arm behind his shoulder so that his hand rested against the center of Harken's back. "Until a mystery is solved, there is always more information to be discovered."

Gone was the perceived aloofness that added to Harken's dread. In its place was this warm and nurturing, personable prefect. Boundarymen were not accustomed to being coddled, but in this case Quarternine's encouragement did the trick to melt away much of Harken's uneasiness about sayzrs.

"These Shanzi are a relatively new organization," said Quarternine. "I regret that I do not know as much about them as I would like, but I certainly have never known them to venture this far north."

"That much is true," said Harken. "And from what we've seen so far, they have all been human in race."

Quarternine nodded as he pondered the facts. "What is it about this particular altercation that would convince such anti-magic fanatics to allow the use of magic to further their cause?"

"We don't have anything solid on that just yet, but the mere fact that they reached our borders is troubling, to say the least."

"So tell me," said Prefect Quarternine, "what more did you tenacious boundarymen uncover?"

"While we were examining the bodies of the two dead left by the Red Bear's second encounter—one of them was a Shanzi commander—we found this spent wand on him." Harken was proud to be able to hand the spent wand to Prefect Quarternine.

"Ahh," Quarternine remarked. "This is good. This is very good. You have done quite well, indeed."

Before Harken could say anything further on the matter, Quarternine had his eyes closed and was passing a hand over the wand.

"It would be a big help to us," said Harken, "if you were able to descry the most recent castings from—"

"Confusion . . . Hold . . . and Web," said Quarternine.

"All right, then, we should be able to reconstruct much of their conflict with that information."

"There is something more you wish to tell me?" said Quarternine.

"Ah, yes. The wand-wielding Shanzi commander had a mark branded under his chin. At first we figured it to be some kind of Shanzi symbol, but none of the others had it. I would describe it as two lightning bolts, or possibly a symbol for twin rivers."

"SS?" Quarternine said.

"Your guess is as good as mine," said Boundaryman Harken.

"And that's the problem," said Quarternine. "Until we can uncover something more to corroborate our theories, it remains just guesswork."

"Could it be something about the Red Bear and his adventuring party?" Harken offered.

"Yes, it could. But in what way do you mean?"

"A prior run-in," said Harken. "It seems the Shanzi had it in for these Terminators, and I suspect that hatred went both ways. I believe the Shanzi were tracking the Terminators—hunting them, in fact."

"So it would seem. But to journey three or four weeks north of the nearest town, just for vengeance?"

"I wouldn't doubt it," said Harken. "From what I've seen, in humans especially, revenge can be a strong motivator."

"Yes," agreed Quarternine. "And it is wise of you to see it that way. But what would motivate them to resort to weaving spells? Would they betray their own belief system just to even a score?"

"And yet there is evidence to support exactly that result."

"And yet," countered Quarternine, "at the center of it all is the map of the psychetropic spheres." Sayzr Quarternine grinned and patted Harken on his shoulder. "You helped to uncover it, but do you truly *see* it?"

"See what?" Harken began to get the idea that Sayzr Quarternine understood more than he revealed.

"The pattern change. To a sayzr, that's always the first clue. And there's nothing subtle about this convergence of so many unusual events."

"So what does it all mean?" Harken asked.

"What indeed. And who or what is behind it? This warrants some meditation." Quarternine stood up and walked toward the stacks. "See what more you can learn about these Shanzi, the Terminators, and that SS mark to see if, in fact, there's a connection. When you're ready, we'll speak again."

As he was leaving, Harken imagined retelling this experience to his fellow boundarymen and couldn't resist venturing a final question, though he knew he probably shouldn't. "How will I know when you're ready?"

With his back to Harken, Prefect Quarternine picked up one of the large tomes from a table and studied the spine of its thick, leather-bound cover, saying nothing. He returned the work to its rightful place on the bookshelf.

CHAPTER 19

TIME OF THE RED BEAR: THE WARLOCK KING

In a radical departure from their usual provocative white, Shanzi agent Cassar stood by the secret meeting cave negotiating his Shanzi demands wearing a dark robe to mimic the attire of his School in the Sky contact. Despite the critical need to conceal their relationship, Cassar wore a white ribbon around his arm as a sign of respect for his fallen brethren, and in defiance of the School in the Sky's directives.

Beru, for his part, said nothing, though it was a slap in the face to the Lord of Light, the founder and master of the School in the Sky.

"The Lord of Light understands that this venture has cost you the lives of several of your men—" Beru replied before cutting himself off. He raised a finger of caution to alert his Shanzi counterpart to keep silent as the black crow that was perched on his shoulder shifted its feet. Knowing that any leak about the Lord of Light working with the Shanzi was punishable by death, even the slightest move from the watchful bird could be unnerving.

The blackness of the crow's eyeballs reflected the paleness of fear in the faces of the operatives. The Shanzi agent shuddered upon seeing his dual image being held in judgment by the crow's gaze.

Abruptly the crow took flight, leaving the two men standing motionless beneath the light of an early moon. The reflection of trees and small mammals passed across the shiny black globes as the crow circled around their vicinity.

Color restored to the men's faces when the crow returned to its perch upon the shoulder of Beru, the School in the Sky operative. Satisfied that their private meeting had remained private, Beru respired deeply and continued precisely from where he had left off.

"But," he whispered forcefully through his soft, pudgy cheeks, "he also recalls that you were cautioned about your mission's proximity to his native village and the dangers of interacting with its villagers. You can inform the Shanzi leadership that their request for reparations is denied."

"We did not interact with the villagers—"

"One villager," Beru corrected him.

"Oh yes, excuse me," said Cassar. "But that was only one villager. And we Shanzi are a highly trained, unified force—"

"One villager is all it takes! This mission was too critical to risk such variables. You were unwise not to heed the stern warnings of his Lightship."

Beru's sternness, it seemed to Cassar, was out of character for his fat, clean-shaven, friendly appearance. The genial feeling he projected emboldened Cassar to play the fearless negotiator. "The Lord of Light should not have placed restrictions on our methods. Not—"

The crow fluttered its wings, tipped forward in rapid succession, and made talking noises with a low and deliberate chirrup that interrupted the Shanzi agent. Despite being unnerved by the presence of the crow, Cassar tried to appear unaffected.

"Not being able to destroy the artifact compromised our tactics and posed greater difficulties for my Shanzi brethren."

"The item would have been of no value to the Lord of Light if the Shanzi destroyed it too soon," said Beru. "And that would have betrayed our alliance."

"Perhaps," said Cassar. "But at least it would have been destroyed instead of remaining in the hands of those who would spread the plague of magic. You were forewarned that we would stop at nothing to rid humanity of such unnatural perversities. For any Shanzi, no sacrifice is too great for our cause."

"No one here doubts the fanaticism of your squadron of zealots," Beru said. "But in order to fight fire with fire and win, you have to ensure yours is the hotter flame. That map was to be our master's edge over his peers. You could have destroyed it *after* the Lord of Light had the chance to study it. Now it is their advantage to exploit."

"Because of the restrictions he placed on our ability to destroy the artifact in the moment of engagement, our hands were tied," Cassar said. "It allowed the item to slip back into the hands of the enemy and caused this setback."

"That should not have been enough of a factor to tip the scales against you. You were an entire Shanzi regiment against a single bloated, slow-moving, dullard dwarve."

"He entered your master's village. He was able to find help from those sympathetic to him and his cause."

"You let him get away, and by doing so, the Shanzi have failed us all. Our master is not pleased. He must now devise a new plan to retrieve the map without alerting his village prefects to the true target of his desire. For that reason, your charge is to report no reward and no reparations to the Shanzi."

"He's your master, not ours," Cassar said with growing agitation. "The Lord of Light is just another warlock, and we Shanzi have sworn to reject the kingship of any magic crafter, no matter how powerful—" Cassar's mouth dropped open at the sight of his reflection in the crow's eyes beginning to shift and change. Though he held his actual face still, in the reflection, his mouth was being stuffed until he choked, and his jaw wedged open and forced apart.

Cassar turned and fled from the harbinger of doom, stumbling through the dark and sinister trees in a panic. When he tripped over a root, he fell into the arms of three awaiting beauties. They were completely naked, their flesh black as soot. The smiling, giggling, white-haired elves wrapped their curvaceous bodies around him and began stuffing his mouth with soil, then took turns pounding it down his throat with a wooden stake. Cassar struggled and squirmed as the laughing ladies took turns hammering the wooden stake deeper into his throat.

Beru saw none of this. There was only what he perceived as the Shanzi operative having been driven mad by the Lord of Light. He watched Cassar rolling around, alone in the darkness, filling his mouth with handfuls of dirt. In a fit, he crammed a thick stub of a branch into his mouth and slammed his head against the ground with all his weight. The body of the Shanzi convulsed and then fell silent.

"It appears I was in error," Beru said quietly, as if addressing the dead Shanzi. "There's no need for you to report the denied request to your Shanzi leadership, after all. For the Lord of Light has spoken, and they will, no doubt, get the message."

—— CHAPTER 20 ——

BRIDGING THE GAP

The bell rang. The last class of the day was over. T'Ralo stood by the main entrance and watched as Rasilla stepped outside. He'd been waiting for her while everyone else had been in class.

Rasilla hugged a few books tightly against her chest and glanced around, seemingly looking for someone.

T'Ralo felt a surge of confidence and stepped toward her. "Could I accompany you home?" he asked, extending his hand.

Rasilla's expression fell, and T'Ralo's heart sank. Clearly, he wasn't the someone she had been looking for.

"Oh, that is so very sweet of you to offer," Rasilla said. "But . . ."

T'Ralo continued to hold out his hand, which Rasilla looked at but did not take.

She squeezed her books tighter to her chest. "But you know, you and I live in opposite directions from the school. I certainly wouldn't want to be a bother."

T'Ralo shrugged. "It's no bother." He knew he should probably give up and leave Rasilla alone, but he had grown accustomed to humiliation and rejection and figured he had nothing to lose. Using his weakness as a strength, he pressed on. "I'd be happy to walk with you. I've got nothing that needs doing and no place to go."

Rasilla raised an eyebrow. "Of that, I am only too certain." She looked past him and smiled. "But I think someone else may have plans for you."

T'Ralo glanced over his shoulder to see his ever-present sidekick coming up the walk. *Please, not now.*

Sissi stepped between them and snatched T'Ralo's extended hand. But instead of taking it to walk with him, she placed something in it. T'Ralo opened his hand to find a wet, sticky, browned apple core.

"Thank you," said Sissi. "I'm all finished with it now."

T'Ralo feigned a smile and threw the apple core into a group of pine trees. He then looked for a place to wipe off his hand.

Rasilla took a few steps backward. Her shoulders ended up in the arms of Glimmer, who had just appeared on the scene.

Before T'Ralo could decide whether to wipe his hand on the grass or his pant leg, Sissi grabbed it again. "Okay, you can walk me home now."

"It looks like you two make quite a couple," said Rasilla. "I certainly don't want to . . ." She glanced down at the browned apple meal oozing through their clasped fingers ". . . come between . . . that."

T'Ralo, who could feel the trace drippings of apple meal between his hand and Sissi's, tried to smile casually at Rasilla. Sissi tugged him away, but over his shoulder he heard Rasilla playfully chastising Glimmer for showing up late and nearly consigning her to an awful fate.

"You are in big trouble, mister."

"What did I do?"

"I almost got stuck having to walk home with you-know-who."

T'Ralo frowned. She couldn't even bring herself to say his name. He glanced back over his shoulder as Glimmer spoke.

"You mean I came between that? I'm so sorry. Maybe I can catch up with them and bring him back to you." Glimmer feigned a move to retrieve T'Ralo.

"No!" Rasilla laughed in protest, tugging on Glimmer's arm. "Don't you dare!"

Rasilla and Glimmer laughed and teased each other.

Sissi, like always, appeared oblivious, and tugged T'Ralo along as she continued on her merry way.

Being a creature of habit, Sissi required her usual detour to cross the Riverton Bridge. The bridge spanned thirty feet and had a railing on either side that attracted many kids who liked to attempt to balance their way across. The consequence of falling usually meant ending up in the river, but this time of year, there was only thick, swampy mud waiting at the bottom. The swamp mud reeked of rotten organics. For Sissi, however, the challenge of crossing along the top of the railing had nothing to do with her visit.

T'Ralo knew she was here to cross the bridge in each direction simply out of routine and her own unique attraction to it. He clambered up the railing and started across the bridge with Sissi walking alongside him.

On the return trip, a cry of sarcasm about the impressiveness of his feat came from Brisshden Thermicss and Phylo Selryn, whose route home always brought them by the Riverton Bridge.

"Why not try it blindfolded?" Phylo challenged.

"He's not going to do it!" Brisshden shouted so that everyone could hear. "Prefect Serren is probably going to fail him in physical skills if he's not thrown out of the academy before the year's end!"

"So what if I get thrown out?" T'Ralo said in his own defense. "I'm a fighter, not a wizard."

The boys laughed in response and soon were on the deck of the bridge with T'Ralo and Sissi.

"Then why did you miss physical skills class today?" asked Phylo. "That pertains to fighting skills."

"I forgot to do my fractal lab assignment, so I was looking for something to bring in."

"Oh yeah," Brisshden said with a laugh, "I saw that. He tried to hand in some tiny bugs." He and Phylo shared a hearty laugh at T'Ralo's expense.

"Well, if you're such a skilled fighter," Phylo said, "you wouldn't be afraid to walk the railing wearing a blindfold."

"I would," T'Ralo said, "but I don't have a blindfold."

"Lame excuse," Brisshden said. "You can use your shirt. You a chicken-balk-balk. You a chicken-balk-balk."

Phylo joined in. "You a chicken-balk-balk, a chicken-balk-balk."

Sissi's eyes lit up. Soon she, too, began singing the song. "A chicken-balk-balk. A chicken-balk-balk." She added a beat to her step and, landing on her toes, did a dance of delight to the tantalizing tune.

T'Ralo didn't take Sissi's singing personally. He knew how compelling repetition was to her. It was easy for her to get caught up in the rhythm of the taunt.

He removed his shirt and tied it around his head to cover his eyes.

He had no doubt that Phylo and Brisshden were watching closely to make sure he did it properly. Wary of everyone's whereabouts lest he be bumped, T'Ralo stood sightless on the rail and waited, giving himself time to sense his surroundings. He was not intentionally drawing from his academy lessons, but physical training with Frendle and Serren were in him.

Sissi, still singing, was in her own world, as usual.

T'Ralo didn't need to remove his blindfold to know Sissi was studying the slopes and angles of the railing supports on the bridge. It was something she always did when they crossed the bridge together. She would bend down and close one eye to view the railing supports, all the while gripping her index finger like a pencil between her thumb and middle finger.

The sound of her voice confirmed her location. "... a chicken-balk-balk. You a chicken-balk-balk."

As much as she annoyed him, T'Ralo was more annoyed by the way these students, like other villagers, treated Sissi as if she was just their amusement. Most of his classmates viewed her as a sort of innocent. Some even pitied her for being out of touch with regular folks. It was an odd sentiment, T'Ralo thought, given that people were generally more out of touch with Sissi than Sissi was with them. It certainly didn't conform to the lessons inscribed over the entrance to the Academy of Sayzr Magic.

Brisshden and Phylo sounded quite pleased to have Sissi take their side against him. But he knew their pleasure was misplaced. The fact that she was simply enjoying a silly-sounding rhythm was lost on them.

"Hey, Sissi?" It was Phylo. T'Ralo could tell by the nasal twang in his voice. "Sissi? Wake up, Sissi! Pay attention, or you'll miss seeing T'Ralo fall."

"He will not fall," Sissi stated flatly.

"What do you mean, he won't fall?" Phylo sounded disappointed.

"T'Ralo is a good balancer. He will not fall unless he is pushed." Sissi resumed her singing. "You a chicken-balk-balk, a chicken-balk-balk."

"Wait," Phylo said. "Are you calling *me* a chicken? Sissi, it's T'Ralo who's the chicken."

"Stop trying to reason with her," Brisshden said. "She doesn't understand what she's saying. But maybe she's right that he just needs a little push."

T'Ralo felt someone—it had to be Brisshden, who sounded the closest—grab his ankles. "Hey!" he shouted. "Don't you dare touch me! That could be seriously dangerous."

"Dare not touch you?" Brisshden apparently didn't appreciate being spoken to that way. "Or else what?"

"Or else I'll just quit," said T'Ralo.

"We won't push you," Brisshden said. "But if you quit, that will only prove you're a chicken."

Despite being blindfolded, T'Ralo continued to walk steadily along the railing of the bridge. No matter what they shouted at him, he maintained his composure. He sensed he had passed the halfway point and would soon be nearing the end of the railing when someone pushed him. Feeling the wind rush past him, he landed at a slight angle with a hard thud that knocked the wind out of him. A second later, he felt the muck rise up to meet him. The mud was up to his chest.

"You . . . will . . . regret that!" he blurted out over his pain. "I'll get you back for that."

"Ooh," Phylo said in a taunting voice, "we're so afraid, because you're twice the size of Brisshden."

T'Ralo, while removing his shirt from his eyes, heard Sissi correct Phylo. "He is not twice the size of Brisshden. Brisshden is much bigger than T'Ralo."

"We know, Sissi," Phylo replied. "We were joking. Our point was that we have no reason to fear T'Ralo, because he's not strong enough to get back at us."

"He will be," she said in her matter-of-fact tone, "when he becomes a master sayzr."

Brisshden and Phylo had a good laugh.

"Well, he better hurry it up," said Brisshden, "because he'll probably be thrown out of school before the end of the week."

"He cannot leave school. I walk to school with him."

"Not anymore. He's failing all his classes, so they must be preparing to ask him to leave the academy."

"But I want him to stay," said Sissi.

T'Ralo smiled grimly as he slogged through the muck. Even in his current predicament, he was concerned about his childhood friend. Sissi had never been very good at seeing the world beyond her needs. She often reacted in confusion—not to mention anger—when the world did not bow to her whims. She simply couldn't fathom such a betrayal.

"We think the school will be better without him," said Phylo.

"But I want him to stay," Sissi repeated.

Phylo just shrugged his arms at her and ran off laughing with Brisshden.

T'Ralo was still struggling to reach the embankment, making slow progress through the deep, foul-smelling mud.

Sissi called down from atop the bridge. "Where are you going?"

T'Ralo was too busy trying to extract one of his legs while dry-heaving to answer her.

"Why are you leaving school?" asked Sissi. "You are not answering me. You have to tell me why you are leaving school."

T'Ralo paused to look up at Sissi, whose face was etched with confusion. "I'm trying to get out of the mud." He was interrupted by another dry heave. "If you want me to answer your questions, you have to help me out of the mud first." Frustrated, T'Ralo returned his attention to the mud that was threatening to swallow him. "Find me a rope or a long stick," he shouted without looking up, "or something to reach me with!"

He continued yelling until Sissi simply appeared next to him, knee deep in the mud herself. She didn't seem bothered by the stench.

"How did you get here so—?" T'Ralo noticed that Sissi was holding on to an under beam of the bridge to keep her weight supported while she moved.

He reached for her hand, and she was able to pull him closer so that he, too, could reach the bridge. The two made relatively swift progress to the safety of the embankment, despite Sissi pausing on occasion to lift her foot and watch the putrid mud squish through her toes. She squeezed her toes together and sang, "You a chicken-balk-balk, a chicken-balk-balk."

In situations like this, when others would complain, T'Ralo held his tongue. He patiently waited to see how far she would take it, and only during one lengthy pause did he have to prod her to start moving again.

Once on dry land, he had to convince her of a change in plans so they could find some way to clean off the malodorous mud. "Sissi, I think we should go swimming at the lake instead of berry picking."

"But we already agreed to go berry picking."

"I know, but things sometimes change, and now we need to go swimming."

"Why are you saying that?" asked Sissi.

"Because we are covered in mud!" said T'Ralo, raising his voice.

Sissi looked down at her legs. "Oh." She tried to brush it off.

"It will not come off that way, Sissi. How can we clean off the mud, Sissi? Tell me how," he demanded in a friendly tone. T'Ralo found it effective to have Sissi vocalize the idea herself in order to feel more comfortable with it.

"By . . . going swimming."

"So what should we do next?" he asked.

"We should go swimming."

"Great. Then that's what we'll do."

As they headed for the lake, Sissi added, "And then we will go berry picking."

So typical of Sissi, T'Ralo thought. She was a genius with the bright spirit of a child half her age who often aimed for desires over practicalities.

"We may not have enough time to do both," he said.

"But I want to go berry picking," Sissi said, raising her voice.

"We'll try to do both," T'Ralo offered.

And off they went together, hand in hand, with Sissi singing along the way. "You a chicken-balk-balk, a chicken-balk-balk." She laughed heartily. "You a chicken-balk-balk, a chicken-balk-balk."

Eventually, T'Ralo gave in and began singing it along with her.

Sissi responded favorably, clearly enjoying the fun and laughter of this song.

Several minutes into singing and playing along the path, she interrupted their interplay. "Wait, wait, wait! Where are you going?"

"What?" he asked. "We're going to the lake."

"No, where are you going?" she repeated. "Are you leaving school?"

"Oh, probably, yes," he said without the least sign of concern.

"But I want you to go to school with me," said Sissi.

"I'm not choosing to leave, but the prefects are going to have to ask me to leave because I cannot pass my classes to graduate."

"You will graduate," said Sissi. "All the master sayzrs graduate."

T'Ralo laughed. "You're not understanding. I'm not going to be a master sayzr, Sissi. I'm not even going to be a wizard." He tried explaining to her that he just wanted to be a swordsman and that, once school was over for him, he would finally be free to join up with an army.

Sissi put her hands to her head, adding mud to the mixture of foreign substances in her disheveled, frizzy hair. "That is not right. I think you will be a sayzr."

"It's nice of you to think of me that way, Sissi. But it's also impossible. Even if I passed the final exam on psychetropes this week, it still wouldn't be enough for me to graduate." T'Ralo picked up a stick and began using it as a sword, attacking the air and rapping it against tree trunks as they stepped along. "Which is why taking the exam would be pointless and why the prefects should ask me to leave school."

"No, that is not right," Sissi insisted. "If you pass psychetropes, you can still graduate."

"No, I can't," said T'Ralo. "I failed everything else, except maybe physical skills, depending on my attendance record, and passing those two classes alone would not be enough to qualify for graduation."

"No, that is not right!" said Sissi. "You can graduate even if you only pass psychetropes. None of the other classes matter."

"What are you talking about, Sissi?" asked T'Ralo.

"The Rules of the Academy of Sayzr Magic," she answered. "Page nine states that scoring with ninety percent accuracy or higher in psychetropes entitles any student to participate in the Chambers Challenge. It is in the rule book."

"What rule book? Where did you get a rule book?"

"We each received a copy of the rules on the first day of school, nineteen years, three hundred and thirty-nine days ago."

"Anyway, what does it matter if I participate in the Chambers Challenge or not? Even if I show perfect accuracy on the final exam, psychetropes is only one class, and I already failed too many others to graduate."

"Not true," said Sissi. "If you succeed at the Chambers Challenge, you automatically graduate. Anyone who can transdimension is eligible for automatic graduation. That is also in the rule book, on page six."

"Sissi, I find it amazing how you pieced all that together—and for my sake, no less. But, assuming you're correct, and assuming further that I studied my brains out nonstop and managed to actually pass the psychetropes final, there's no way I could achieve anything close to ninety percent accuracy on more than sixty thousand profiles."

"Sixty-six thousand three hundred and sixty," she emphatically corrected him.

He rolled his eyes to the sky. "Even worse, then," he said. "Nobody else has a mind like yours, Sissi. While it may seem easy enough for you to memorize and recite all sixty thousand—all the different psychetropic profiles—what comes easy for some people can be very difficult, and sometimes impossible, for others."

Although playing the naysayer, he was actually interested to know if Sissi might have some clever solution to offer. She held a distant look in her silvery eyes, as if she were processing some riddle. Though it seemed as though she was preparing to speak to the point, she remained quiet.

Something about her little enigma of a friend brought about an impossible conundrum for Sissi. A twister of infinities stormed through her mind.

She'd ventured down infinite tunnels of logic twisters before. As overlapping and continuously shifting psychetropic pairings raced through her mind, she tried to map out the various events and people involved, exploring the infinite possibilities for solutions to multitiered problems.

For a being like Sissi, getting caught up in infinities proved to be a frustrating and sometimes dangerous place to go. She once dwelled for days on a problem that she had to be pulled out of by none other than Prefect Sparzd. The broader the parameters, the greater the risk for a creature like Sissi to get overly involved in running samplings of infinite permutations of intersecting events and personalities in an effort to map out a desired pathway—the means to an end.

People were accustomed to Sissi's peculiar behaviors and often let her be when she was "doing her thing." On that one particular occasion, she was caught up in a mental process for four days before Sparzd recognized a need to intervene. Once her mind was torn away from the task, she was forced to come to terms with all she had absentmindedly missed during those four days, all the regular routines and daily patterns. She realized there was a bad side to her hyper-focused calculations and knew enough, from then on, to watch herself.

After about a minute of silence, Sissi started talking to herself, almost inaudibly. "Sixty-six thousand . . ." Once again, her voice trailed off.

T'Ralo continued waiting, expecting her to respond in some fashion, to offer some idea or potentially useful bit of advice on how to think and remember, at least a little bit, the way she could.

Then Sissi's voice finally returned as loud as ever. She spoke out robustly and with verve. "A chicken-balk-balk, you a chicken-balk-balk, a chicken-balk-balk, you a chicken-balk-balk . . ."

—— CHAPTER 21 ——
A TEMPEST OF FATES

T'Ralo squinted into the thinning fog, which was no match for the morning sun. Up ahead, Sissi appeared through the mist. She sat on the fence that penned the corral off the south side of her home, where she was waiting for him to walk her to school. She wore a simple pink dress, well cleaned and showing fewer traces of old stains than her usual attire. T'Ralo immediately recognized her tightly laced, leather boots as a futile effort by her parents to contain the free spirit that would inevitably be returning home from school bare-footed.

"T'Ralo!" she called out with her customary enthusiasm.

T'Ralo offered a noncommittal wave.

After greeting him, Sissi hopped off the fence and into the interior of the pen, where brown and red hens dashed about to evade her steps. She chased after a small bunny and eventually cornered it between the side of the cottage and a rabbit hutch that had been converted from a chicken coop. Sissi's mother was there assisting with the caretaking of Sissi's new pet.

"Is he not the cutest little thing?" Sissi asked as she nearly strangled the frightened bunny rabbit by pressing it against her cheek with excessive force.

The bunny kicked itself free, stumbled when it struck the ground, then darted across the pen to the end opposite Sissi.

"What happened to your squirrel from the other day," T'Ralo asked. "Uh . . . Mr. Puffins?"

"He stopped being fun to play with," Sissi said. "He started sleeping a lot. Then Mom had to set him free." Sissi took off after the bunny again.

T'Ralo politely regarded Mrs. Haanna. They exchanged greetings and spoke a little about her daughter. He explained to Sissi's mother that he did not expect to remain at the academy much longer and that Sissi would be forced to make some adjustments.

Mrs. Haanna asked him to consider remaining as her escort to and from school for the last twenty-six days before graduation.

The topic moved to how Sissi loved her animals to death—literally.

"She seems to have a new pet every week," he said to Sissi's mother.

"She has been improving," said Mrs. Haanna. "Lately they have been lasting longer. She managed to go a full two weeks with her last pet."

"Maybe you should not allow her to keep these animals."

"Then she will never learn," said Mrs. Haanna. "What she learns about caring for animals, I believe, could translate to caring for other people. And just look at how much she adores them," she added with a mother's ensorcelled smile.

The rabbit bounded sharply to the right, avoiding Sissi's grasp.

Sissi's momentum sent her stumbling face-first into the powdery dirt with her arms fully extended. A cloud of dust rose from her hair when she stood, and her face, arms, and chest were covered in the ruddy soil.

T'Ralo watched as Sissi's mother found a broom and attempted to sweep the mess from Sissi's pink dress. With insouciance toward her mother's efforts, Sissi returned to be with T'Ralo, forcing her mother to try to keep pace while swatting at her with the broom.

"We need to go now or else we might be late for school," said Sissi.

"Oh yeah, we wouldn't want that," T'Ralo said sarcastically.

Sissi had already run off, and T'Ralo, the soon-to-be flunk-out, was now the one left having to chase after Sissi, this time with the backpack she had left behind.

This school day was not unlike the previous day, except that Sissi insisted T'Ralo attend every class with her. He went along with the request just to placate her, even though he held no illusions about being permitted to finish out the day.

He was surprised when Prefect Sparzd singled him out for achieving the second highest grade on the homework assignment based on his having handed in nothing. Sissi's work provided the requisite sittropes, naming common interactions and trials between people that were used in the puppet master's theatre. Although Rasilla's thirty-six-page thesis on the jester character topped the class in length and verbosity, the highest recognition for psychetropes went to Sissi who, unlike T'Ralo, actually did the homework and explained as part of her single-page submission that puppet show characters could not be properly mapped because they were not real people with real minds capable of being molded and influenced by life experiences.

The moment T'Ralo was expecting finally came during the last quarter of Prefect Sparzd's class. With the exam on the psychetropic spheres only six days away, Prefect Sparzd called T'Ralo to his desk. He handed T'Ralo a slip of paper and instructed him to report to the headmaster's office.

Prefect Sparzd leaned back in his chair and folded his arms guardedly as Sissi approached his desk.

"I need to use the necessary," she pleaded.

What she really wanted to do, Sparzd suspected, was to accompany her little friend to the headmaster's office. He could see it on her face, which was contorted with agitation. The nonstop movement of her squirming legs as she crossed and uncrossed them in a dance of urgency, he regarded as nothing more than a feeble, over-exaggerated performance.

Without taking his eyes off her, Sparzd calmed his mind and tried to read her.

She looked back at him but revealed nothing.

Sparzd usually made a conscious effort to conceal his reactions and emotions, but there were times when doing so became difficult, even for a sayzr. At the moment, he couldn't hide the frustration he felt. When a subject was being read, the reader essentially opened a window to that person's life and assigned various psychetropes in an attempt to map out the experiences and perceptions that shaped that person's psyche. One of the consequences of opening such a window was that the reader also had to remain open and, in so doing, typically revealed their own true self. Nonetheless, a successful read was not necessary to recognize Sissi's ploy as a pretext for wanting to help her little friend resist expulsion. Sparzd refused to permit Sissi to leave the classroom for any reason.

"If the headmaster wanted you to accompany that student," Sparzd said, revealing to her what he knew about her true motives, "he would have requested it. If you really just want to relieve yourself using the necessary, then you can go at the conclusion of class. The need should still be there."

Sissi appeared to be studying Sparzd. "I am sorry, Prefect. You are right, of course. I had been pushing him to apply himself for your examination all week. Not having to endure a test on the thousands of psychetropes will probably be something of a relief for him."

Sparzd nodded to be polite. "Students, like all people, have aptitudes for different things."

"Prefect Sparzd, is it difficult to determine which of the sixty-six thousand three hundred and sixty classical psychetropes to cover for the examination?"

Sparzd grinned. "It might seem impractical to test such a broad topic in only three hours, but I have an approach that will do justice for the class. We all have our own way of doing things, Magistra Haanna. So you need not worry about your little friend. Trust that he will be all right in finding his own way. And you need not worry about me. Now return to your desk."

Prefect Serren, the physical skills instructor, could feel the long, cool shadow cast by the apparatus looming behind him. The apparatus, which he knew inside and out, was comprised chiefly of two flat, rectangular towers, each fifty feet tall, facing each other from twenty yards. On the right side was a levered switch. On the left, an equipment rack of spears, poles, discs, and a variety of objects. An errant squirrel meandering behind the prefect sprung along the grass as it passed between the two slabs.

Serren was introducing the senior class to the next crop of students who would be entering Sayzr Academy. They had assembled behind the school, atop a grassy hill where he held class. T'Ralo was not present among the graduating class, and Serren made no mention of him or his absence to the mittles. Just as the students preparing to graduate ranged in age twenty years apart, the new students were between ages thirty and fifty. For occasional nelves (non-elves), the ages were quite different, such as between six and ten for human children.

"The natural world can mislead creatures of sight toward figments," Serren said. "You mittles will soon be transformed into full-fledged students of sayzr magic, and hopefully, chambers magic here at the academy. Over the course of the next score, you, as the entering class, will come to understand the empty spaciousness of solid objects and the physical barriers of empty space. Today's demonstration is as much about physical skills as it is a lesson in the divine contradictions that exist in Nature."

Serren gestured to the rack of equipment beside the apparatus and invited a volunteer from the group of visitors to don a modified chest plate and attempt to pass through the empty space between the towering slabs. The shoulders of the chest plate had fins that fanned upward to shield the wearer's head on either side and a padded headband affixed to the front and back of the armor to support the head in place. In case the wearer collided with a broad object, such as a wall, the fins were designed to prevent a blow to the head from any direction and the headband to avoid a broken neck.

A mittle named Breggern, who Serren had earlier heard boasting to his peers, volunteered for the demonstration—or so it appeared. Serren, having read the moment when Breggern had commanded a large portion of his class's attention, waited until the boy was in the midst of his boast to request an able volunteer.

The round mittle looked like a silver plumb wearing the full chest of plate armor. At first he moved like a plumb, almost rolling down the hill until he awkwardly adapted to the weight.

After reaching into a barrel of various-sized iron balls, Serren selected one as large as an adult fist and said, "Never take what appears to be empty space for granted." He tossed the iron ball underhanded between the two slabs, and the ball whipped to the left and stuck to the face of one of the towering plates with a loud clank. "We are as blind as bats!" shouted Serren. "They have adapted, and so must you." He turned to Breggern Bishbn and signaled for him to proceed. "Forces exist everywhere, Mittle Bishbn. Plan your strategy for passing through."

The shoulder fins plainly blocked Breggern's peripheral vision. Judging by the way he was swaying back and forth, Serren knew the boy was attempting to visually establish the center point.

"Have you a plan to share with us, Mittle Bishbn?" Serren asked.

"I will run through at the center to try to balance out the opposing magnetic pulls," said Breggern.

"A sensible approach," said Serren. "What approach would you have taken, Mr. Trezpin?"

Students at the academy never knew when they would be called upon for some directed purpose. In this case, Serren had put Glimmer on the spot, not just before his peers but as an example to mittles preparing to enter as the next class. In doing so, he was paying Glimmer a compliment, but also placing on him a heavy burden.

Glimmer answered cautiously. "Given that we are not permitted to pass over the field or tunnel below it, then attempting to pass through at the point where the two opposing forces are equal seems like a logical move. I am less certain about his method for accomplishing that. Perhaps it will work for him, or perhaps a more reliable means could be devised."

"Mr. Breggern Bishbn?" prompted Serren.

"I also plan to reinforce my approach by running with enough velocity to cancel out all the opposing forces," said Breggern.

Members of the graduating class chuckled.

"*Cancel*?" Serren repeated. "Now, that would be an impressive feat."

The silver plumb mittle appeared at a loss.

"We typically do not possess the option to cancel a natural force, let alone all of them," Serren explained. "However, you might find creative ways of obeying the laws of Nature that counteract or overcome any of the numerous forces to which you may be subject." He then turned to address the entire group of mittles. "Even as you evolve over the next score of years, from blindness to sight, beware of blind spots developed in the dark—"

Members of the senior class joined him in completing the familiar aphorism: " . . . that may follow you into the light."

"Yes," nodded Frendle. "But my comment was not intended to discourage you," he said to Breggern, "so please, carry on."

Breggern, looking focused, took several steps backward and then braced himself to lunge forward and sprint down the middle point between the two slabs. Before completing his first step within the magnetic field, he was quickly consumed by the overwhelming force of the left slab. His momentum twisted him upside down so that his back slammed into the magnetic plate and he hung like a plum on a limb next to the iron ball used in Serren's demonstration. Breggern, the boasting mittle, groaned and tried to wiggle himself free to no avail.

Serren stared down at the other mittles, who struggled to withhold any laughter lest they be chosen to go next. The prefect gave them ample time to demonstrate their restraint and experience their own humility before calling for another "volunteer," only this time, with less finesse. "Mr. Trezpin, will you please volunteer on behalf of the academy to see if you can, in fact, 'devise' a better plan?"

"I would love to volunteer, Prefect Serren," he said.

The class laughed, and Serren snuck a grin back at the graduating class that he kept concealed from the mittles.

"Good luck, Mr. Trezpin."

Glimmer donned a suitable chest plate, modified just like the one the mittle wore. He took a moment to contemplate the puzzle and then raised a finger to direct a question at Serren. "May I use the iron ball that you threw into the field?"

"Yes, Mr. Trezpin. All of the tools and equipment here are at your disposal. If you think of anything else that might be helpful to you that has not already been provided, please let me know." Serren pulled down on the switch at the end of a post protruding from the ground beside the right slab.

The iron ball and the mittle fell like fruit to the ground below.

Serren gestured for Glimmer to retrieve the ball. The silver plumb moaned as he lay on his back. Glimmer stepped past the mittle as he began righting himself to his feet.

Once Glimmer was well free of the field with the iron ball, Serren reactivated the magnetic plates.

The mittle ran for the edge of the zone once he realized the prefect was reactivating the magnets, but throwing his weight forward only resulted in an inversion as he was forcefully pulled in, this time slamming into the plate upside down on his belly and facing the magnetic slab. The cluster of mittles struggled again not to laugh.

Glimmer began by approaching the field on his hands and knees. He gradually nudged the iron ball closer to the fields, hoping to detect their weakest, outermost pull. After a few more rolls, he withdrew himself and stood up, having thought better of his approach.

Glimmer knew well how to focus on a solution and permitted nothing of the mittle hanging on the wall, his crawling around on the grass, or a false start to penetrate his concentration. He paced outside the field for a spell and then reached out with his feelings to draw from Nature's Djin. He quieted his mind. Knowing that Nature worked on multiple levels, upon layers of similar patterns like fractals, he opened up to and consumed a greater awareness. When the Djin spoke to him, his awareness identified a mark of Nature, a commonality that existed within the present situation. He realized that just as the electromagnetic force field prevented penetration by certain metals, so, too, did his mind compartmentalize perceived distractions from his focus on a solution. If metals susceptible to magnetism were analogous to his distractions, then finding a way to allow either one to pass through could lead to a solution for the other. Glimmer Trezpin, the true natural, was much at ease about running through a mental exercise with no foresight as to where it might lead. He was fortunate to feel at home trusting in the fruits and promise of Nature. Though many observers mistook this as blind faith, to the likes of Glimmer, empirical evidence justified letting go and trusting in the guidance of Nature's Djin to chart him successfully through life.

The clear choice was to begin with the matter he had most control over: his own mental deflection and containment of the three biggest distractions. Glimmer had to open up his mind to the extreme and instead embrace and allow the three distractions to occupy his mind so that he could be cognizant about what they were. The only way to do this was to change his perception of the three ideas from negative to positive. The mittle on the wall was, on the one hand, amusing and a sign of failure, but how long did a humorous event remain funny? And if for so long, then there would be plenty of time afterward to delight in the experience of an amusing event. As for the failure and humiliation, it might be exactly what Breggern needed to one day become a master sayzr. After all, people learn from their mistakes. And in line with this observation is the sayzr aphorism, 'the secret to success is failure.' Glimmer magically turned one of the distractions into an inspiration.

What else was in the distraction compartment? The fact that he was crawling on the ground and being perceived by some people—in this case, the mittles—as symbolic of a lesser being: base, or common, and certainly not glamorous. He was more embarrassed that he had recklessly miscategorized this idea. Glimmer was well beyond concern for appearances. Once he permitted his mind to focus on it, it became self-evident that third-party perceptions were no deterrent to using any means necessary to succeed. The second distraction transformed into a confirmation of his powers.

The third distraction, a false start, boosted his humility and inspired him to remain fearless of failure and to continue to embrace creativity.

Now he could turn his attention to the iron ball. If he overcame his distractions by allowing them to enter the focus of his conscious mind, how might he relate that solution of intangibles to the present task? What pattern must be followed—and how—in order for the tangible, iron ball or his plate armor to penetrate the magnetic fields and exit out the other side without being overcome by their forces? He could not be certain of the path through the magnetic fields, but could he somehow permit one of these metal objects to enter his body?

The chest plate was out of the question because it was designed to be worn on the outside of the body, not the inside. And given the size of the ball, taking it in was not an appealing prospect.

He glanced back at the equipment rack and decided to revisit the bucket of iron balls. He selected a smaller one the size of an acorn, and opened his mouth to receive it. He knew that it must have seemed absurd to the mittles, for even he could not imagine how following this pattern of allowing a metal object enter something, in this case, himself, could possibly be helpful. But he had had plenty of prior experience following Nature's patterns only to discover unexpected solutions, and was fully prepared to see what might be revealed by following a known success pattern that was relatable to the current problem. With the smaller iron ball inside of him, he returned to face the fields.

As Glimmer went through the motions and crawled toward the magnetic fields, a revelation began to unfold. Glimmer closed his eyes, relying instead on the little metal ball for guidance. *We are blind as bats*, he thought. When he reached the larger ball he had used as his marker, he knew he was still centered at the edge of the field and nearing the zone of influence. As he crawled forward, he soon felt the ball in his mouth being tugged to the left—only to the left. The point of equilibrium was not at the center point between the two magnetic slabs. He picked up the large ball from the center point, and sidestepped on his knees until he detected a balance between the opposing force fields. Then he set down the larger ball to mark the spot of equilibrium. He withdrew again, opened his eyes, and paced the distance to the right slab.

From the equipment rack, he borrowed a pole slightly longer than the distance he had paced out and aligned it parallel to the face of the right slab so that the end of the pole reached the center of the slab face. By holding onto the end of the long pole outside the field, he would use it like a giant protractor to guide him across the fields—and at least to support him from falling to the right.

After walking the long pole up to the iron ball marker, Glimmer proceeded through the magnetic fields with his eyes closed, again allowing the little metal ball in his mouth to serve as his eyes and shape the fields for him. He would tilt his head slightly from one side to the other in order to detect his path based on the pressure of the ball on his tongue and against his cheeks. The path he was following was like a seam in the magnetic fields, the line of equilibrium.

With his eyes closed, Glimmer imagined the path of equilibrium as the common wall shared between two joined bubbles. At the same time, it was also like walking just outside the edge of a violent windstorm. His armor shook and rattled, twisting at his body as each magnet exerted its influence. Whereas the tip of the pole would trace an arc across the fields, Glimmer adjusted his grip up or down the pole according to the path as indicated by his iron sensory ball. He was midway across the magnetic fields when the pole was perpendicular to the face of the magnet to his right.

As he began to pass the midpoint, something unexpected occurred. The more he continued in a straight line, the more the ball pressed against the right side of his mouth. He stopped. Something was wrong. The pole indicated a straight line across the fields as being one way, but the sensory ball in his mouth called for a drastic course change to the left. Glimmer knew enough to settle this contradiction in favor of the sensory ball from which, unlike the long pole, his perceptions were informed by a sightless, rather than a sighted, creature. When he tilted his head leftward, it relieved the pressure of the ball against the right side of his mouth. Glimmer maintained his faith in the sensory ball, though it seemed nonsensical that the magnetic force from the right could be increasing.

He let go of the pole and altered his course to the left. Now the path of equilibrium, he imagined, was more like the common walls between groupings of bubbles. After he veered to the left, the sensory ball began to press more and more against the back of his mouth and then eventually diminished along with the violent storms tugging at his armor.

Glimmer turned and opened his eyes to a round of applause from the mittles and his class.

Sissi did not applaud. She was too busy pacing with agitation behind the group of mittles, muttering phrases like, "You cannot do this, Headmaster Ghostas" and "I found a way." Some of the mittles who overheard Sissi perceived it as jealousy, as though Sissi was claiming to have known the solution all along and wanting credit for it over Glimmer.

Prefect Serren waved his hand, and a shimmering distortion appeared to reveal a third magnetic plate set about thirty degrees from the right slab on the side reached by Glimmer. "The natural world can mislead creatures of sight toward figments. Take heed, young mittles. Over the course of the next score of years, you should grow to understand the fabric of the infinite universe like the back of your hand or any other object of familiarity. It, too, consists of seams, like a shared curtain wall between discernible systems, be they the size of an atom, a planet, a solar system, galaxies, and so on. That you may never see it is entirely irrelevant. Those of you who still cling to your sense of sight like a security blanket, take heart in knowing that what we are able to observe of infinite fractal verses dictates what the remaining, unobservable infinite universe must necessarily look like."

The common walls between groupings of bubbles, thought Glimmer, *of infinite fractal sizes.* By quieting his sight and relying on an alternative sensory perception, he had avoided figments that would have been fatal to his cause.

As he loosened his chest plate, Glimmer glanced back at the apparatus.

Breggern was still upside-down and struggling to wriggle free from the magnetic plate. He would have to ask his fellow mittles how Glimmer had avoided the same fate.

It was a perfectly humiliating start, Glimmer thought, for an arrogant albeit talented mittle on his journey toward a sayzr's mastery.

— CHAPTER 22 —

A MURDER OF CROWS

An inverted twister of blackness lifted off the ground as swiftly as it had touched down, leaving in its path a composition of corpses. As if pulled away by the swift hand of a magician, the spiraling murder of crows revealed Warlock Beru Zixhal in a tatter of black robes standing beside a man kneeling on the ground with his head tucked under his arms. Surrounding them were seven dead men, the remnants of a clandestine conference that had been taking place by an ancient ruins overhanging a cliff face. Flying off into the distance with the spirits of the vanquished beneath their wings, the released crows ascended to the heavens, leaving only one of their kind behind. The robust crow remained steadfast atop Warlock Zixhal's shoulder.

"Arise, board member Gwellin, for you are not of these men." Gone was the amiable, pudgy face of the Beru from twenty years ago—the Beru once known to the Shanzi in the time of the Red Bear. This day, Warlock Zixhal appeared with dark, sunken eyes, and his sharp, gaunt facial features matched his grim demeanor.

Gwellin cautiously lifted his head but did not stand up. "You . . . you killed them all."

"Exchanging bribes and pledges only jeopardizes your acceptance into the Federated Northlands. If you truly wish to secure a seat on the Federation's board of governors, I have a plan that will see you personally installed to serve in that role. But first, you must be made aware of the growing threat that lurks among your kind. There is a monster afoot, and it is taking hold. When its powers are fully realized, it will have the capability of enslaving you all."

"You mean everyone in my entire village, including the sayzrs?"

"No," said Warlock Zixhal. "I mean everyone, everywhere."

"Oh. All right. All right."

"Hiding your doubts because you fear me is futile, for I know your thoughts on this matter."

"Please," Gwellin pleaded, shielding himself with his hands. "Forgive me. It's just that, we normally rely on our village sayzrs to see such things. Especially of the magnitude you describe."

"You can be certain your academy prefects already know of it. As does your Governor Multhrobe. And in time, he will reveal it to you."

Gwellin delivered a puzzled look concerning the ominous warnings from the dark messenger. He tried desperately not to do anything that might upset the unidentified assailant or the intimidating crow that chillingly fixated on him with its black, reflective eyes.

"I am referring to the girl child, Sissishal Haanna," boomed Warlock Zixhal. "You must rouse the community against the Sayzr Academy, first, by focusing on their misuse of the flunky student, the girl's companion. Even as a pretext, that should serve to impress the governing board of the Federated Brakken Northlands. But, in all likelihood, the prefects will be forced to release the boy to you. That should upset the girl child. And when that happens, the prefects will be hard pressed for excuses to shield her outbursts. You will then be able to shed a light on the dangers of Sissishal to the broader community."

With a single caw, the black crow menacingly lurched forward on its perch.

"Do this," Zixhal continued, "and your community will prosper from earning a seat on the Federation's board of governors. Fail and you shall pay the ultimate price for a sayzr's hubris. Heed my words, or risk losing everything to that monster being foolishly harbored by your academy prefects."

"What would you have me do?"

"As a political advisor, you have the governor's ear. Use your skills in the art of the dialectic. But you must be subtle in planting any ideas about organizing against the academy."

"How will that ensure me a seat on the Board of Governors?"

Warlock Zixhal revealed the slightest hint of a grin. "A board seat requires someone to sit in it, and Governor Multhrobe's time is already consumed by his current post. He will need to appoint a confidant to assume that role on behalf of the wood elves, and you are the obvious choice."

"But, to go up against the academy sayzrs . . . it's suicide. We could never defeat—"

"To march against them is to succeed. You will claim your victory either way. Nevertheless, we foresee that they will be forced to release the boy to you. Our own predictions are consistent with prophesy. So let it be written, so let it be done.

Gwellen opened his mouth to speak but no words came forth. He raised his finger then put it down."

"Out with it!" barked Zixal.

"And if, for some reason," asked a quivering Gwellin, "the boy is not expelled?"

"Then at least our campaign against this . . . Sissishal, will be underway."

Gwellin's lips widened to a cautiously devilish smile at Zixhal's plan.

"When you have completed the task of confirming Multhrobe, you will be contacted with further instructions about your demonstration."

"And you are . . . ?" inquired Gwellin.

Warlock Zixhal stretched out his arms to allow the inland winds to fill his black robes, then stepped off the edge of the cliff, along with the crow, and was gone.

CHAPTER 23

FROM THE PAGES OF SAGES

The scent of mud and manure blew over the curtain wall of the academy as T'Ralo exited the rear outer courtyard. Three sheep greeted and bleated past before allowing him to proceed along the stone walls that were stacked low and wound their way up Nester Hill.

Up ahead, T'Ralo spied a man who wore black leathers and was seated against the wall. The man said nothing as T'Ralo approached. Thick stubble evenly covered the man's cheeks and firm jawline. His rugged good looks reminded T'Ralo of the great heroes he had read about in storybooks. A fair moment passed, with the man staring at T'Ralo as if sizing him up.

T'Ralo waited well beyond an awkward silence before speaking up. "Is your name Karmin Porris?"

"Where is your sword, young apprentice?" Karmin's voice was smooth, with a confident calm that didn't disappoint his storybook appearance.

But T'Ralo was thoroughly confused by the unexpected question. "I was just told to come here and meet you. Nobody told me what it was for. Why do I need to have a sword?"

Karmin shook his head. "They said you were interested in learning to be a sword fighter. I was asked to instruct you."

T'Ralo's usual insouciance couldn't mask his excitement, and he freely allowed the smile on his face to confirm what Karmin had been told. "I don't have a sword of my own, but Prefect Serren has practice swords I may be allowed to borrow."

"It's just as well." Karmin waved it off. "The first thing we teach is surviving a sword fight, which doesn't necessarily require a sword."

"No sword?"

"You can address me as 'Master Porris.' I'm not yet a master, but it will make things easier between us. And no, swords are for sword fighting, but being fleet of foot is more often the best method of surviving against an attacker with a sword. So let me see you run."

Before T'Ralo had time to think, Karmin raised a blade over his head and shouted, "Run!"

T'Ralo took off running with Karmin chasing after.

"Good!" Karmin said after a few moments of dashing around. "If you ever get into trouble and are lucky enough that running away is an option, your speed may very well save your life."

T'Ralo resisted the urge to roll his eyes. He began to accept the entire experience as yet another letdown by the academy.

But Karmin appeared indifferent to his lack of enthusiasm. "The second lesson of survival is rock throwing," he said.

"Master, I do not mean to sound disrespectful, but when are we going to get around to actually using a sword?"

"When you can hit that wooden post seven out of ten times from twenty paces, and hit it on the first throw seven out of ten sets."

"But that could take forever," T'Ralo protested. "And I already received instruction using a sword through the academy."

"If all you want to do is swing a sword around, you're free to do so, but you'll need extreme patience and my instruction if you want to live. Learning to be an expert, or even a below-average swordsman, takes a long time practicing the same repetitive motions—time that cannot pass in your favor if you're dead." Karmin sheathed his sword and picked up a stone. He pumped his throwing arm three times before rolling the stone off his finger and tossing it against the wooden post.

"I should be able to do that." T'Ralo picked up three rocks at a time and began to throw them at the post.

A miss. A miss. The third toss hit the post.

Karmin interrupted him. "One out of three will not do. High accuracy is an imperative. Even if you cannot knock out your opponent, a rock in the face will likely give them pause long enough for you to outrun trouble. High accuracy will serve you well when you are nervous or rushed, or when your proverbial post has legs and is charging after you."

T'Ralo felt stupid and considered excusing himself from the lesson. He was supposedly learning to be a great sword fighter, yet each lesson seemed geared toward teaching him to run away like a coward. He knew well enough from being in the academy for so long not to be hindered by expectations, but that did little to stop his preference for actually wielding a sword.

As humans go, Master Porris seemed like a neat guy, and not at all like someone to be trifled with. T'Ralo tried again and missed three out of three. He then picked up three more rocks.

Another miss. Another miss.

Karmin caught his wrist before he could throw the third. "Let me show you what you keep doing wrong."

There's a wrong way to throw a rock? T'Ralo thought.

Karmin took the stone from T'Ralo and bounced it up and down in his hand. "Feeling the weight of the stone will give you a better sense of the forces involved and what is required of you to send the rock a specific distance to an intended target. It is typical for people to be more accurate on subsequent throws as you were, largely due to this same phenomenon. But your probability of success, even on your first throw, can be drastically improved simply by handling every rock before you throw it. Even in the heat of battle, it is usually worth trading off the extra time to get a feel for your projectile in exchange for greater accuracy."

Master Porris handed the stone back to T'Ralo, who pumped his forearm up and down a few times, as instructed, and then tossed it directly against the post. He smiled at Karmin.

Karmin did not smile back but instead appeared to be waiting for T'Ralo to throw more.

Which T'Ralo did, pumping each one before tossing it. After he struck the post with seven out of ten stones, he paused to face his master.

"Not bad. But a seven-out-of-ten accuracy requires you to hit *at least* seven out of ten, not *at most*."

T'Ralo frowned.

"You should be grateful, young one. It took me weeks just to attain the accuracy you already have. Any natural ability you can translate to aid you in sword fighting is a gift."

—— CHAPTER 24 ——

THE ART OF NOTHING

The thick sideburns adorning Hampern's ruddy cheeks looked like lamb chops in a pool of blood. A large, bulging vein along the front edge of his temple pulsated as he shook his fist and shouted at Headmaster Ghostas.

Ghostas, feeling defeated by the barrage of complaints, shrank into his office chair. As he peered into the ugly, contorted faces of the village leaders, he longed for the routine of solitary study in his post-dismissal sanctuary, his office.

The warm embrace of the red carpet tamed errant sounds as it ran the length of space from Ghostas's desk, up two steps, and to the opposite end of a one-chair reading room whose walls were lined with a modest library. The smell of fine parchment and leather-bound books populating the shelves soothed the senses for meditation. The entire room was relatively plain and simple, especially for a sayzr, but he liked it that way. Ghostas recalled well the yearnings of his youth, before he had become a sayzr, and noted the irony of attaining the power to have everything and anything he wanted, only to discover the few and the common were the only things worth having.

Today Ghostas had been denied the caress of the customary quiet that replaced the cacophony of students after their departure from the campus. What little buffer his desk provided was eroded by Hampern, a member of the village board of advisors, who had come to defend the primary governing document of their entire civilization, the Declaration of Rights. Standing next to him was Governor Multhrobe, and to the governor's right was Gwellin, another angry board member.

"Gentlemen, please!" Ghostas said. "Do you not see that I understand and share your concerns?"

"Then why would you hesitate to free him at once?" Gwellin shouted over him.

"Yes!" the governor shouted triumphantly louder than the others. "You must agree to free him immediately!"

"I agree with you." Ghostas raised his hands in a failed attempt to quiet the rowdy bunch. "I agree with you. You see, Governor Multhrobe, this is what I was warning you would happen. You were supposed to keep this a secret."

"A secret!" Hampern barked. "I am a member of the board of advisors!"

"These are political matters that concern us all!" shouted the governor. "If no one else does, certainly our own governing board of advisors has a right to know!"

"I agree with you about the need to free the boy," Ghostas said, struggling to be heard over all the invective, "but I would not use the word 'free.'"

"You need to listen to the headmaster," said Prefect Quarternine, raising his voice to match the others. "We're not accustomed to this. You should have made a proper appointment."

"And we're not accustomed to the Sayzr Academy treading on our most sacred rights," Gwellin countered.

"I can assure you the boy is not being kept here against his will," Ghostas said.

"Does he know why he's still here?" Hampern asked. "Do his parents? No! You did not tell any of them."

Ghostas finally stood up to address his visitors. "Gentlemen, we can send for the young boy right now and have him expelled from Sayzr Academy today." His statement earned their attention. "In fact, he would have been expelled months ago had it not been for a number of prefects identifying the potential for grave ramifications to our cause, our society, and this village. If your position to expel this student remains unchanged, I can accept that. But as the elected leaders of our village, you have a right and an obligation to learn what these potential dangers are. If you will permit me to speak uninterrupted, I should like to impart this critical information to you."

The politicians muttered to one another.

"Yes, yes, Governor Multhrobe has already informed us of your secret monster," Hampern grumbled, "this . . . this . . . peculiar progeny that you've been harboring here like some dangerous animal."

"Then you can let me know if I have left anything out!" insisted Ghostas.

Hampern, perhaps perceiving that Ghostas had just issued an ultimatum, backed down.

Ghostas, pausing to allow a moment of silence to gain momentum, was determined to carry on a calm discussion and thus spoke in a quiet tone. "On the one hand, we can ask the boy to leave the Sayzr Academy with only twenty-six days left before graduation. If we do, he is almost certain to enlist with a warring army, suffer under the rule of commanding officers, and possibly get himself killed, which, I can assure you, would be contrary to his parents' wishes. So the first thing to consider is that all of this need not be about benefiting that other student. In fact, we have already made arrangements to provide the boy with his own private lessons in swordsmanship in the event he is to remain at the academy."

The village leaders remained silent while Ghostas pulled a file from his drawer and placed it on his desk.

"Then there is the matter of this other student you aptly referred to as a peculiar progeny. Upon graduation, she will be known to us as Magistra Haanna. While it has proven difficult to determine the kind of sayzr or even person she will be, she has yet to cause anyone harm or to do anything to warrant being condemned a criminal, a monster, or a danger to society. Nevertheless, it is true that we have taken certain precautions in the event, however unlikely, that she poses some sort of threat to herself or to others.

"I cannot emphasize enough, however, that the possibility of her becoming dangerous is not the only consideration weighing in favor of preserving this . . . symbiotic relationship. Whatever it is about this boy's profile and manner of relating to Ms. Haanna that comforts her, the point is that she enjoys his companionship, and his presence in her life helps to keep her grounded. Given our poor prospects for graduating a master sayzr upon reaching the end of the twentieth academic year for the current class, and Ms. Haanna being the only certainty at present for this class to produce a master sayzr, there is at least a strong argument—even if not strong enough to weigh against the alternative—but a strong argument in favor of not taking any risks that might upset Ms. Haanna's path."

Ghostas's words were followed by silence, which seemed to indicate that something of these other considerations was getting through to the village leaders.

But then Gwellin spoke up. "The argument, you mean, is to not upset Ms. Haanna."

"For fear of invoking her retribution," added Governor Multhrobe.

Ghostas raised his hands again. "Please. Let us refrain from inflaming this discussion. This is an institution of learning, not a political stage. There is no need to resort to yelling or attacking an innocent student with hyperbole."

"You said it yourself that she could pose a danger," the governor countered. "We would like to know more about this danger and how we can protect ourselves."

"Very well," said Ghostas, tugging his shirtsleeves with finality. "Should Ms. Haanna ever demonstrate, to our satisfaction, any irresponsibility or abuse of her powers, we prefects of the academy as members of the council of sayzrs are prepared to move in to contain her in our own way. We will protect her as we do all our students, and if ever it became necessary for any of our students, we alone would insulate them and others from any harm."

A quiet confusion stalled the governor's momentum. "So where does that leave us with respect to the young boy? Are you proposing we leave the girl at your disposal and the boy at ours?"

"No," said Ghostas. "I already told you: I favor following our traditional model, which calls for expelling the boy and not catering to the anomaly of one peculiar student. I believe we should allow Ms. Haanna to succeed on her own merits the same as every other student. The only thing I am formally proposing is that we make the correct decision and that the decision be as informed as possible. I alone cannot be the one to make that decision. For the safety of the village and the security of our students, it is vital that we all agree to support whichever path is taken."

"And how, pray tell, do you propose we ensure which is the correct decision?" asked the governor.

"I have summoned the grandmaster sayzr himself to offer his insight and his blessing to our course so that you may return to your political posts reassured and spread that reassurance to the other leaders. If we expel the young boy from the academy despite all the potential repercussions, it is imperative that we not learn of any plot against Ms. Haanna or her family. And if it happens, we will know of it."

Their eyes widened at the mention of the grandmaster sayzr's involvement, for a visit from the grandmaster was a rare occurrence.

"Now that you have been made aware of this approach, you will understand that our entire discussion here today was primarily for the benefit of the grandmaster, to apprise him of the situation firsthand."

"Firsthand?" asked Gwellin.

"Yes," said Ghostas, gesturing behind them. "The grandmaster sayzr has been sitting over there in my reading area since you arrived."

"Since we arri—" Gwellin turned around with the others.

An angled shadow peeled away from the grandmaster's face as he leaned forward in a wingback chair. His gold-embroidered red robes draped to the floor, and a small leather-bound book whispered a puff of air as he closed it with one hand. A heavy wooden staff punctuated the regality with which he filled the chair.

"But we did not tell you we were coming. How did you know we would—"

Ghostas gave Gwellin a look that reminded him of whom he was dealing with.

"Oh. Right. I beg your pardon."

While respect for the master sayzrs of the academy had been waning in recent years, particularly from self-absorbed, self-aggrandizing politicians, a grandmaster sayzr still carried the highest clout of legends and heroes and was regarded as a symbol of the historic pride and greatness of their society. Contributing to this view may have been the grandmaster's aloofness, which stood in stark contrast to the comparative commonality and accessibility of schoolteachers. It mattered not that the prefects of Sayzr Academy were all masters of chambers magic, that they were capable of great tricks of the mind, or that they each held the title of sayzr, since they were, nevertheless, schoolteachers.

"Please excuse us for failing to notice your presence, Grandmaster." Governor Multhrobe bowed so deeply he was bent at the knee.

Gwellin and Hampern followed suit.

"You each saw what you needed to see in order to serve your cause," said the grandmaster, who grunted while using the staff to pull himself to his feet.

"There is no shame in elves being dedicated to their trade, and I commend each of you for your service here today."

"Thank you," said the three politicians, who slowly rose to face the grandmaster sayzr.

The grandmaster stood and nodded his approval before addressing everyone in the headmaster's office. "You have all demonstrated, quite well for me, I should think, a clear understanding of the grave matters at hand. I was impressed by the passion evidenced here today for upholding our sacred beliefs and traditions." He made his way to the door and then rested his staff. "I especially want to thank our headmaster for arranging this illuminating meeting so that I could be educated about the competing views." He then lifted his staff about a foot off the ground. "I now feel confident in everyone's understanding and ability to handle the situation, whatever the outcome."

"So we have your blessing, Grandmaster, to do as we discussed?" asked Hampern.

"*Do?*" inquired the grandmaster sayzr. He stepped back inside the doorway, closer to Hampern. "No, no. That is just it. You must not *do* anything. Everything is fine enough as it is. You have already done a praiseworthy job in carrying us to this point." With that, the grandmaster turned on his heels and was out the door.

Hampern turned to face Ghostas with his arms out to his sides in question. The governor and Gwellin also shrugged at Ghostas. This was obviously not what they were expecting. Here was what looked to be a political triumph gone awry.

Ghostas was also stunned by the grandmaster's response.

"We cannot have this," stated Gwellin.

"This simply cannot be," said Hampern.

"Please allow me to have a moment with the grandmaster," said the headmaster as he hastily sidestepped the administrators and hurried out of the room.

The grandmaster sayzr had made it as far as the open courtyard before Ghostas finally caught sight of him. Ill prepared for the grandmaster's speed, Ghostas had to double his efforts in order to catch up with him.

"Grandmaster!" shouted Ghostas.

The grandmaster slowed his pace but continued toward the main entryway. "Oh, Ghostas. Have you come to escort me to the front exit?"

"No, I mean, I can, but . . ." Ghostas despaired but recentered himself. "Grandmaster, I mainly came to ask what you are doing by allowing the boy failure to remain here. Surely you must be concerned about inciting civil unrest where the popular interest is for freeing a child being kept here under false pretense? As well as for risking scared villagers turning into an angry mob set on putting their torches to Sissishal or her home. Even Sparzd sees the need to allow Ms. Haanna to succeed or fail on her own, and surely you recognize the need of measures to avoid inviting trouble to this institution and its students."

"No." The grandmaster sayzr continued to outpace Ghostas by a step.

"No?" asked Ghostas as he rushed along to keep pace with the grandmaster. "But the consensus amongst the masters has been to uphold our traditions and our laws and respect the will of the village leadership. Excuse me for questioning your stance on the matter, Grandmaster, but they are probably in my office right now plotting some sort of protest and an unofficial revolt against the academy."

The grandmaster made a slight gesture with his free hand as if brushing off the idea. "Nonsense. Too many villagers know why they are here. More likely, they will go after the headmaster directly and browbeat him into submission so they may return home as triumphant heroes. Whoever he is, I sure would not like to be in his shoes." He turned to peer over Ghostas's shoulder and added, "Oh look, it would seem I am right again."

"This is no laughing matter. You cannot—" Headmaster Ghostas glanced back to see the governor and advisors literally jogging after him from a hundred yards behind. "This is not good. This is unacceptable. As headmaster of a village academy, I am duty-bound to do what is safe for the community."

"*Do*? Now why am I hearing that word again? You of all people, Ghostas, should know better than to do anything."

"Not always. And they will be upon me in but a minute. How can I justify refusing their stern pleas when a simple solution is at our disposal. I tell you, this is one of those times we must intervene. I have the consensus of the master sayzrs."

"No, Ghostas!" The grandmaster stopped beneath the main entryway and spun on his heels to face Ghostas. He pounded his staff to punctuate the point. "We are all masters, but you know me. We are all masters, but it is my family who founded this academy, and it is my likeness carved into one of the statues in the Garden of Residents. We are all masters, but it is I whom you call grandmaster and I whom you summoned to intervene and resolve. I am the greater seer, which means you must trust in my view. You have to trust me, Ghostas. No matter how bad it may look to you and the others, everything is on a productive course. I am sorry if you cannot see it, but you must comply with my vision."

"There could be trouble," said Ghostas.

"Our primary function is to foster new master sayzrs. Even one or two of them should be enough to undo whatever damage befalls the village over this course. Restoring the balance could be their first duty. Any of our newest sayzrs can see to righting the course and preserving our people."

"Do nothing, and the ends will justify the means?"

"That is what I am seeing, old friend," said the grandmaster.

The village leaders were within forty yards.

"Dread is upon me," said Ghostas.

"You have my blessing to use magic on them," said the grandmaster with a grin. He tilted his head and peered at the clouds. "There are some rare and unfamiliar patterns afoot. It is a dark shroud indeed, but overall, I do detect a positive direction."

Ghostas could see there was something more the grandmaster was puzzling over. "What is it, Grandmaster?"

"I sense something vaguely familiar that I have not known since . . ." The grandmaster patted Ghostas on the back. "Everything is good the way it is." He then stepped outside the entrance and headed off. "Do not change anything!" he shouted over his shoulder. "And be certain to alert me if anything significant develops."

The grandmaster sayzr walked briskly down the gravel road with his pant legs exposed. The gold-embroidered tails of his red robe surfed the wind current to match his speed.

— Chapter 25 —

Mutations and Permutations

A stream of students poured out the main gate and pooled around the forward lawn. Beyond there, evergreens lined the road running down and away from the Sayzr Academy. While most milled about, waiting to join their friends, Brisshden Thermicss and Phylo Selryn floated off down the path, no doubt up to some planned mischief.

Rasilla, Glimmer, and Matyr waited specifically for Salyndra. They would gather today as a foursome to visit the quarry, where cliff diving and rope swinging offered entertaining ways to test their nerves.

Sissi was among the mix of students, as well, but visibly agitated. If she wasn't rocking her steps back and forth, she was walking in a circle and mumbling to herself. To an eavesdropper, it might have appeared that she was rehearsing a grave plea to some person of authority, replaying a conversation she'd already had or imagined having in the future.

A small group of mittles standing nearby noticed her peculiar behavior.

To Sissi, a facial expression was like a mask, and whenever she was deep in thought, she would lose track of which mask was covering her face and, as a result, how others might perceive her.

The mittles observing her became increasingly nervous. Sissi was staring back at them, unwittingly wearing a look of such contempt that a few mittles took a cautious step backward.

Sissi marched over to them but stopped short of lashing out at anyone. She studied them as though they were inanimate objects, once dynamic beings now frozen in time. They were new to the academy. Her time was ending. She scanned their masks. Everything was okay to them because they had no expectations. Sissi, on the other hand, had developed relationships with certain people, established a daily routine, enjoyed a working system for her schooling, and acquired certain expectations based on past experiences.

And now she was suffering for it.

As someone who possessed too many negative traits to ever transdimension, Sissi was far from Sayzr Academy's typical graduate. Her gift for psychetropes was her only saving grace for becoming a master sayzr. Otherwise, to Sissi, change meant only loss and the chaos of the unknown. The group of mittles had something she wanted: a freshness, an innocence, a sense of comfort, and an overall contentedness. These things Sissi desired from them were much harder to take away than an apple. Sissi eventually discovered that her object of desire was not a thing that could be physically taken but rather an intangible that proved far more difficult to get her hands on.

Fear and anger washed away in a flash as her special companion, her friend T'Ralo, emerged through the archway as one of the last students to trickle out.

"T'Ralo, you are still here!"

T'Ralo looked up to see Sissi running toward him. "Yes," he said with a broad smile, "and I'm as surprised about it as you are."

"Does this mean you will stay in school with me?"

"It means that I at least want to." He felt exuberant—but still apprehensive.

They held hands as they walked the path together. He told her about the sword training he was receiving and, most importantly, from whom he was learning. He wanted very much to continue his training for as long as he could manage and was hoping Sissi might be able to help him stay in school.

By the time they reached the Riverton Bridge, he knew he would have to wait until Sissi finished with her bridge-crossing routine before he could prod her for more information. Instead of accompanying her, he just sat on the ground at the bridge entrance while Sissi did her thing. He was too overwhelmed with excitement and nervous energy to do anything else.

Sissi strolled down to one end of the bridge and then turned around and crossed it again. All the while, she was pinching her index finger between her thumb and middle finger, gripping it like a pencil and stroking it as she studied the bridge railings from the corners of her eyes. She appeared transfixed by the railings and each railing support as she passed by them. This time, something new had been woven into her pattern. She began singing quietly to herself as she strolled along.

T'Ralo remained seated until she completed her return trip and was ready to continue their journey.

As they headed for the quarry for swimming and diving, he attempted to discuss the subject of school and sword fighting with her. "I don't want it to end. But with the final exam on psychetropes at the end of the week, I may only have a few days left to learn anything from him."

Sissi did not respond. She was still mumbling a melody to herself.

T'Ralo squeezed her hand to remind her of his presence. It did not cause her to look up, but she did acknowledge him, in her own way, by singing the song louder so that he could share in it.

"A chicken balk-balk, you a chicken balk-balk . . ."

T'Ralo sighed and rolled his eyes. "Is this going to become a regular thing with you?"

It might not have bothered him so much had the song's origins belonged to something other than a taunt against him. As it was, it remained a metaphor for a rather negative experience. Fortunately, he was able to compartmentalize it. T'Ralo could partition mental processes and winnow out the effects of negative emotional stimulants to enhance his focus and effectiveness. It wasn't something he did without thinking, and it didn't always work. It was like using a muscle: the more serious the problem, the harder he had to work at it. In this case, he allowed himself to disregard the history behind the song and just play along with its silly, catchy rhythm.

Sissi smiled when he joined her.

"A chicken balk-balk, you a chicken balk-balk. A chicken balk-balk, you a chicken balk-balk."

One thing T'Ralo failed to contain was the fear of losing invaluable training from Karmin Porris. It tore at his mind even as they sang together. He tried bringing it up a few times. "Hey, Sissi." But getting Sissi to shift her focus was not easy, and calling her name was not always enough.

He resorted to what was set before him, the pattern at hand. He embraced Sissi's interest in the song like the momentum of a stream being gradually diverted. "A chicken balk-balk, I am a chicken balk-balk, of psychetropes balk-balk."

"No, no," Sissi protested. "Say it right."

T'Ralo replied using the same sound pattern as her protest. "My psychetropes test," he said in a tone that sounded mocking, "I will fail it tonight."

"It's not tonight," Sissi said, correcting him. "The psychetropes test is on Sunday."

He'd gotten her.

"Then I'll fail it on Sunday and be thrown out of the academy, Sissi. I'll lose my fencing class, and we won't be able to go to school together anymore. I was hoping you could maybe figure out something else from the academy's rule book that might help me stay in school—like skipping the test, or delaying it so I need not fail right away."

Sissi shook her head. "You will not fail the test because I figured out the solution."

T'Ralo stopped dead in his tracks. "What?"

Sissi calmly repeated herself. "I figured out the solution."

"You mean, you can teach me to think like you and memorize sixty thousand psychetropes?"

"Sixty-six thousand three hundred and sixty," Sissi corrected.

"Okay, fine." T'Ralo was growing impatient. "But did you figure out how to teach me to remember like you?"

Sissi stared at the ground. "No."

"Something in the rule book, then?"

"No."

"No?" asked a disappointed T'Ralo. "Then what is your solution to my learning..." T'Ralo took a breath. "...sixty-six thousand three hundred and sixty classic psychetropes by this Sunday?"

"Prefect Sparzd will not have enough time to test us on all sixty-six thousand three hundred and sixty psychetropes. So you won't have to learn them all."

T'Ralo waited for more, but Sissi said nothing. "Not your best stuff, Sissi."

"What did you say? I couldn't hear you."

"Nothing." T'Ralo chose his next words more carefully so as to embrace what was set before him. He repeated her statement. "Prefect Sparzd will not have enough time to test us on all the psychetropes."

Sissi smiled at him and nodded approvingly.

"If I need to score at least ninety percent on the test to stay in school, is there any way I could do it? Or avoid it?"

"Yes," Sissi said, as if it were T'Ralo who was the one not paying proper attention. "That is the solution I figured out for you. You only have to learn from the original psychetropic sphere, the Ancient Sphere developed by the ancient elvenmen."

"You mean the oldest version? The very first one? What good would that do me?"

"The Ancient Sphere is comprised of only five hundred traditional psychetropes."

T'Ralo shook his head in confusion. "So then you're suggesting I could somehow pass the test by learning just five hundred psychetropes?"

"Of course not. Simply passing the test would not be a solution for you."

"Oh. Sorry."

"To qualify as a solution, you need to score ninety percent or greater. I was talking about achieving one hundred percent accuracy on the exam. And no, you do not need to learn all five hundred traditional psychetropes from the Ancient Sphere. You only need to learn three hundred and sixty-six of the traditional psychetropes. You can rule out the remaining one hundred and thirty-four because they do not apply to human or elven cultures. If you could manage to memorize the three hundred and sixty-six traditional human and elven psychetropes from the Ancient Sphere, you would achieve one hundred percent accuracy."

Though Sissi appeared completely satisfied with her explanation, T'Ralo remained uneasy. He began thinking that if Sissi really knew what she was talking about, then there was something he must be missing. He challenged her. "All right, then, suppose I do memorize those three hundred and sixty-six traditional psychetropes, but then Sparzd tests us from among the thousands of others from the later revisions. How will that help me?"

"He won't. He is only going to test us on the Ancient Sphere."

"But we cannot know that." T'Ralo was losing his patience and hope. "Why would you ever think to rely on that, Sissi?"

"I read him."

T'Ralo had had enough and sat down on the dirt trail. "Wait—what? Now you think you read Sparzd?" He dropped his head into his hands, his hopes completely deflated. "Oh no. Come on now, Sissi. This is not playing a game to me. This is serious, and what you're saying isn't even possible."

"Yes, it is."

He sighed and looked up at her. "Sissi, please concentrate on what I'm saying. We both know Sparzd is a master sayzr—and a master of psychetropes, at that. It would be impossible to read him."

"Evidently not." Sissi stared at the ground and twisted a circle into the soil with the ball of her foot.

"Sissi, how could you possibly read a sayzr, a true master of psychetropes?"

Sissi shrugged. "I tricked him."

T'Ralo considered that Sissi might sincerely believe she was reporting the truth, but he knew better. Whatever she thought had happened between her and Prefect Sparzd, if there was any reading going on, Sparzd was the one doing it. "You cannot so easily trick a sayzr, you know. And of all the sayzrs to trick, how could you possibly trick Prefect Sparzd?"

"I tricked him into thinking I was trying to trick him," said Sissi.

T'Ralo froze. His mouth hung open as he struggled to work this one out. "That sounds incredibly clever, even though I still don't understand it." Though his mind was barren of reason, he found himself wanting it to be true. "If you tricked him into thinking you were trying to trick him, yet you truly were trying to perform a trick, then you succeeded in no trick at all. Right?" He asked the question with great uncertainty about his own reasoning.

"Wrong," said Sissi. "I thought you were smarter than that. There were two different tricks in play, and I used the failure of one as a diversion to mask the other."

"Wait now. That almost makes sense to me. What were the tricks?"

"I tricked him into thinking I was trying to trick him into letting me out of class so that I could help you."

T'Ralo squeezed his head, still straining to understand her. "How did you do that?"

"Soon after you left, I was up at his desk giving reasons for him to excuse me from class, such as having to relieve a full bladder, feeling sick, needing to vomit."

"So then were you really trying to get his permission to leave class or not?"

"I did not care to leave the classroom at all."

T'Ralo groaned. "Sissi, this still makes no sense to me. If you didn't want his permission to leave class, then you could have simply remained in your seat."

Sissi shook her head as if shaking off the distraction of T'Ralo lagging behind. "Even if you are among the least stupid people I know, this conversation would demonstrate there's not that much of a margin. The point of that trick was not to succeed. It was to direct his attention at my efforts. Then, as he focused his concentration on trying to read my sincerity and anything else he struggled to uncover, I was able to read him without his realizing it." She picked up a long stick and handed it to T'Ralo. "Maybe it would be good for you to learn fencing."

"Because," T'Ralo said, still piecing it all together, "while reading, the reader is vulnerable to being read."

Sissi clapped. "The reader is vulnerable to being read," she said, confirming the rule and applauding enthusiastically. "Hey, T'Ralo, you remembered something from class." Sissi loved patterns and code and was drawn to the comforts of repetition. "The reader is vulnerable to being read."

"Yes, but even if Sparzd was too focused on reading you to notice you reading him, might the read itself not reveal to him what you were up to?"

"It is a possibility. But in this case, I don't think he was able to read me. He looked frustrated by his attempt, the same as with prior attempts."

T'Ralo shook his head in utter disbelief. "So you're saying that you tricked a master sayzr, performed a successful read—against Sparzd of all people—but that Sparzd somehow failed to read you?"

"That is what I have been telling you all along."

"What could make Prefect Sparzd unable to read anyone, let alone one of his own students—a mere pupil?"

Sissi shrugged.

T'Ralo shook his head again. "Sissi, if what you're saying is true, then that would mean you have the abilities of a master sayzr. It would mean you're a sayzr."

"Do you think your brain can remember three hundred and sixty-six psychetropes?" asked Sissi.

"Is that the only solution you have for me?"

Sissi smiled and nodded with her usual enthusiasm.

"I'm not sure what to think about all this," said T'Ralo, "but I'll try it." He handed the stick back to Sissi. "I also need to find my own sword, a real one."

Sissi swung the stick, trying swordplay, slapping it against a few tree limbs, thus mimicking T'Ralo. But she didn't appear satisfied with it as a sword and eventually converted it into a walking stick. She dragged the stick most of the way to the quarry, leaving behind a trail in the dirt that traced their path.

T'Ralo picked up throwing stones and made a target of tree trunks that appeared ahead in order to work on his accuracy.

Sword fighting, which had once been about swinging a sword, now wore a different face: rock throwing. This was turning out to be a strange day for T'Ralo. He had yet to fully understand the sense of it, but Karmin Porris had instructed him to learn rock throwing as a path to becoming a successful sword fighter. For now, he understood each related to fighting: sometimes a person fought by swinging a sword, and sometimes a person fought by throwing a rock.

This reminded him of the way Sissi communicated. Sometimes she related to people as though she was as sharp as a sword, and other times she seemed as dull as a stone. He had come to recognize these two, distinct forms of communication, but he failed to understand what Sissi was doing differently in each paradigm.

CHAPTER 26

WILL TO POWER AND WILLPOWER

Governor Multhrobe stood silently before the special committee and pretended to search his thoughts. He already knew what he was going to say. He had rehearsed his remarks earlier. But pausing before giving an address was a time-honored ritual. It gave him time to calm his mind, and it gave his listeners time to focus their attention solely on him.

His audience was comprised of a few dozen local merchants and tradesmen, preselected for service based on their eagerness toward improving their wealth and stature. He had invited them here, to this closed session, because he knew each one of them could ill afford to abide by the grandmaster sayzr's decision. They had invested their time and wealth in the future, not a murky past.

"I called this meeting of the distinguished committee on Federation membership," the governor began, "to review a matter that could reflect poorly on our application for induction into the Federated Brakken Northlands. As a people, we stand poised at a historical turning point. Acceptance into the Federated Northlands opens doors to us that until now have been closed. Our greatest men will be properly recognized, and we'll finally have the opportunity to expand our trade reach. We can ill afford to risk losing this opportunity by our failure to enforce our sacred Declaration of Rights, no matter the source of its breach."

By the time the governor finished speaking, he felt confident that most, if not all, of the committee members were in favor of releasing the deceived student from the Sayzr Academy. The boy's enrollment was both unethical and invalid. Though there would likely be some division as to how to go about accomplishing that goal, the governor knew his constituents: their hopes, fears, and grumbling stomachs would lead them to unanimous action against the Sayzr Academy leadership.

── Chapter 27 ──
Of Treats and Cheats

T'Ralo's first study session with Sissi took place in the main room of the Haanna home, where Sissi's mother had cleared the dining table to make room for Sissi's hand-drawn maps. There were twenty-one in all, with no more than twenty-five psychetropes plotted around the large circle drawn on each page.

Sissi began by separating out fifteen of the twenty-one maps. "Here. These are the psychetropes that pertain to elves and humans."

"Why is this one labeled with fewer psychetropes than the others?" T'Ralo asked her.

"A sphere is three-dimensional," Sissi explained. "I can only work in two dimensions, so I drew circles to represent planes of a sphere and organized them just like the original prime material maps. Of those fifteen maps, all but one have twenty-five psychetropes listed, the last one having only sixteen because, as Prefect Sparzd explains it, even when they were first developed, the ancient elvenmen knew there was more work to be done and that additional psychetropes worthy of inclusion would eventually be discovered."

T'Ralo pointed at the page to the left of Sissi. "This one looks . . . strangely familiar."

Sissi smiled at him and nodded as she spun it around on the table. "You're looking at it upside-down."

"Upside-down?"

"If you want to see her, that is—the Lady Vynscella." Sissi drew an imaginary circle with her finger around a pattern of symbols that loosely resembled a humanoid figure. "She's one of the most common among the human and elven people. She can tell you many secrets about a person's parental relationships."

"Wow. Did you come up with that?"

Sissi nodded. "The Lady Vynscella was fabled to be the protector of children. She was like a mother to all. And it looks like a lady to me. See here, and here?" She pointed out its female characteristics.

They had been studying for an hour or two when something broke T'Ralo's concentration: the aroma of baking cookies. He smiled at Sissi.

"My mom is making treats," she said. "But you have to keep working hard on your studies if you want to earn a cookie." It sounded as though she was parroting some rule previously laid down by her mother.

Most meals were prepared and eaten in one of the village's three dining commons, with dinner being the most popularly attended event. In a typical home, a woman so desiring could specially prepare her own ingredients for bread or other baked dishes and bring the item to the nearest dining common to be baked. The Haanna residence was unusually well equipped for a variety of culinary delights as a result of Sissi's mother's years of service at the dining commons. She had an ember box with a skillet top, which was formerly used in the kitchen of one of the dining commons, and not one but two clay pots for baking.

T'Ralo smiled again at his study companion. "Sissi, are you aware that you communicate in two different ways? Most of the time, you communicate in a way that seems more natural for you but less clear for others. Your thoughts often seem . . . elsewhere . . . to the point where you leave out important details, as if you assume people can read your mind. The trouble is, your thoughts are so unique it's like you speak a different language. Other times, however, you speak more direct and precise, like everyone else, and talk in a way most people can understand. I usually notice this when you're motivated to make a point or explain some concept, like tonight, when you explained your maps, or earlier, when you told me of your test-taking strategy."

With her elbows on the table, Sissi rested her cheeks in her hands. "No matter how unique every individual person may be, I notice there are still certain things everyone responds to in the same way. There are common ground reactions to certain words, phrases, and inflections. For example..." Sissi released her cheeks and dropped her elbows from the table. "...If I fold my hands in my lap, sit upright, speak sharply and astutely, and introduce a statement with the word, 'Incidentally,' followed by a palpable pause before completing the vocalization, it commands from people their greatest attention and most capable understanding of what I am about to communicate to them."

"A spell!" T'Ralo announced. "If that's the case, why not speak that way all the time?"

"As you said, it's not natural for me. I have to consciously think to do it, and the effort it demands can be annoying."

T'Ralo nodded. "It's your world versus their world. For you to enter someone else's world, you have to change your focus. In your world, everything makes sense. Everything is familiar and normal. When you enter someone else's world, meaning and priorities seem out of sync. The opposite is true for anyone trying to understand your world."

"You are the only person, next to my mother, who has ever entered my world to speak to me and understand me on my terms," Sissi said matter-of-factly. "On rare occasions, Prefect Sparzd has done it, too, but he was unaware that he had done so."

"I do something better than the prefects?" T'Ralo asked with chaste modesty. "I would have never thought such a thing possible."

He shared a laugh with Sissi and then glanced over at Mrs. Haanna, who was standing beside the skillet and stacking warm cookies on a plate. T'Ralo realized she'd been listening. Her lips quivered as she used the crook of her arm to wipe at her tears.

"You mustn't tell anyone," Sissi whispered. "It must remain our secret. If Prefect Sparzd ever learned of it, he might learn other things about me—like about how I helped you study for his test."

T'Ralo smiled. "I don't know what to think, Sissi. You say some incredible things sometimes." He lowered his voice to a whisper. "But if you truly read from him that there's only these three hundred and sixty-six psychetropes on the exam, that would be a miracle."

"I didn't read that," Sissi said. "I only discovered he would test from the Ancient Sphere. Ruling out all the nonhuman and non-elven psychetropes was my idea. Just a guess."

"Just a guess?" he whispered loudly. He was about to get all worked up but took a calming breath. "Oh well. This whole thing seems like your guesswork to me, and I know of no better option."

Mrs. Haanna served each of the children a warm cookie. She then wrapped several more and put them, along with a rhubarb pie sweetened with pine nuts and honey, into a basket.

T'Ralo's eyes sprang wide with surprise. "Wow. Thank you. Shyton's light, why are you giving all this to me?"

"You are our special guest this evening. This is our way of saying thank you for being a good friend. You are always welcome here."

T'Ralo examined his gifts and sniffed at the goods. "Are you sure about all this?"

"I am sure it's not enough. T'Ralo, when the prefects first explained to us the value of a special friend for our daughter, it was as if anyone would do. I have known for some time now that you were particularly good with Sissi, but what I just heard her say . . . tonight . . ." Mrs. Haanna covered her mouth to hold off the tears. "If there is anything else you ever need, I insist upon your telling me so that I can do what I can to help you."

Sissi wore a silly, wide smile. Then she nudged the air, as if nudging him for his attention, and gestured with her fist as if swishing a blade.

"Oh," T'Ralo replied sheepishly. "Well, I have long pursued a swordsman's career, and a grand opportunity recently presented itself. Sissi has been helping me with it, but as she is now reminding me, I am in dire need of a sword of my own. So if you happen to hear of anything—"

"The old shed!" remarked Mrs. Haanna. "Mind you, it may not be much of a sword if it's still in there, but I seem to remember once seeing one among all the clutter. Most everything in there has been worn or rotted by the weather, but you are welcome to it if you can find it in there."

T'Ralo stumbled as he stood in haste. "May I look? Tonight?"

Mrs. Haanna chuckled with delight. "You certainly may."

T'Ralo ran out the front door and leapt off the porch toward the woods, where the forgotten shed was covered by an overgrowth of plants and trees. Some of its siding had rotted off, and the roof was more hole than roof. He realized it was getting late—and dark—and that he'd best fetch a lamp in order to see inside the old shed.

He turned back, leapt up the porch, and burst through the front door, only to find Sissi's father, whom T'Ralo assumed had just entered through the back door.

Before T'Ralo could ask, Mr. and Mrs. Haanna smiled in unison as Mr. Haanna held out a lit lantern in his hands. T'Ralo returned the laugh, took the lantern, and ran back to make his way through the thicket to the old shed.

He spent a few minutes navigating his way through the debris of broken farm tools, part of a chair, a wagon wheel, and a barrel with rusted strapping. The shed was dusty and full of cobwebs that glowed in the lantern's light. He used part of a handle that had once belonged to an axe to break past some of the webbing and knock other objects out of the way. It smelled musty. Layers of mold and dust coated every surface. In the middle of a large, warped picture frame rested the silhouette of a slender something that resembled a scabbard.

T'Ralo brought the light closer and spotted the hilt of a sword. Without thinking, he grabbed the hilt and hurried out of the shed.

Back inside, he washed his hands of slime and mildew in a washbasin. The scabbard had been covered by a leather skin that had rotted long ago.

Mr. Haanna took a whiff of the scabbard and started coughing. He then removed the sword. "You're in luck: 'tis only the scabbard that's foul."

They discarded the scabbard and kept the sword. The blade was pitted with rust and in dire need of sharpening, but it was long and heavy, and it felt impressive enough to T'Ralo.

CHAPTER 28

ART OF THE CRAFT

T'Ralo was glad to finally have a sword to hang from his side, even if Karmin Porris never asked or mentioned anything about it. That part certainly troubled him, but not for any reasons to do with vanity. If his teacher showed no interest, then that probably meant he thought T'Ralo was not ready to use a sword.

"Remember well that fencing is an art form," Karmin said during one of their lessons. "Though we may strive toward artistry, we do not seek to become artists. We are swordsmen who live by the sword, and that is why we teach swordsmanship over fencing."

A highly skilled fencer could put on a better show, but he was less likely to survive a real battle than an average swordsman. This was so because of the fear of death and the unpredictability of battle. Pushing him to gain the skill of rock throwing with perfect accuracy, T'Ralo realized, was Karmin's way of helping him cope with the unpredictable.

"Ah-ha!" shouted T'Ralo after hitting his target ten out of ten times. He rested his hand on the hilt of his sword in an attempt to suggest he was now ready.

"Well done," said Karmin. "Now try it with your left hand." Once again, he seemed more intent on teaching T'Ralo patience than actual swordsmanship.

"My left hand?" repeated T'Ralo.

"If you want to live," said Karmin.

"I can throw with my right arm if I really need to hit something."

"Not if your opponent has sliced it with his blade or broken it with a club."

T'Ralo knew better than to argue. He spent the next fifteen minutes averaging one out of twenty with his left.

"Look here," said Karmin, raising his sword overhead at an angle. "This is a standard block for an overhead attack. The angle ensures your opponent's weapon is deflected away from your body." He then dropped the tip down to his left side and kept the hilt higher than his head. "This is the same move to deflect an overhead attack from the left side. Notice that you can adjust the deflection angle to compensate for the force of the attack being deflected. If the force is too great to deflect whilst holding your ground, you may have to step to the side as part of the defense. As you will later learn, this seemingly vulnerable predicament can be used to your advantage to step aside whilst simultaneously slicing your opponent's exposed side. For now, let's stick to the basics. Now you try it."

They ran through three basic defensive blocks: the overhead deflection, the front slap-away, and the below-the-waist block. There were six movements in total, one complete set for each side of the body from head to toe. These moves were combined with the flexibility to meet the attack with an equal and opposite force, or to absorb it completely, or even dodge it, as necessary.

"Think of your sword like the bars of a cage," said Karmin. "Nobody can hit you as long as you are locked inside your iron box. If you move your sword fast enough, and smart enough, it need not occupy every space at the same time in order to work like a cage." Karmin whipped his sword back and forth rapidly to illustrate his point as T'Ralo tried to push his blade through Karmin's iron fan, to no avail. "But you must take heed not to tire yourself out. A common mistake is expending all your energy in the panic of a fight. Your opponent need only wait you out and strike at you once you're spent." He stopped fanning his blade and gracefully blocked T'Ralo's sword with the minimal effort required. "Good form maximizes power with the least effort. Balancing form and efficiency with strength and energy is the heart of the art form."

While observing the poetic movements of his master, T'Ralo began to see them for what they were—a set of choreographed patterns. It was like watching a dance for the sword being performed by . . . a blade dancer.

T'Ralo then asked the question he'd been pondering. "Master? If you're not a real master, then who is your swordmaster?"

"Geltin."

T'Ralo felt ready to burst. "Swordmaster Geltin! You mean—I cannot believe this. He's known to be the best. The best of the best."

"All the swordmasters from your village are among the highest in all the lands. Swordmaster Geltin is uncommonly talented, and I am privileged to learn from him. As are you, for in a way, you are also learning from Swordmaster Geltin . . . through me."

"Could I meet him?"

"After you have demonstrated patience and commitment for a few years, I might be willing to introduce you."

"A few years?"

"Seeing as how that's not a question one with patience would ask, perhaps you'll be lucky enough to just bump into him on your own."

"Sorry, Master Porris. I am just excited to be properly trained, and I never imagined you were—"

"You didn't think much of me until you heard the name Geltin spoken."

"I'm ashamed, my master. Who am I to know a good teacher from an exceptional one? It's just that I have not done well here, and as a result, things have not gone well for me at the academy of late. Being treated with favor to a master's teaching in the fencing arts is the last thing I would have expected to receive."

"Not done well?" Karmin looked at T'Ralo in disbelief. "You have made it to your twentieth year, where I never made it past the third."

T'Ralo's eyes widened.

"You didn't know I was a former student of the academy," Karmin surmised. "That should tell you something. You've already surpassed where I was when I first started my training. True, you may never achieve my level of skill with a blade, but given where you are today, it is certainly possible."

T'Ralo could not control his broad smile. "When will you become a true master swordsman?"

"When my time comes, and I am ready. Which includes teaching a piece-less novice like you how to be proficient with a blade."

"What does my being piece-less have to do with anything?"

"Any master swordsman from our village could travel to the nearest city and earn a small fortune in a matter of weeks training the promising and eager populace. Remaining here to teach students of little means removes wealth as a motivator and symbolizes a budding swordmaster's genuine commitment to the art."

"I doubt that I could thank you enough for so graciously accepting me as your—"

"Actually, in your case, I did not do any of that. You see, a master swordsman is usually allowed to select his own students. In exchange for blindly agreeing to teach you, I managed to receive certain compensation." Karmin smiled, gesturing to his black leggings of finely crafted leather with short layers of chain overlapping their way down each leg. Over each forearm, he wore bracers of the same design. This three-piece armor matched Karmin's old leather vest as well as his quiet ruggedness.

T'Ralo couldn't help but wonder if a replacement vest to match the chain enhancements of his latest acquisition was in the making. "I should have been asked to leave a long time ago. Why instead did they arrange for me to have this opportunity to train with you?"

"I do not know."

"How long will I get to train with you?"

"Until they tell me otherwise." He gestured for T'Ralo to continue practicing. "As long as you remain enrolled here, it is up to the academy. If you are expelled or graduate, then it would be left to me. I would have to evaluate your skills, your character, and your progress to decide whether to keep you on as a student."

"I fear I am more thrilled to be training with you than I am worthy."

A ghost of a smile touched Karmin's lips. "You just abide by what I tell you, and let me worry about the rest."

—— CHAPTER 29 ——
THE MOB RULES

Headmaster Ghostas stood directly below the inscription in the arched entryway to the Sayzr Academy and waited.

Down the road and just coming into view, a cadre of villagers armed with torches, pitchforks, swords, and clubs wound its way toward him. Governor Multhrobe did not lead the pack but was among them. His presence suggested this was his doing.

"What's this?" Ghostas asked as the crowd neared the entrance.

"We are here to free the boy you are keeping under false pretenses to serve that monster you are experimenting with," said the man at the front of the pack.

"Oh?" Ghostas drew out his words in order to project an aura of confidence. "And what would any of you know of such things?"

"We know it violates our Declaration of Rights!" shouted the man.

"And jeopardizes our acceptance into the Federated Northlands!" shouted another.

"I see. And if we were accepted, our village would earn a seat on the Federation's board of governors?"

"That's right," said the first.

"And what would that gain us?" asked Ghostas.

"Peaceful relations, for one thing, and trade agreements. It would allow our stagnant community to grow, advance, and prosper."

"Stagnant or stable?" Ghostas replied.

"See here," advisory board member Gwellin said, stepping forward,

187

"this is first and foremost not about the Federated Northlands. This is about righting the wrong against an innocent student in the name of our Declaration of Rights."

"I think not. I think you all want more. More trade, more money, and above all, greater status and respect. But from whom? Outsiders to our village? Humans? Maurice, my old friend, we embraced you as our governor not because of your title. You did not enjoy that status prior to being elected governor. Rather, we embraced you because of who you were before you were governor. The same goes for all of you. Be careful what you wish for, as only from a great height can there be a great fall."

"That's not what this is about—" began Governor Multhrobe.

"I know what this is!" Ghostas shouted over the governor. A grayness spread itself across the bright sky as clouds filled the air with cool humidity. "This is a political stunt to garner greater local support for your cause and raise awareness of this event to impress the Federation board of governors."

"It matters not," one particularly committed committee member said, hoping to prevent Ghostas's words from casting a shadow over their noble cause. "Today we are taking the boy from the school and returning him to his home."

"Why did you not just meet the boy at his home before he could even arrive here? Not theatrical enough for you? You needed a greater confrontation to appear as though you all participated in some historical achievement in preserving our laws?"

Doubt appeared to stir in some of the men, who looked to the governor and the village leaders from the advisory board.

"The boy's home is not the problem," Hampern countered. "The problem lies here, at the Sayzr Academy."

A light drizzle began to fall from the sky.

"We did not come all this way to be tricked into retreating when every day that passes is a grave injustice to our sacred values," said Governor Multhrobe, who gestured for the men to continue their advance on the school. "We don't want any trouble with you, Headmaster, but if you do not step aside, we will do what is necessary to enforce our laws."

The drizzle became a trickle, and eventually, a light rain began to dampen the path, causing the dirt to stick to the soles of the men's shoes.

Ghostas stood firm as the mob closed the fifty-foot gap between them.

Other men might have recoiled in fear, but he felt his resolve strengthen as the crowd drew nearer. For every step the men took toward him, the intensity of the rain increased. For every snarl they threw at him, the swirling gray clouds darkened above them. Soon the wind picked up and sent howling currents against them.

The men struggled to advance on the muddy path, which had become saturated with rain. "We shall overcome!" several of them shouted, prompting all to join the chant. "We shall overcome!"

The torrential downpour formed rivulets of water running down the path. One hundred yards away in either direction, the sky remained clear, the ground dry, and the weather unchanged. As the crowd pressed forward toward Ghostas, wind gusts wrestled with the arms of men brandishing weapons overhead. The rivulets, now rivers, caused a few to lose their footing and slip back or fall to a knee.

Ghostas held his hand raised and open before the men. He, too, was getting soaked by the rain. The rivers became rapid, and soon the mob was strewn down the path and several lay off to the sides on what had now become a riverbank. The mob had been scattered and were in no position to march against the school as a unified force. Clubs and doused torches were washed downstream as most of the men were preoccupied with helping each other out of the river.

When the clouds broke, the sun returned and the river ran shallow along the path. The water that remained soaked into the earth or pooled in place.

"Do not be discouraged, friends and neighbors," Governor Multhrobe called out to them. "We are a great people, on a great cause, on this great day, and these waters are nothing more than the tears and blood of the academy losing its hold against our righteous path, our just laws."

The men began to regroup into formation. Those who had lost their weapons took up rocks and sticks.

"No, Maurice," Ghostas warned as the reformed mob began to advance again, undaunted. "It is a fool's errand."

Ghostas turned to see Prefect Quarternine approaching. He was holding a scroll, already unrolled, in his hand. Quarternine placed one hand on Ghostas's shoulder and held up the scroll so they could both read it.

Ghostas studied the scroll, which showed the test results from Prefect

Sparzd's psychetropes exam. There, among the top scorers, was T'Ralo's name.

Ghostas turned to Quarternine and searched his face for clues. "Can this be?"

"It's official," Quarternine said. "Sparzd assures me the boy passed on his own merits."

Ghostas accepted the unexpected gift without further question. He took the parchment and addressed the mob. "Gentlemen, lay down your arms. The boy has earned his place at the academy. His test score here shows that he has passed Prefect Sparzd's class."

"It's a trick!" shouted some of the committee members.

"It is not a trick!" boomed Ghostas. "It is official. The boy has earned his place."

"It's only one class!" shouted another man.

"It matters not. Such are the rules of the academy. Are you going to storm the school for following its own rules?" challenged Ghostas. "Our classes let out in just a few hours if any of you feel the need to speak with the boy."

Governor Multhrobe turned and faced the other way. His voice was soft and heavy with disappointment. "He's right. Our cause is moot. Stand down."

A relieved Ghostas traded smiles with Quarternine. He understood the governor's frustration. The governor and his constituents felt they deserved better treatment when kingdoms and other communities were growing and prospering around them. Why should they not participate in the same bounty?

At the same time, Ghostas was wary of the emotions stirred up by the entitlement the governor and his followers felt. Only a conjured rainstorm had stayed their anger. Ghostas watched as a dispirited Multhrobe trudged down the path with heavy shoulders.

— CHAPTER 30 —
OF GODS AND SPHINCTERS

Deep purple robes faded to black in the twilight-darkened corridors as Headmaster Ghostas turned down the hallway to his office. Up ahead in the darkness was a sliver of light, alerting Ghostas that his office door, normally locked, was now slightly ajar.

Erring on the side of caution, Ghostas began an abrupt incantation. It was a chant as old as the ancients, and its magic amplified the deepness of his voice, which registered in the extreme low and hollow bass range, vibrating the stone walls on a microverse particle level.

At the proper frequency, Ghostas entered the wall. Traces of his form, nigh invisible, trickled like a shadow along the stone surface and then crossed the hallway at the floor by his door and up again to the opposite wall.

Rather than cloaked in secrecy, the figure poring through reports on Ghostas's desk sat with a casual bearing and hood resting below the shoulders. The figure plucked a red folder from the lower drawer and read its contents, then issued a soft chuckle.

Ghostas emerged from the portion of wall behind the figure seated at his desk and reconstituted his particles to his prior form. He immediately recognized the figure in his office. "Grandmaster?"

"Ah, Ghostas. I intended no alarm but judged it a poor time to disturb your recent endeavors. So please pardon my intrusion, but there was no time to waste. With this tempest of fates upon us, I was seeking further insight into the direction of its culmination."

"So you admit to the turbidity of the Djin," said Ghostas.

The grandmaster ignored the comment, instead pointing with a devilish smile to the paper inside the red folder. "A sphincter?"

It was the final thesis written by T'Ralo and concerned where all life on Earth fit into the larger context of the omniverse. His clever perspective explained the paradoxical reports of a universe that was at once expanding and contracting. He postulated that the planet, and indeed the entire solar system, was but a molecule-like particle that made up the flesh of the active sphincter of a cosmolongous, canine-like beast existing in one of the megaverses relative to their own. Whilst in the middle of defecating, relative to the outer edge of the canine's sphincter, as fecal matter forced open the mouth of the anus, the ring of flesh between its perimeter and center folded and collapsed like the squeezing together of an accordion. On the other hand, relative to two points on the lip of the mouth of the sphincter, as the rim stretched around the girth of a protruding stool, the distance between those two points became greater. The thesis concluded that over a period of several billion Earth years, the canine-like creature would finish its business such that its sphincter would close and Earth would be destroyed.

"Brilliant or childish, it's impressively unflattering." The grandmaster chuckled again. "Your decision to keep this from circulating publicly is certainly prudent."

"When last we spoke, you sounded far more certain of your senses," Ghostas said, not wanting to change the subject away from the business of the Djin.

"And nothing has changed," said the grandmaster. "At least for the time being, and certainly not enough to warrant action. However, it is as if we've reached a pinnacle, and at any moment things could fall in any direction."

Ghostas noticed his orderly desk in disarray. "So it warrants constant monitoring. But from my office?"

"An obvious source of information I may not be privy to, and the best place to meet up with you to discuss recent events and exchange what has been revealed to us that the other may not yet see."

Ghostas wasn't buying it. There was something odd about the grandmaster snooping around his office. "Where would you like to start?" he asked, trying not to reveal too much as he took a visitor's seat on the opposite side of his desk. There was no hiding the peculiarity of the grandmaster's intrusion, but in the stalemate of perception between two sayzrs, it was unreadable whether the mysterious behavior was motivated by malevolence or just the wisdom of the grandmaster concealing events for the greater good.

"Among the events that have come to pass," the grandmaster said, "what concerns you most?"

"Our village leadership being lured by a growing human presence and a culture that worships decadence and annihilation in its insatiable pursuit of wealth, dominance, and control as an end rather than as a means to an end, and above all, a self-destructive disregard for the laws of Nature."

"I understand even our own Governor Multhrobe was at the center of their cause?"

Ghostas nodded. He had every reason to trust the grandmaster's motives. Still, it was awkward for the two of them to probe the depths of each other's eyes for knowledge of what the other was thinking. "We grew up together, but then we grew apart after he left the academy and I continued on with my studies here."

"It is indeed a serious threat," agreed the grandmaster. "Lost to the humans, our ways could be, if even our most trusted administrators succumb to these perverse, self-aggrandizing values."

"Could it truly be that the strategy of the ancient elvenmen has run its course?" Ghostas wondered aloud. "That strategy has kept us protected from a jealous and destructive enemy under the same cloak of distraction for ages. What will become of us and other people who accept the infinite, accidental miracles of Nature? History's greatest ruse, after all, was at once a solution and a threat to wizard-kind. And now, in our own time, the manifestation of that threat is upon us."

"Hmm." The grandmaster nodded thoughtfully. "One cannot help but wonder how differently things might have played out had the ancient elvenmen given them sphincters instead of gods."

What was once the distraction of a different subject became omni-relevant. Sayzrs had a way of doing this.

"I'm afraid it's too late for that," said Ghostas. "Their boundless egos would lead them to war before they accepted such a story of humility over the glorious favoritism of an all-powerful, intelligent being. And if they learned that that ancient tall tale came from our village . . ." He shook his head. "Gods or no gods, they would hunt us down to root us out, thereby undoing the entire purpose of what our ancients set out to do."

The grandmaster stood from his chair and walked casually around the desk. After stopping behind Ghostas, who was seated on the opposite side, he placed a reassuring hand on Ghostas's shoulder. "There is a path to extinction for all cultures," he said as he quietly raised the Cerebral Staff over the headmaster's head. The black orb of the memory-stealing staff began to glow. "In our case, whether by war or attrition."

With the black orb of the staff pulsating, the grandmaster seized upon the opportunity to simultaneously probe for key information. "Where have you hidden the ancient scrolls recovered by the Red Bear?"

"I . . . don't know," Ghostas replied weakly.

"What is the contingency plan for Magistra Haanna?"

"I don't know," said Ghostas.

The grandmaster was running out of time. He formulated a final question. "Who does know these things?"

"We drew a sayzr's lot."

The grandmaster burned inside, for he understood, only too well, the precautions of a sayzr's lot. For each task to be completed in secret, stones were placed inside of identical boxes, with only one stone, the task stone, specially marked. The sayzrs drew from among the boxes, then parted company to open their boxes in private. Thus, only the sayzr who received a task stone would know of it, and the details of the performance of that task would remain a secret. In this case, only one prefect was the keeper of the Red Bear scrolls, and only one prefect knew the details of the plan and arrangements for Sissishal.

Headmaster Ghostas's short-term memories were subtly being replaced by the implanted memories of the Cerebral Staff. The whites of his eyes turned black and then slowly returned to normal. With the remnants of his pre-manipulated memory still lingering on his tongue, Ghostas had to struggle to finish his final thought.

"The plague of humanity . . . it seems . . . has spread to our village." He dropped his head into his hands. "I am not alone among the prefects in feeling this concern—that we may be heading into . . . the dark times."

Chapter 31

The Age of Entropy

Infinity is as much about boundlessness as it is about limitations, for it evokes the very subject of understanding. Eternal pluralities speaking as one comprise the Djin. The Djin, sometimes described as the song of Nature, or voice of God, speaks to the senses of all living things. Those with awareness who are tuned in to the Djin can use it to great advantage.

Amongst the omniverse of infinite infinities, across all relative realities, where time equals space, the forces of Nature engage in a dance of harmony and opposition. A cosmic soup of particle rearrangement plays out across gradients of creation and destruction as energies accumulate and dissipate. Some perceive this as interplay between light and dark forces. Out of this push and pull, intelligent formations occur, and those born of the dark clusters are the Incarnates of Evil.

Neither living nor thinking, a cosmic corpus of energy patterns and rules transcends physical creation with consciousness. From a throne of divine contradictions, black holes, and colliding galaxies, it begins again. After eons upon eons of exile, the great cosmic beast of dark forces awakens to regurgitate extra-dimensional daemon hordes to reign over a new age of entropy.

The beam of light carrying the dark surfer across time and space complained as it was torn from the fabric of space. The escape route, a space bridge, occurred adjacent to the eye of a black hole that had just swallowed what was formerly an aging galaxy.

Harnessed by its master, the light beam traveled under demonic direction. Ripzeal artfully rode his beam of light, surfing among gravitational forces that clashed like choppy waves between the flood of planets that had been pulled from their orbits and were clustering into a massive whirlpool. The dark surfer waited to catch the perfect wave. He rode his beam in the opposite direction, skipping past the doomed planets as if using their gravitation zones like stepping stones across a river. By so doing, the dark surfer remained among the outer rim of the affected debris. The beam sailed smoothly within the gravitational sphere of a nearby planet, zooming toward its surface in the diametrically opposite direction of the cosmic whirlpool's pull, even as the planet itself was hurtling toward the center of the black hole.

It was a moment of near equilibrium, the beam of light neither gaining nor losing meaningful distance relative to the event horizon of the black hole. Ripzeal skimmed off the gravity of this planet and onto the next, banking his light beam to catch the next opposing wave. An angry ocean of planets and space debris, some colliding, some combining into larger masses, gave a twisting physical body to the intangible gravity zone of the celestial sinkhole.

Ripzeal spotted his next target: the dominant gravitational wave rushing toward him. Its source was a planet multiple the size of others he let pass and moving faster than the average debris swirling around the dark, daemon-induced vortex. With the proper trajectory, this dominant planet of sufficient mass and velocity would provide the force to pitch Ripzeal's light beam back in the direction of the black hole.

After charting his path to circumvent the dominant planet's opposing pull, Ripzeal made a radical cutback off the lip of the gravity zone of his last planetary stepping stone. He then allowed his light beam to be drawn into the zone of the dominant planet from the side opposite the black hole. The daemon-harnessed beam was allowed to succumb to the forces of the black hole as it hurtled toward its center at a shrinking forty-five-degree angle.

The vortex's pull tugged the dominant planet out of round until its hole-facing side began to pull apart from its rear hemisphere. To the dark surfer, this mattered not, for his timing was accurate. Traveling at a combined speed greater than half the speed of light relative to the eye of the black hole was a temporary moon orbiting the dominant planet and on a collision course with a similar, opposing coupling. As the pathways of each of the dominant planets neared, the original dominant planet arched to within a ten-degree angle to the hole's pulling forces when Ripzeal banked his beam of light away, just in time before the two "moons" collided with a combined speed approaching that of light. Out of their collapse erupted a radiant space bridge that shot Ripzeal and his possessed light beam—not just from the eye of the black hole but from the very fabric of space—into the external abyss.

The radiant tail speeding across the external abyss blinked in protest against the extraction. Its reluctance faded to renewed vigor once the beam was freed from the deceptive curvature of the fabric and the fraction of its particles. Plunged into the pristine emptiness that existed between the infinite ribbons of space, the possessed beam gleefully transferred the demonic energy across the vacuum of the external void, skipping over the ribbon valleys and stealing time by essentially skimming from one cosmic wave crest to the next. In this way, entropy could outpace creation.

The absorption of all energy and the annihilation of all living things were not without opposition, and in one cluster of galaxies the creation of creation created guardians of the light to fight against the dark forces, slowing and redirecting them while nurturing the powers of creation. Serving as guardians of the light, these beings became known for their role as guardians, and their role as guardians became their namesake. Known throughout the galaxies, the Asguardians of Asguard were great warrior-farmers who explored the galaxies, protecting other life forms from destruction by the Incarnates of Evil. As space farmers, they set in motion the cosmic conditions for the existence of life, even from such distant beginnings as an exploding star.

After returning the beam to its original space-time, the dark surfer dropped out of the external abyss and into the next wave crest, piercing the ribbon like a free radical. Ripzeal's struggle to remain with his beam of light revealed phantasmagoric traces of his physical form. One of the curved horns twisting around his face radiated vibrant green, indicating a galaxy rich with photosynthetic-based habitats, a plague upon his master's work. For the dark surfer, this particular ocean of particles would be shark-infested.

The sharks rushed in to neutralize the dark surfer by swarming his presence like white blood cells overwhelming a virus. In an apparent attempt to outspeed the Asguardians, Ripzeal banked a turn by a nearby star system. An object, miniscule in comparison, was hurled toward the demonically possessed light beam by one of the pursuing Asguardians. As he weaved his way through a slalom course of asteroids, the dark surfer evaded the warrior-farmer's projectile—a short-tailed hammerhead—which curiously continued to speed ahead of Ripzeal in a straight path. Despite the obstruction of the asteroid field, the Asguardians managed to keep pace with the dark surfer by blasting apart interposing asteroids with the intense heat of their star-bladed weapons.

The short-tailed hammerhead disappeared into the gases of the nearest star. The curious object caused a major solar flare that enveloped the dark surfer, exorcizing his demonic energy from the light beam. Knocked off his beam, Ripzeal, the dark surfer, was transmuted into a physical being, rolling and tumbling as he ricocheted off the occasional asteroid. The major assault was on. The warrior-farmers launched a storm of photons that burned holes into the body of the transdimensional intruder.

Though the gradual disintegration by Asguardian photons accumulated from annoyance to severe damage, the daemon acted as daemons always did, as nigh-intelligent creatures programmed to act on instinct and lacking in free will. Undaunted, the daemon Ripzeal strayed not from his purpose. Multidimensional life forms such as daemons and Asguardians enjoyed immortal qualities such that a damaged body in one dimension, once rejoined with the plurality, could be repatterned based on the other forms and corrected. Death worked much the same way, except that replacing an organic body in a particular realm took a bit more time and effort.

To avoid interference with his cause when passing through Asguardian territories—those rich with intelligent life forms—Ripzeal employed different strategies for extirpation. Here, the subtleties of self-destruction were far more difficult for the Asguardians to control, so with signature methodology, the dark surfer designed to possess choice life forms as agent embodiments of himself to carry out his master's bidding.

The daemon's stomach nostrils puckered to volcanic-like mouths as he stroked them to a forest of erections, animating all the tortured corpuses absorbed throughout time—and now ornamenting the daemon's limbs, face, and chest like embroidered tattoos. The bedizenment of howling spirits cried out their soul-stealing pain with writhing, lustful gyrations to an eventual climax of eternal anguish and despair. The albino elephant trunks became engorged as Ripzeal continued running his fingers through his pus-dripping abdominal snouts, calling forth a storm of its rains.

Through these orifices, Ripzeal regurgitated a plume of degospores. The eruption of greenish clouds from his stomach nostrils carried his seed on solar waves and otherwise dispersed his degospores throughout the galaxy. Most of the daemon pollen would die out, succumb to the crystallization of its freezing point, or burn up under the Asguardian shark attack or by the heat of active stars as it drifted along various paths through space. Carried by a meteor, a portion of the cloud of degospores would eventually come to fall like volcanic ash on a small blue planet, creating in one isolated area a carbon-like blizzard that would engulf the inhabitants of a single town, raise the dead, and bring forth the daemon spawn.

Swarms of Asguardian warrior-farmers, powerfully equipped with their signature adornments of legendary craftsmanship, necessitated that the dark surfer take evasive maneuvers. Many a civilized culture modeled their traditional-styled armaments and ceremonial pieces after the magic items of their gods. Ornamental headdresses worn by world leaders, those in positions of power, or to symbolize status—be they earned by deed and of feathers or inherited by blood right and of precious metals—were all derivations of the brilliant Crown of Puissance. The Crown of Puissance enhanced strength, a particularly important enchantment even for a mighty Asguardian when this attribute becomes diminished by form alterations necessary to enter certain realms. The radiant golden appearance of the Crown of Puissance was most closely mimicked by the gold-picketed crowns of kings and feathered war bonnets of Indian chiefs, especially those adorned with the prized golden eagle feather.

Indestructible artifacts forged in the heart of the hottest stars in the omniverse comprised most of the Asguardian armaments, including the star blades of the warrior elites, the Asguard Urdii, and Miljorn, the hammer of creation's fourth life form. Two of the Urdii accompanied Ripzeal's sharks. Two Urdii were all that was required to cross star blades and create a white, daemon-incinerating nova ray. On either side of his feet, flamewing-like jets propelled Ripzeal around a small moon. The dark surfer just barely escaped the Jollite Javelin, now wielded by Gedtor, leader of the swarm. The javelin's trajectory was torn from Ripzeal's course by the gravitational pull of the moon. With Gedtor leading the pursuit, Ripzeal began gathering up asteroids and surrounding space debris in a hurried attempt to concentrate their inherent power. To aid in his endeavor, the dark surfer swelled to planetary proportions, increasing his mass to amass even more material within his growing sphere of gravitational influence.

Gedtor swiftly retrieved the Jollite Javelin as he rounded the moon with matching speed. Gedtor accelerated around the moon and rose on Ripzeal's horizon before realizing the daemon's ploy—too late to reduce his speed. The sector of space congested with a congeries of space particles, where the daemon-conjured, verse-relevant gravitational force simultaneously defended, distracted, and attacked Gedtor and the Asguardian swarm.

Rather than catching up to it, Gedtor was pulled into the daemon's massive abdomen, now multiple times the size of Gedtor. If Gedtor increased his size to match the daemon's, it would only aid the daemon by hastening the creation of a black hole. Asguardian hubris, however warranted, and zeal for battle thrust Gedtor directly into the heart of its trap. It was nigh intelligent and acted with mindless purpose—on instinct—but with the ability to create and adapt to achieve its purpose: to serve its master in eradicating such unfortunate byproducts as life and, among life, mutations so perverse as to result in free-willed intelligence. It was a daemon entity. It was known to have destroyed other Asguardians. It was Ripzeal, the dark surfer.

Having ruled out size-matching, Gedtor's incredible might served him no better to force himself away from Ripzeal, his arms merely sinking into the daemon's soft abdomen. On the other hand, growing to match the daemon's size could have permitted him to hold the daemon in place for them both to be destroyed, either by white nova rays or their mutual implosion, black holes be damned. But the idea of a single daemon undoing the greatness that was Gedtor was untenable.

The Urdii, now joined and with a clear shot at the dark surfer, were unable to form the white nova ray without also destroying their Asguardian pack leader. With one arm, Gedtor held off a planet cluster from compressing him against his own limbs and with the other reached out to command the return of his intelligent hammer. The enchanted indestructible forced its way through all physical material in its path, tunneling through small moons and asteroids, cracking some in two and smashing smaller obstacles into space dust until it reached the hand of Gedtor. In an effort to bring aid to Gedtor, the Urdii blasted their own path through the clusters of asteroids by striking obstacles in their way with their superhot star sabers.

The sharks continued to swarm around their deadly prey, only now with the understanding that this was the very daemon that had terminated a handful of their Asguardian brethren by the same strategy now being employed against Gedtor. In the last Asguardian era, Ripzeal had caused extreme gravitational pull from a growing mass cluster and crushed some of the Asguardian warrior-farmers under the compression of an implosion of mass-excessive bodies. If it had done it before, it could do it again—this time against Gedtor, Fourth of Creation.

Gedtor, with his mighty hammer Miljorn in hand, struck an opening in the hot, compressed stone that caged him and tunneled a course away from the belly of the beast. Finding leverage for his awesome strength, for the Crown of Puissance, Gedtor climbed Miljorn's path like a ladder through the solid material. He managed to force his hands into the wall of rock by leveraging his body against the strength of the opposing wall. Inside the dense material that formerly belonged to a single moon—the moon first paired to Ripzeal—Gedtor managed to smash away an arm's-length sanctuary to create a temporary air pocket, one that held for a sufficient moment. Gedtor slapped his godly arms together, and the Thunderclap of Gedtor released a verse-relevant shockwave, causing a sub-cluster of the galaxy to expand.

The expansion released Gedtor from Ripzeal's being, and the demonic forces of gravity were rendered null by dispersion. The scattered school of sharks attended to Gedtor's strategy—one also at once a defense and offense. It was an ideal setup for his capable companions: leaving Ripzeal alone and exposed in open space. Ahead of the others, the Urdii rebounded and reunited. Taking aim at the dark surfer, the Urdii crossed star blades, and in an instant—blinding light. It was a planet-quaking explosion abruptly muted into a bright, spherical pulse. Out of the pulsation, out of the silence, the white nova ray singed shoulder material off the daemon.

The discerning eyes of a daemon deftly identified velocitants destined for collision, the conditions of bridging. Unlike his last crossing, velocities within this sea of debris required a more complicated pairing of orbiting systems. Among the space particles, he identified a satellite rock orbiting its host at roughly one-hundredth the speed of light, twenty times that speed relative to its host's host, and roughly three times faster still, relative to the host planet of its host's host—an asteroid, around a moon, around a planet, carried by the tide of Gedtor's shockwave. With a combined speed faster than half the speed of light, this satellite rock was on a collision bearing with yet another such rock in a similar orbiting system. The impact, at just the right time and at just the right point in their respective orbits, would yield a collision of matter approaching the speed of light.

Ripzeal reverted his mass and accelerated his being, attempting to transform into energy and possess a new beam of light to escape his attackers and their attack.

Urdii aim was steady and true. The nova ray began boring a hole through. The faster Ripzeal traveled, the fewer photons could reach his body to burn him out of existence, and the less of a physical corpus remained to be harmed. The process of nova ray disintegration slowed exponentially. Mathematics favored the dark surfer. Ripzeal rode this wave of advantage to an ethereal state. Ultimately matching the pace of the ray, he caught a beam of light and banked a turn out of harm's way. In a blink, the gateway collision launched the dark surfer out of the material realms and off their ribbons, dropping the daemon and his light beam into the external abyss.

Fellow farmhand Kokli placed a reassuring hand on Gedtor's shoulder as the Urdii and other sharks returned from the hunt. "Time was, it took our brethren, but this time it failed to take the Fourth of Creation. In the future, it will be our prize to take it, the daemon Ripzeal."

One of the Urdii shouted in celebration. "Hail to Gedtor, son of the First, for solving the daemon's gambit!"

—— Chapter 32 ——
The Chambers Challenge

"My feet are killing me," Sissi complained, as she had done for the last half hour of the trip.

Most of her fellow students ignored her.

Finally, five hundred yards from the base of a sheer rock cliff in the Black Forest Mountains, the prefects brought the class to a halt, allowing everyone to rest.

Sissi plopped herself down on the grass and stared absentmindedly at two caterpillar-like land formations fifty yards from their camp. The cave-like tunnels appeared as mounds of grass and boulders, littered with graffiti from years of visitors scratching their names, dates, and sayings into them with chalk, coal, and other stones. The group paused to appreciate the awesome mountain whose unseen peak reached beyond the cloud cover as the midday sun splashed its golden tan across the face of the cave-pocked cliff.

Sissi, still facing the caterpillar mounds, propped her blackened feet up over the skinny trunk of a fallen tree. "My feet are killing me," she repeated.

Once again, she earned no sympathy from the others, including Rasilla, who recoiled with a look of utter disgust at the black dirt and pine tar layering the bottom of Sissi's feet.

Sissi's eyes were drawn to the objects of Rasilla's scorn, and she noticed a few pine needles dangling from the balls of her feet. A torn, dead leaf covered one of her heels.

Rasilla stepped over the fallen tree and passed by Sissi to stand behind her.

As Sissi continued staring at her black toenails and filth-encrusted soles, a plan began to take shape in her mind.

"Be sure to hydrate," one of the chaperones said as the other students dropped their carrying packs and settled in.

Prefect Sparzd took up a position behind the group and facing the caves. "Welcome to the Chambers Challenge, everyone."

Sissi frowned. He was standing in the wrong place, directing the class's attention away from the spectacle of the cliffs.

"You have just completed the three-hour hike," Sparzd announced.

The students shouted back with a mixture of moans and cheers.

"At least until it is time for us to turn around and do the return hike home," the prefect added.

Sissi cocked her head to one side when she heard other students chuckling. Was Prefect Sparzd making an attempt at levity? If so, she thought, this was unlike him. She would have to acquaint herself with this unfamiliar facet of his personality.

"We realize it has been a hot day," Sparzd said, "so we will give you a few extra minutes to rest and refresh yourselves as needed. There is much about to cloud a distracted mind, so please be mindful of your responses to any negative input."

Base camp was littered with students who had broken their earlier formation and were now organizing themselves freely—some in small conversational groups, others not talking at all, and a few who were discussing the day's events with the other prefects and chaperones. Glimmer Trezpin stood silently like a crane, tall and strong and leaning on a long walking stick.

After several minutes, Prefect Sparzd returned to his orating position to prepare the group of hopefuls for the commencement of the sacred trials.

Meanwhile, Sissi's sore feet hadn't stopped troubling her. She sat reclined with her wiry arms hyperextended as if her elbows were on backward. As she arched her back, she tilted her head to look up at Rasilla, who was still standing behind her. Rasilla bore little resemblance to the Shanzi that Sissi had encountered as a little girl. This would be nothing like reading a simpleton human with the aid of a map. Not that she needed a physical map anymore. In her mind's eye, she summoned the perfect, three-dimensional image of the psychetropic spheres. But, manipulating a trained sayzr without her knowing it, posed an entirely different challenge. Rasilla, she informed herself, was going to require extra effort. Rasilla did not seem to notice Sissi staring up at her. Sissi studied the nervous look on Rasilla's face. Then, without taking her eyes off Rasilla, Sissi looked at Rasilla again, and then again.

"You must not allow yourself to be distracted, Rasilla."

Rasilla glanced down at Sissi.

"You have no cause for doubt," Sissi assured her. "All evidence suggests you will succeed in this day's challenge."

"You really think so?" Rasilla clearly liked the sound of what she was hearing.

Sissi proceeded to answer but wasn't just talking. She was moving as well. One movement in particular involved placing all her rear weight on one arm so that, with her free hand, she could run her index and middle fingers through her hair in a circular motion and tuck it behind her ear. This hair-tucking movement, combined with other subtle actions, created a multi-metaphor. Among the many messages it conveyed to Rasilla were "trusted girlfriends," "beauty," "we are special," "you are special," "everyone is/should be paying attention to us," and "our little secret."

"Most definitely," said Sissi. "According to my calculations, you have consistently scored in the highest percentile of the entire school in every course, study, and test."

Rasilla's eyes grew lively and vibrant with every word from Sissi.

"In fact, in comparison to known master sayzrs, you have clearly demonstrated all of the same unique traits," said Sissi, swirling her fingers to re-tuck her hair behind her ear. She waited for Rasilla to fish for more.

"Thank you, Sissi," said Rasilla. "You truly noticed all those things about me? I mean, you really think I have a good chance at succeeding in the challenge?"

"Being gifted as you are, with so many broad and varied skills, it is not a chance—it is a probable certainty. Possessing a high degree of proficiency in all the same fields of concentration known to a master sayzr can't help but result in you becoming a magistra yourself." Sissi was building Rasilla up for the cogency of her argument. "And I have witnessed the evidence of your having such abilities in all the fields of concentration, except for healing."

"Oh, yes—wait. What?" Rasilla's excited expression began to melt.

"Oh, it's probably nothing to be concerned about," said Sissi. "It's not as though you were given much of an opportunity to try." She twirled her hair behind her ear. "I mean, if someone in the village is seriously ill, they go to see a known healer. They will not waste time visiting a school on the off chance they will bump into that one student among many who can help them."

"The shine of stars, Sissi. You make a good point! I'm starting to think they should have given us a chance to practice more on our healing skills."

"I agree with you, Rasilla," said Sissi. "It may not matter so much for a talent like you, of course, but for most other students, it seems only fair." Sissi wet the tip of her pinky finger by feigning a nail-biting action and sliding her tongue just slightly through her teeth to meet the tip of her pinky. She then slid her wet fingertip along her hairline, tucking her hair even tighter behind her ear.

"I suppose you could be right. I only wish I had your faith in me, Sissi," said Rasilla. "But, as you say, I don't have much experience in the healing arts. What makes you so confident that I would make a good healer?"

"Just look at your hands, your elegant fingers," Sissi said, pretending to brush one of her eyebrows straight with her ring finger. "They are long and graceful, yet firm and strong. You have the hands of a healer. But most importantly, you have a healer's spirit."

Sissi captured Rasilla's full attention by discussing how exceptional Rasilla was and what made her perform so exceptionally well. It was exactly the type of conversation Rasilla enjoyed having. Sissi knew Rasilla would invite her to continue.

"A healer's spirit?" Rasilla said as she squatted down on her knees to speak more closely with Sissi. "What makes you think so?"

"You are the most caring, compassionate, and selfless person I know," said Sissi.

"I have always done my best to be that way with all people," said Rasilla, "even the ugly ones. Although not everyone always thinks so. Which is why it is so nice to hear that someone actually noticed."

"Whoever doubts your altruism must be blind," Sissi stated bluntly. "Why, just a few moments ago was the perfect example. I was complaining about my severe aches and pains, and you were the only person to look my way with a genuine look of concern for me."

"Oh yeah, well, of course, for goodness' sake," said Rasilla. "You really mean it? No one else paid you any mind?"

"Not one other person," Sissi confirmed with a tone of self-pity. She further emphasized her point by gently closing her eyes as she spoke. Then, with a look of excitement, she opened her eyes wide and asked in a manner designed to mimic Rasilla's speech patterns, "Can you believe it?"

"I can't believe it!" said Rasilla with nearly the same tone and modulation.

Sissi sat upright and placed her hand around Rasilla's wrist. "Well, the important thing is that we make certain you succeed in today's challenge. Agreed?"

"Yes, of course," said Rasilla. "We should work as a team."

"Good, because the only thing that can stand in your way is the distraction of anxiety and doubt," said Sissi.

"Yes, yes!" Rasilla whispered loudly. She took Sissi's hand between hers. "How do you think we should handle that?"

"It is vital that we remain positive," Sissi said. "To do this, you need to focus on the positive evidence of all your abilities in common with our master sayzrs. Instead of doubting your abilities as a healer, I will allow you to prove it to yourself by pouring all your focus into working on me. Why rely on faith when you can enjoy the power of proof?"

"You would do that for me?" said Rasilla.

"We girlfriends have to stick together," said Sissi, staring affectionately at Rasilla while placing her other palm over Rasilla's such that they were cupping each other's hands. "Besides, you would be helping me out, as well, because my feet are still very sore. Who better to receive healing hands from than the most beautiful and talented woman I know? Particularly a woman I can trust to put everything she has into performing the task better than anyone has ever seen."

"I should get started right away," Rasilla insisted.

Sissi's voice returned to its usual matter-of-fact tone. "Just work on my right foot, Rasilla. That one hurts the most. Master Morris Multhrobe," Sissi called out, without so much as a pause for breath, "what everyone says about the governor's son is true: you and Rasilla have the same healer's hand traits." She lightly smacked her lips, as if having just finished a most satisfying meal.

"I declare that Morris Multhrobe and Rasilla Vandono make the perfect healing couple. Why not join us, Morris? Rasilla would love you to pair up with her in rubbing my tired feet."

Morris was stupefied. Familial mannerisms and politic-speak drew his full attention to Sissi, while any negativity about nearing her sweaty, odiferous feet was washed away by something immensely intoxicating. Never before had Morris heard his name mentioned in the same sentence as Rasilla's. His mind, his desires, his ego were suddenly flooded with this wonderful concoction. And it was not just any combination of favorable meanings, but one that specifically described their pairing as perfect, labeled them a couple, and voiced the phrase, "Rasilla would love you."

A satisfied-looking Sissi gently rubbed her belly as Morris knelt alongside Rasilla and diligently worked his fingers into Sissi's left foot.

"You are doing great, Morris," said Sissi. "If your work ends up complementing Rasilla's, she cannot help but to be impressed with you."

Morris glanced over to compare his results with the foot Rasilla was attending to.

"Careful, Morris," directed Sissi. "There's that pain again. It's too bad you have nothing sharp to shave down some of that hardened skin." She formed a snarl and clenched her jaw at the corner of her mouth.

This led Morris to come up with the creative idea of using his teeth to gnaw at the corns on the bottom of Sissishal's feet.

As prelude to the Chambers Challenge, Prefect Sparzd addressed the class, offering reassuring eye contact with each student to bolster their confidence. ". . . And remember to quiet your minds by remaining restful and open to receiving the Djin of Nature—"

Sparzd stopped his speech abruptly when he noticed an incongruent pattern among the crowd at the same time he was having trouble locating the eyes belonging to a prized student.

An agitated Sparzd stepped down, and the crowd parted in front of him, revealing Sissishal with her back to him.

Rasilla was using her fingernails, now clogged with black filth, to vigorously pick Sissishal's toenails clean.

The master seer felt the blood drain from his face. He did nothing to conceal his horror. "Rasilla! Morris!"

Hearing Sparzd roar at the two using their first names sparked everyone's attention. The students seated on the grass turned and craned their necks in unison. But Rasilla and Morris remained under Sissishal's spell.

Sparzd acted quickly to snatch a wineskin from the nearest student and squirt water into their faces.

Rasilla and Morris were visibly riled by this interference but barely paused in their ministrations to Sissishal.

Sparzd finally stepped over to Rasilla and smacked her across the face.

Rasilla leapt to her feet, bewildered. The same went for Morris.

"Who are you?" Sparzd screamed at Rasilla and Morris. "Are you not Rasilla Vandono? Are you not Morris Multhrobe?" He seized Rasilla's wrist and violently shoved her heavily soiled hand in her face. It was black, her nails were dirty, and a few were broken and split apart. "Was this your choosing? Did you act on your own volition, or did you allow Magistra Haanna to play you? What were—"

Sparzd's words were cut off when he caught a glimpse of someone entering one of the twin caterpillar-like caves. He looked around for confirmation and saw by the grave look on Karmin Porris's face that he'd spotted it, too. The momentous day, normally a time to bray out, seemed to be unraveling.

Rasilla looked down at Sissishal's feet and then back at Sparzd with ever-widening eyes of awareness. "Oh! Oh! Sissi! Oh!" She lashed out at Sissishal.

Sparzd was ready to restrain. He hoisted Rasilla by her waist as she flailed and kicked to get at Sissishal.

After handing Rasilla over to Karmin, Sparzd turned to Morris.

Morris's cheeks burned blood-red. All had witnessed that undignified image of Morris. Streaks of Sissishal's filth ran across his lips and down his chin. He shook with rage as he spat out pieces of dead skin from between his teeth.

Sparzd held Morris at bay and then instructed two of the other chaperones to accompany the boy into the woods, where he would be allowed to cool off while under guard.

Next, Sparzd conferred with the remaining prefects. But before doing so, he had tucked his trembling hands into his robes so as not to spread the contagion of fear to others, and to allow himself time to gain control of his wits. Had anyone else caught a glimpse of someone entering the sacred chambers of enlightenment? The others shook their heads no. It appeared that only Sparzd and Karmin had seen anything. Sparzd hoped that by directing the prefects' energies to matters other than Sissishal, it would help to deescalate their reactions. It proved to be an effective technique, even on himself.

Sparzd took a moment to gather himself. All that remained was to calm the students so they could focus on the matter at hand. He held up his arms to address them. "I ask you all to settle down and remember the grave importance of the Chambers Challenge. What was done just now is over. I also remind each of you of your pledge not to use magic on a fellow student without their consent. We will resume shortly with the challenge, but first, I ask you to please speak up if you noticed anyone leaving the group or entering the caves."

The students looked around at one another but found no one missing.

When the chambers themselves were investigated, Sparzd and the others found no one inside. Either he was seeing figments, he concluded, or whoever had entered the caves had transdimensioned.

CHAPTER 33

INCARNATES OF EVIL

A storm of the dark surfer's degospores entered the atmosphere, causing a green pollen cloud to rain down upon an unsuspecting town. Stalled horses shifted and pounded their hooves with nervous complaint. Hungry bovines and billies bemoaned the blackweed where daemon seed soaked the soil.

At one of the town wells, a schoolteacher's expression took on a bewildered state as the green cloud settled around her. She released the pail of water she was fetching for her class, and the rope whipped wildly around its spool as the bucket of water plummeted back into the blackness of the well with an unseen splash.

In the cemetery, a widow visiting her husband's grave was busy tidying up his resting place and dusting off his tombstone. She removed a black ribbon from her hair and gently placed it before the grave mark. From a basket of dried, cut flowers, she removed a rusty spoon and, kneeling before the tombstone, scooped a shallow pit in the dirt in which to plant the flowers. She held a crumbling divot at the ready to fill in the hollow as soon as she centered the flowers in place. When the end of the stems struck the sandy soil at the bottom of the shallow pit, it caused the sides to slowly erode, and she paused to watch it partially refill itself. Though the miniature landslide seemed to be caving in, the hole was widening, not shrinking.

The widow postured her neck at the curious soil trickling down the ever-widening funnel of a sink hole. To save the dried flowers from being engulfed in the deepening hole, the puzzled widow reached for them with a quick hand and gripped their gathered stems just in time for her own hand to be gripped and pulled into the dark hollows . . .

The miller's apprentice cut himself off in mid-question and dropped a heavy sack of grain. The sack split open when it hit the floor and coughed up a plume of corn dust. He was shocked by the horror of the miller, who was staring directly back at him, seemingly indifferent to his arm being chewed up by the crushing wheel and his blood splattering in every direction under the compression of the heavy stone.

Wearing the same brown dress she always wore, one crudely tailored from burlap sacks, Mary Walton, eight years old and the youngest in the family, sat alone. An often forgotten presence in the Walton household, Mary sat in a dark corner beneath the open steps to the children's loft with her crutches resting against her cot, watching. She watched as her family enjoyed their dinner. Annie and Gabriel fought constantly and never listened to Mommy, but Mary, unseen, would quietly listen and remember. She had to in order to teach herself about the world. She watched how Mommy prepared food, listened to adults speak of things and give advice to others, and pored over any old school papers she could get her hands on from her older siblings.

She lifted a lame leg from the cot and placed it onto the floor in order to face the table directly. There was an empty place setting for one more, but that was Daddy's seat. Daddy was so late for dinner this evening that he had missed the prayer of thanks. It was not like Daddy to ever miss the prayer of thanks, but the sun was setting, so Mommy had been forced to proceed without Daddy and without the prayer bread he brought back from the market every Thursday evening.

Mary's older siblings, Annie and Gabriel, pestered each other impatiently as Mommy filled their plates with mash. They always made a fuss while waiting.

Mary, on the other hand, was used to waiting. There was no room at the table for her, and because she was the youngest and needed too much assistance, she waited like the dogs to be fed from the table leftovers.

Despite being younger than Annie, Gabriel was a firstborn son, which meant he was first and favored in all things, even ahead of Mommy. Clearly aware of his position in the family, he abused it whenever he got the chance.

Mommy smacked Gabriel's hand as he reached for the carrot stew. "Wait your turn!" she admonished him for the thousandth time.

Annie shot Gabriel an exaggerated smile for getting caught by Mommy.

Mommy speared a turnip onto Gabriel's plate just as Daddy walked through the door with an awkward gate, a contorted expression, and eyes staring up at the ceiling.

Gabriel laughed heartily.

Daddy did a silly walk up to the table. He also made a funny face. His face and hands were dirty, and he had a patch of sod hanging from the side of his mouth.

Annie's face soured when Mommy skipped over her to spear a turnip onto Daddy's plate.

Mommy gave Daddy a strange look. "What are you playing at?" she asked. "And why don't you have the prayer bread with you?"

Daddy didn't answer her. Instead, he reached for her arm and placed his hand around Mommy's wrist.

Mommy sat upright as if something had suddenly caught her attention. Then, overshooting the bowl of turnips, she speared Annie's arm with the serving fork.

Annie stood up, wide-eyed and screaming.

With the handle of the fork in hand, Mommy pulled Annie's arm closer to her and then leaned over and bit into Annie's fingers. Annie's bones made a funny noise as they crunched between Mommy's teeth.

Gabriel sat with his mouth agape.

Annie stopped screaming and stared at her brother with an eerie grin as

Mommy continued chewing off her fingers. When Mommy paused to finish the pieces of Annie that were in her mouth, Annie lunged across the table and pounced on Gabriel, sinking her teeth into his face.

Mary placed her hands over her ears and closed her eyes as tightly as she could, but when she reopened them, the dogs were barking outside and her family members were still doing monstrous things to each other.

Annie turned toward Mary and held her in her gaze. She was first to advance toward Mary, with Mommy following close behind.

Mary's cot was already up against the back wall, and she had nowhere else to go, so she rolled onto the floor and crawled underneath the cot, reeling her legs in behind her. She instinctively cried for help, as if Mommy would stop being the monster. "No, Mommy!"

It was a simple matter for the Annie and Mommy things to upset the cot and get their hands on Mary, but the dogs had gotten in the house and were tugging successfully at the garments of the Annie and Mommy creatures.

Mary shuddered, having never heard her dogs growl so viciously. With a wooden crutch in each hand, she seized the opportunity to crawl under the dinner table and then managed to sneak out the front door amidst the chaos.

Mary made her way through neighborhood shadows and the cover of night to avoid various clusters of humanoids she discovered walking around in a seemingly unbalanced manner, not unlike herself. Her heart hammered like an angry fist against her chest wall, causing soreness with every beat. She ducked behind a wheeled cart and squeezed her eyes shut in a failed attempt to stop the tears and the terrors. She didn't understand what had just happened to her family, but she desperately hoped to find her uncle, the Reverend Walton, to help fix everybody.

The home of a family friend was just ahead of her. It looked peaceful enough to suggest the adults inside might still be normal. Maybe they could help her find her uncle. The reverend would know what to do.

Mary summoned all her strength to stop herself from crying so that she could move about in the moonlight without attracting too much attention. Using the back of the cart for extra leverage, she pulled herself up and placed all her weight over her crutches so that she could slide her legs in below until she was balanced over her feet. With her crying somewhat contained, she unsteadily traveled down the side of the cart in the direction of the house.

An unseen cat prowling around the wheel of the cart screeched when struck by Mary's stray crutch and bolted away into the darkness.

Mary fell hard when her feet and the feet of her crutches caught on something sizable, like a heavy sack, which sent her scooting across the dirt and separated her from her crutches. The abrupt impact with the ground hurt. Mary's arms were scraped up, and her flushed face was bleeding. Falling was a sore point with Mary, and for as long as she had been given crutches to allow her to move on her own, she had been especially hard on herself, no matter that anyone with normal legs could trip on an unseen obstruction in the night.

Mary shakily searched the ground, feeling in the blind for her crutches. The second crutch eluded her until the moon dimly peaked between drifting clouds. In the dark, Mary was able to see the shiny outlines of the annoying, foiling obstruction that had tripped her.

The mound moved. It lunged at her with all determination. It was a creature, like her parents, that had gotten pinned beneath the wheel of a heavy cart.

Mary fell back and dropped the crutch. Her shriek tore the night.

The creature swatted at Mary with its arm but missed. It then reached for Mary's crutch to reel her in.

Mary wiggled backward in a panic, dragging the crutch under the weight of her legs. The creature missed when Mary bent at the waist and shifted the crutch to the side. The crutch slipped away from her legs, allowing the creature to go after it again. Mary's arms were too short to reach for the crutch, and she was farther away from it than the creature.

The creature landed its hand only slightly out of reach. In a fit, it stretched its limbs outward. Its fingers dug into the dirt like a team of draft horses marching up to one side of the crutch and well within reach. With a simple pivot of the wrist, the creature's fingers pounced at Mary's crutch but drew back only soil. Mary had managed to pull the crutch away in the last instant, using her other crutch as a reaching hook. She scrambled frantically on all fours to the house and crawled beneath its covered porch. From her new hiding place, Mary tried desperately to suppress the sounds of her crying. She pulled her legs in and hugged her knees to her chest as she began praying for help—for divine intervention and for her uncle, the Reverend Walton, to come find her, to make everything all right.

Mary was scared for herself, for her family, and for the people of her town. Weighing upon her thoughts was Molly, her rag doll and only friend in the world. She had left Molly behind in her hasty escape. She thought about how scared Molly must be and hoped Molly was still safe from the monsters. Molly was a good hider, but even if she was safe, Mary knew that Molly must be missing her mama. Molly needed Mary, and Mary found strength in that.

Mary stared into the blackness of the night for answers. It was cold. The air temperature hadn't changed, and droplets of sweat bejeweled her ruddy cheeks. Yet somehow, in her bones, she felt a coldness that couldn't be burnt out. The town itself also seemed cold and oddly foreign to Mary. The midnight demeanor of once-familiar neighborhood homes took on a menacing look. Normally graceful, the trees in her town appeared twisted and knotty. Nothing was the same. Nothing could be trusted.

Light from the hilltop schoolhouse beckoned just a few blocks into the distance like a beacon. Being too young and feeble to attend community school, Mary did her learning on her own, but she knew about the school and knew it was normally empty at night. Despite being relegated to the corner of her home and isolated from life in general, Mary insatiably took in all she could of the world. Her thoughts turned to her brother and sister returning home earlier today with tales about how their teacher had run away, never to come back. It had earned them each a smacking. "Normal people don't just run away," their mother had told them.

But Mary was on the run. Mary wondered if the schoolteacher might also be running. Maybe the teacher, or other people, had locked themselves inside the school, just like Mary was hiding under the porch. If she was lucky, she might find normal grown-ups there. A normal grown-up could help her find the reverend, save her family, and rescue Molly.

The stroke of midnight began the emergency mass on that Holy Thursday in the dank basement of the church, their hidden retreat from an infected town. Doused shadows danced in the candlelight that illuminated the faces of the devoted. The Congregation of Thor's Light sat in attendance and listened as their preacher's sermon took an uncharacteristic turn.

"Death!" the preacher cried out. "Death! Death to all who oppose the

Great One! Intelligence is the perversion of dispersal. Ease your pain and your struggles. Allow your inner turmoil to fade away. Free your mind of annoying choices. We must prepare for the Glorious Thursday by returning to the fold and reunifying ourselves with the Great One. Join me, and together we can resist the perversions of dispersal and combine our bodies and souls to be accepted back into the fold of the singularity from whence we came."

The choir leader dropped a silver tray of sacraments she was carrying from the chancel when she noticed the pale, exposed brain protruding from the back of the preacher's head.

The preacher turned, calmly raised his decorative trident, and ran it through her neck. He returned to face his congregation. "Rest and peace await us all within the folds of the singularity. We must cry out to let the Great One hear our devotion. Please, oh Lord, grant us passage to the One. Accept our pledge to the singularity."

The congregation spoke in turn. "Please, oh Lord, grant us passage to the One. Accept our pledge to the singularity."

The preacher walked around the room with his trident stick in hand, rewarding only the most earnest devotees. "Return us to the One. I pray the Lord my soul to take."

"Return us to the One," the congregants repeated in unison. "I pray the Lord my soul to take."

After selecting a congregant leaning back in her chair with eyes shut tight and fingers pale with clenching, the preacher buried his trident stick into her throat and laid her to rest upon her own pool of blood. "By the grace of the Great One, you are released from the shackles of life."

Mary squeezed her eyes against the tears running down her cheeks. Her fear of leaving her resting place beneath the porch wrestled with her fear of the corpse, still pinned under a wagon wheel and not more than fifty yards away. Mary scanned in the direction of the corpse and found it in the moonlight. She quietly licked at a stinging wound on her wrist. Her face was flushed, but her spine shivered. When the corpse moved, so did Mary.

Set apart from the nearest buildings, the community school forced Mary to venture out into the open. Aided and betrayed by the night, she struggled not to trip in its darkness or to be detected in its moonlight. Where the hill steepened, she fell to her hands and knees and crawled. The bitter aroma of grass crushed by her stained knees underscored the bitterness of crawling. The crawling position was a humiliating reminder of her inadequacies. But tonight was different, and she understood that concealing her presence by crawling might just save her life.

The schoolyard began at the back of an outhouse about forty yards from the school. The ground was level enough for her to be upright again, but with the outhouse as her only cover, Mary cautiously peeked around it for a look at the school and continued to stay low.

An orange cat weaved in and out of a run of pickets fencing off the crawl space below the school. Mary took it as a good sign that the cat seemed unafraid to hang around the schoolyard.

Lulled by the inviting dance of the winding feline, Mary approached the warmly lit school. She lowered herself to her knees, once more, to climb the stairs on all fours. A creaking door and squeaking floor announced her presence despite her floor-level entry.

The room was dark, but she could just make out the teacher's desk, dimly lit by the lantern hanging on a wall hook by the front window. After reaching one of the student desks nearest the door, she righted herself over her crutches and stood in attendance in the empty classroom.

"Ms. Beadle?"

Mary listened to her timid voice echo off the walls. The lanterns surely made it seem as though someone should be here—or at least that someone had once been here, possibly using the school as their hiding place. Whatever the case, it was Mary's hiding place now. Mary pressed her weight against a project table lined against the front wall and moved it, inches at a time, to block the front door. As soon as the barricade was fully in place, the light in the room flickered. It was only for a moment, but it cast a brief shroud of darkness around Mary before it was gone again.

Mary looked around the room, this time counting each lantern that hung on the walls. There were three, including one on each of the front and rear walls. At the head of the classroom, to the left of the slate board, a third lantern hung nearest the corner formed by the closet. The true corner had been boxed in by a supply room build-out, but just outside the leftward-swinging door to the supply room hung the lantern. The supply room door was ajar, enough that it blocked a portion of the lantern. Mary stood frozen, unable to recall if the supply room door was closed when she first entered.

"Ms. Beadle?" she asked, her voice echoing. "Is anybody there . . . there . . . there?"

Mary heard a faint scraping noise, like the scuffling of shoes. She watched, with a fright, the orange line of light disappear along the door hinge, from her sight.

"I see you," Mary said as she started toward the supply room. "It's okay. I'm not a monster. I'm still me."

Again from the supply room came the scuffling sound of shoes. The dark space between the door hinge was soon replaced with the lantern's orange. Whoever had peeked from behind the door, blocking the light from shining through, withdrew and retreated to the inner sanctum of the closet room. The unassuming figure displayed disinterest, and Mary took comfort in its acting afraid of what Mary might be. Its behavior gave Mary the strength to approach the half-open door.

"Teacher? Is that you?"

Mary could hear herself breathing, but no one else. She stood before the closet, certain that someone or something was inside. It had to be someone hiding in the darkness, just behind that door, afraid to make a noise.

With the loose door already ajar, Mary knocked it fully open with a wooden crutch, allowing the lantern light to flood the closet around her.

Ms. Beadle's back was turned. A white bonnet with blue polka dots and a matching blue dress came into view as Mary entered the closet.

"Ms. Beadle!"

The orange cat appeared on the scene and stroked its body against the edge of the door, causing it to swing shut behind Mary—sealing her into the darkness.

CHAPTER 34

BY THE NUMBERS

The cardinal rubbed his temples as he read the delivered papers. He didn't feel particularly comfortable with the developing direction of recent reports, and he had a hunch he wasn't the only one in his office who felt that way. When he was finished, he handed the report back to the magistrate, who stood alongside a scribe on the other side of the cardinal's desk.

"As his majesty's trusted advisor," the cardinal said, "I can do little more than report the truth about what we are seeing here."

"Forgive me, Cardinal," said the magistrate. "I know of no other way, unless . . ." He held the scribe in his gaze. "What does the general have to say about all this?"

"The general, I am certain, would remind you all, as well as the king, of his grand victories," the scribe said.

"Yes," agreed the cardinal. "And while he fixates on his greatest victories and greatest battles, which have resulted in his greatest individual losses while securing and expanding our territories to the west, he overlooks the smaller but persistent losses holding off the unholy monsters that infest our eastern borders along the Brakkens."

"It is no secret I have been a longtime supporter of General Zog," said the magistrate. "But I also agree that we can no longer afford to ignore the simple math that shows we are bleeding out more men, money, and resources from perpetually holding off those ungodly creatures descending from the Brakken Mountains. There seems to be no end to their numbers."

"So," the scribe said, "even though winning these little skirmishes has never been a problem for our soldiers, we are ultimately losing this unholy war through the slow drain of our own successes?"

"That is precisely what we are saying," confirmed the cardinal. "The proof is in your own reports. And we have the dwindling exchequer to show for it."

"And I guess the dwindling territories to the south," the scribe said humbly.

The cardinal nodded his acknowledgement. "Yes, two other regional kingdoms vie for control of those territories now. Between holding the borders to the east and expanding them to the west, the Ptolamarch Empire has spread itself too thin to even present a show of force on our existing southern border."

"I now receive complaints daily from my counterparts in the southern Ptolemarchy that Zog has committed no troop support to secure their kingdoms," said the magistrate.

"Then Lord Dayworth's plea is true?" asked the scribe. "Our southern kingdoms are vulnerable, and we could lose them to an invasion at any moment?"

The cardinal exchanged glances with the magistrate and then turned to the scribe. "You must not repeat any of this to anyone."

"Of course," the scribe said with a bow. "What do you suppose is stopping them?" he asked nervously. "Why haven't our enemies to the south already sacked those kingdoms of the Ptolemarchy?"

The cardinal met the magistrate's gaze once more.

"We cannot be certain," answered the magistrate. "Presently, they are immersed in fighting with each other over the territories they have already taken from us. But it's only a temporary distraction. Once they have resolved their differences through war or treaty, they may turn their attention once again to our borders—and perhaps even join forces to share in the conquest of the Ptolemarchy and its spoils." The magistrate painted a grim picture.

"True as that may be, there are other factors securing our borders," offered the cardinal. "One must never underestimate the power of perception. The sheer size and historical dominance of the Ptolemarchy Empire makes for a powerful deterrent to any would-be conqueror." He gathered the scrolls and his logbook in preparation for his meeting with the crown. "If pushed, we could always redirect our armies and resources to the south, which is something they certainly have to consider and would prefer to avoid."

"So that's it, then," concluded the magistrate. "We might do something grand to demonstrate our superiority."

The cardinal paused. He liked the sound of that and raised an eyebrow to communicate as much. "It might be worthy of suggestion to his lordship to invest in bravado over brawn." He tapped a finger thoughtfully against his chin. "We do have the Olympic ceremonies coming up. Perhaps this season we could put on an even bigger show. One part razzle and two parts dazzle!"

CHAPTER 35

ENIGMA

Floating among the swirling fog was like being lost in a dream. He listened . . . and waited. The Djin introduced him. One or all? Corporeal or incorporeal? The surreal surroundings registered in him that the air was thin. The atmosphere felt humid and cold. He was flesh. He was on foot.

Fortunate to make it back at all, T'Ralo reappeared above the cloud line at the peak of the mountain by the outpost. He recognized the observatory through the clouds well enough to know what it was, though few villagers ever actually visited the inhospitable location of the outpost.

A hundred yards away perched an enormously long, green tent protruding from the mouth of a cave. Three people sat outside at a table, never looking up from the large diagram they were studying.

T'Ralo decided to check inside the tent to see if there was anyone who might help him find his way safely back to the class.

Heat blew in his face as he passed through a rolled-up entrance in the side of the tent. A shroud of turbidity cloaked the interior. At first glimpse, it appeared as though a thick fog cloud had seeped inside and remained trapped by the tent. The burning smell of a smithy filled his nostrils, and in the distance, the low clanking of a forge could be heard. But as the pattern of the shroud came into focus, T'Ralo realized the tent was choked full with active spiderwebs.

Below the scaffolding that reached to the ceiling were rows of long workbenches lined with workers dutifully rolling something wispy and transparent. Men with staves raised the giant webs into the air by their centers, allowing them to collapse evenly around the wooden poles before whisking them onto the workbench in alternating directions. They set these gatherings on a prior layer of webs laid out in a circular spread slightly juxtaposed at intervals. To ensure a pure roll, not a single web was stretched or allowed to be torn from its original structure.

With everyone too engrossed in their task to notice T'Ralo, he developed a creepy feeling that he was somehow present but not physically present. His earthly senses told him otherwise. It was a dream, perhaps.

He walked toward the back of the tent to the cave and continued following the sounds of a blacksmith's hammer. It was here that T'Ralo could definitively see spiderwebbing being infused into iron links. Like laundry drying high on a line, the carefully rolled webbing was transformed into silvery strands by a vaporizing process that allowed tiny droplets of steam to carry the slightest traces of liquid metal to coat the strands like morning dew. Smithies overseeing this slow, intricate operation seemed unaffected by T'Ralo's presence.

"Who are you?" someone behind him asked in a peculiar voice.

T'Ralo turned to face a red-bearded gnome wearing black goggles above his wide eyes.

The gnome dropped his notebook and produced a cudgel with a green glowing head. This caught the attention of the smithies as well.

"Sorry, Salmsalm," one of the startled smithies said to the gnome. "We didn't even notice him."

"How did you get in here?!" Salmsalm squawked at T'Ralo, in his low, gritty voice.

"I was trying to find my way back to class," answered a nervous T'Ralo. Apparently it was no dream, and at least someone here believed he was physically present.

The gnome tilted his head to one side. "Class? What class?" He pointed the cudgel in T'Ralo's face. "How did you find this place?"

"My name is T'Ralo. I'm from the academy. I was at the Chambers Challenge. I entered the caves and went . . . somewhere . . . then ended up here."

Salmsalm reached into his pocket with his other hand and pulled out a leather strap decorated with an inset of stones on one end. The two outer stones glowed light blue. The one in the middle turned from yellow to green to light blue. The uniform triplet of light blue stones seemed to satisfy the gnome, though the concern on his face remained.

"You had best come with me," said Salmsalm as he pocketed the leather strap.

Inside the observatory, a young-looking supervisor by the name of Kirshaw sat T'Ralo and Salmsalm down at his office desk to understand the situation. "With all the measures taken to conceal this place, you cannot even see the observatory from the sky."

"But everyone in the village knows about this outpost," T'Ralo said. "Why bother trying to conceal it?"

By this time, Prefect Frendle had tracked them down and was shown into the office by one of the astronomers.

Kirshaw exchanged greetings with Frendle and the astronomer. "Master Frendle," he said, dipping his head in respect to the prefect. "I see you've met Vincid, one of our youngest and most promising stargazers. I was just about to explain to our unexpected visitor the sensitivity of what he has just learned about our operations here."

"How much has he seen?" asked Frendle.

"Everything, I'm afraid," said Kirshaw.

"I found him in the drying room." Salmsalm's voice rattled.

Kirshaw turned to T'Ralo. "How we elves craft together the finest armor in all the lands is a process so coveted that we protect its secrets, even from our own kind, to ensure that its preservation remains a secret. Elven chain is as much a part of our proud history and culture as the sacred chambers and the knowledge of our sayzrs—and a mite bit older at that."

"I suppose if anyone is going to find a way through the magic that secretes this place, it might as well be a master sayzr," said Vincid, the young astronomer. "It is his birthright to know. Eventually, we'd be informing him about it anyway, would we not?"

"You gave us quite a fright," said Kirshaw, "but now it is our great honor to be in the presence of our newest generation of master sayzrs."

A pained expression washed over Prefect Frendle. "Yes," he said and hesitated. "About that . . . We are not entirely certain this one is quite worthy of that designation."

Kirshaw looked confused. "But I thought—"

"As you have witnessed thus far, we are experiencing some highly unique happenstances." The prefect held up his hand. "A moment, if you please?" He turned to address T'Ralo. "T'Ralo, may I ask what you were doing inside of the tent?"

So many people were suddenly interested in T'Ralo, and all at once, that he knew it had to mean trouble for him. He wanted to keep what he had discovered inside the caves to himself, but if Frendle decided to read him, his knowledge would be revealed. Then again, this was all part of the Chambers Challenge, which was like a game. He couldn't be in trouble for something that had happened as part of a game, could he?

He offered a sheepish smile. "I was looking for help to get back to the rest of the class."

"Why not just travel back to the chambers the same way you departed?" asked Frendle.

"I wasn't sure how."

Frendle smiled and patted T'Ralo reassuringly on the shoulder. "Make no mistake about it. T'Ralo here is a remarkable student in his own right. He has shown us some amazing things these last few months. But a master of the ability to transdimension he is not. And T'Ralo, you must never attempt to transdimension on your own, for without mastery supervision, you could be destroyed or lost forever."

Kirshaw stood from his desk. "I, too, must admonish you to pay heed not to speak of anything you have seen here of the making of elven chain mail. It is more than the privileged knowledge of every master sayzr. Our operations here are the communal birthright of every elve, represented in the shared knowledge of a few select villagers. We shall now count you among those few. Perhaps your destiny lies in a lifetime of service with us." He returned to his seat. "I can see you have questions."

T'Ralo, after waiting for Frendle to nod his approval, began with a simple question. "If this is an ancient elven secret, then why is *he* here?" he asked, pointing at the gnome.

"That is a long story," Kirshaw answered. "But Salmsalm has made great sacrifices to preserve our people and our way of life. He has more than earned this honorable exception, which is, at the same time, a great burden, for he has pledged his lifelong commitment in service of our cause."

"May I ask how you get water droplets to carry melted metal?" T'Ralo asked.

"Who, more than a graduate of the academy," answered Kirshaw, "can appreciate how reducing the particle size of a substance down to the next verse can yield drastically different physical properties for that same substance than from what we are accustomed to seeing relative to our own verse?"

"You are lowering the melting temperature so that it can bind to the webs on a micro-particle level," said T'Ralo.

"And so that it does not scorch the web," Kirshaw said with a nod.

"Like most magic," Frendle added, "it loses its luster once you know how the trick is performed. We have seen instances where others have tried to mimic elven chain mail, and some researchers and craftsmen have even come close. But absent the intricate details and time required to complete the process, what they have ended up with, at best, has been an inferior copy that underperforms—and with fatal results."

"The rolling process alone is a secret art form that no one has ever discovered," said the astronomer.

"Preserving maximum web strength during rolling is a painstaking endeavor for our harvesters," added Kirshaw.

"Can you teach it to me?" T'Ralo asked.

"This one has an inquisitive spirit," said Salmsalm. "That is a good thing. But until you have fully pledged your services to what we do here at the outpost, let us consider your knowledge of our harvest and drying rooms to be well enough for the time being."

"Would you like a tour of the observatory?" asked the young astronomer. "I mean, seeing as how you are already here." He turned to Kirshaw. "He's come this far. Would it not be a shame for him to miss out on this rarest of opportunities?"

Kirshaw smiled and turned to T'Ralo. "Allow me to properly introduce you to our resident genius astronomer Vincid. He is leading us in a number of momentous breakthroughs, the full breadth of which we may not yet know for hundreds of years to come."

T'Ralo looked to his prefect for permission.

"You have thirty minutes," said Prefect Frendle.

— CHAPTER 36 —
LIGHT OF TRUTH

The tour couldn't last long enough to satiate T'Ralo's fascination with the projects going on at the outpost.

Up a curved flight of stairs that traced the arc of the dome to the second story of the observatory, Vincid stood behind the enormous telescope, holding a prism up to the light. "I guess I don't fully understand it," he said, projecting a rainbow onto the wall. A storage shelf next to his workbench displayed prisms, lenses, colored liquids, thermometers, and a host of other measuring instruments.

T'Ralo tilted his head back, enthralled by the encapsulating dome, and wandered over to the natural light beaming through a narrow opening in the observation curtain.

Vincid pulled down on a lever, and a hissing noise began to seep through lines of piping along the floors and walls. "But whether you're a master sayzr or not, you did something that obviously came close. And now, with your knowledge of the things we do out here, it would be a natural choice for you to join us at the outpost."

T'Ralo didn't know what to say. He was unaccustomed to being fussed over. He appreciated how Vincid was immediately accepting of him and that he held him in apparent high regard. His mind spun from everything he'd seen thus far.

Vincid next showed him their recent discovery of a planet whose surface was made entirely of water. Pressurized steam whistled from copper pipes, and gears turned as the observatory doors spread open and the entire room rotated into position.

Vincid pulled another lever and adjusted the enormous telescope for T'Ralo to see. "This water-world acts like a mirror, reflecting light waves back into space. If we could isolate the wave patterns—in particular, those pertaining to our planet—and descramble them back into a sensible code, we should be able to review the past. It would be like traveling back in time. Just imagine witnessing an important event in history from thousands of years ago and being able to compare what was retold to what really happened."

"I've learned about so much in just this single visit," T'Ralo replied, "that I'm not even sure where to begin to comment on what you've just shared with me. Such a historical achievement would certainly advance the way of the sayzr. But possessing such knowledge has to be dangerous. Not all people would appreciate the light of truth. Are you not concerned about inviting trouble if word of this discovery spreads?"

Vincid's face lit up. "Hey, I like that. 'The light of truth.' I can't wait to share that with my fellow hydro-punks. You see, you really do belong here. Come now. Why not join us?"

T'Ralo removed a copper hand telescope from the shelf and played around with it. "I don't know. Maybe you're right. I mean, this entire place amazes me." He extended the telescope and stared out the opening in the dome into outer space. "Just watching you work open those doors was like nothing I've ever seen." He looked up from the telescope and glanced around the room, taking in all the copper pipes, fittings, gears, and levers. "Who made all this stuff?"

"Everyone at the outpost is a bit of a hydro-punk," Vincid answered. "We build all sorts of machines powered by water. Anything you can power from hydrogen and oxygen has got to be righteously harmonious, right? If you join us, you, too, could take part in helping to build machines like this."

"I don't know if I'd be much help. It looks complicated."

"All we're doing is speeding up the particles on a microverse level. We let Nature do most of the work for us. Like you said earlier, the properties of any object are related to its verse relevance to any other object."

I said that? T'Ralo didn't remember sounding so smart, but he wasn't about to correct Vincid on that point. "How did you come to find a planet made of water?"

Vincid stood to formally present his explanation. It was then that T'Ralo realized with something of a shock that Vincid still thought of him as some type of great wizard and, apparently, believed T'Ralo might be testing him.

"We may not all be sayzrs," said Vincid. "But we certainly know how to use a sayzr's teachings. We simply follow the patterns that are presented to us and read Nature's code. That's practically the sayzr credo, is it not?"

T'Ralo thought it incredible to have someone like Vincid actually trying to impress *him*.

Vincid pointed to the rainbow projected on the wall. "Anyway, looking closely at this rainbow, in between the spectrum of colors are those black lines of code that reflect the energy patterns of specific elements."

"Yes, the uniform particle code. They teach particle code at the academy so students can learn to read certain spells and, ideally, weave their own patterns into the fabric of the Djin. According to the prefects who ran our UPC class, with the right code or recipe, a spell-caster should be able to conjure any object. So you searched the skies for a pattern of light that was predominantly encoded with the energy signatures for water?"

"Hydrogen and oxygen," acknowledged Vincid. "And we found it—the water-world."

"I guess what I meant to ask you was what made you go looking for such a planet in the first place? I would think a search like that could take a lifetime to complete."

"It was just a notion I had: to try to see something of Earth reflecting back off an object in space. Given the way of the sayzr, to 'interfere' as little as possible, a great body of water was just one of a handful of ideas floated amongst us in an effort to devise a solution on our own." He handed the glass prism to T'Ralo, walked back to the center of the room, and leaned against the enormous telescope. "I suppose they don't want to tread upon that whole 'necessity is the mother of invention' business, but even in general, there seems to be a strong reluctance among sayzrs to demonstrate their magic abilities."

"You're telling me. After twenty years at the academy, the closest thing I've ever seen to anything truly magical happened today, when I somehow ended up here. When it comes to chambers magic, it seems the prefects expect us to take everything on faith."

"But sometimes they will help with more than just words of insight."

Vincid smacked his hand against the side of the enormous telescope. "And with the help of our master sayzrs, this device allows us to process spectral information quickly. It's more than just a large telescope. With this remarkable tool at our disposal—and a little luck—I was able to find what I was looking for in just a few hundred days."

"What if instead of water we discovered a planet made of something even more reflective, such as mercury?" T'Ralo asked.

"That might considerably advance efforts to descramble returning waves of light into a clear picture of the original event," Vincid answered and then smiled.

T'Ralo wasn't certain whether Vincid was looking for approval or just flattering him.

"If such a planet is out there where we can discover it," the young astronomer continued, "perhaps we should dedicate some time to searching for high concentrations of the signature pattern for mercury. Bear in mind, of course, that it's mostly atmospheric interference we have to undo."

No, T'Ralo decided. *He's just trying to flatter me to get me to join them. At least he likes me and values my input. Here is someone who believes in me, even if that belief is misplaced.*

"It is time," said Prefect Frendle as he stood in the doorway.

It was difficult for T'Ralo to say goodbye to his new friend, but once again, someone from his village was setting restrictions upon him and controlling his life.

Just as they were a few steps out the door, Vincid ran to catch up to them. "Here." Vincid handed T'Ralo the copper telescope he had been playing with earlier. "Until you formally decide to return to the outpost and make your life here with us. Keep looking up."

T'Ralo nodded to Vincid with deep appreciation.

Outside the observatory, Frendle took T'Ralo's hand, and they departed. As they walked alone, Frendle complimented him on his pointed questions to Kirshaw about the hidden forge.

Something deep inside T'Ralo told him that Frendle's comment, though sincere, was somehow reserved. It was as if he was holding back and being careful not to say too many nice things about him. The thought was barely an impulse, and T'Ralo didn't know what to do with it, so he buried it from whence it came and forgot about it.

As he pondered the thick fog overhead, T'Ralo thought back to a few minutes earlier, when he'd had a clear view of outer space through the handheld telescope. Between the assistance of sayzrs and the cleverness of people like Vincid, the seemingly insurmountable task of descrambling light waves from outer space seemed a realistic goal, well within their reach.

CHAPTER 37

AFTERMATH

The heavy door vents were closed, sealing off the conference room from the observation deck. Headmaster Ghostas had conjured a scrying pool through which the council of sayzrs observed the Chambers Challenge unfold. From their remote location, the audience of sayzrs drawn to this historic event surreptitiously reveled in the spectacle of how this peculiar graduating class had resolved itself at the Challenge—in a manner unforeseen.

Having arrived at the post-Challenge gathering later than usual, Prefect Frendle stood to address the members of the Sayzr Order who served on the counsel of sayzrs with the summary report on the Chambers Challenge.

"It was a uniquely rough and altogether miraculous passage for two remarkable students who, undistracted by Sissishal Haanna's disturbance, disappeared inside the chambers of enlightenment having transdimensioned. One was the naturally gifted Glimmer Trezpin who, by transdimensioning, established himself the master sayzr of his class."

This was not news, as they had all witnessed the same event. What was to come next, however, concerned matters of unique interest to the sayzr council and would have implications for the entire Sayzr Order.

"In a peculiar twist of fate," began Frendle, "the mystery person who entered the chambers of enlightenment turned out to be T'Ralo—the first nonmaster in known history to accomplish a transdimensional journey."

Frendle offered no further explanation about this phenomenon, nor did the sayzrs require one. It was a common characteristic of Nature underpinning the teachings at Sayzr Academy that the right combination of events, throughout eternity, can ultimately lead to success. Proof of random design is everywhere, but because much of the observable world reveals only Nature's "successes," it required an insightful observer to see it true. Unsustainable species may go extinct before they are ever discovered, and imbalanced stars collapse without leaving their mark among the observable constellations. Never before had this phenomenon been known to generate transdimensioning by indeliberateness, and this topic warranted the council's deliberation.

"Where Master Trezpin can employ his skills at will," continued Frendle, "T'Ralo's accidental success lacked the understanding needed to be reliably duplicated."

"He was fortunate to have returned at all," offered Headmaster Ghostas.

Frendle nodded in agreement. "His unexpected trip was so haphazard that he never quite made it back to the caves."

The discussion turned to how Sparzd and the other prefects could have had such a blind spot surrounding T'Ralo. The only other deliberate force at play that the council of sayzrs could conceive to explain their clouded vision was the new magistra, Sissishal.

Prefect Sparzd stood to explain. "It would appear he is no more a sayzr today than he was a month ago. And, while the specifics of Magistra Haanna's influence over us all these past few weeks may forever remain a mystery, it was nevertheless at play. With her corruption of events behind us, we must remain steadfast in our mission to graduate only sayzrs."

Sissishal's little friend T'Ralo was unanimously dismissed from the academy. He would also be prohibited from attending the graduation ceremony, ostensibly to avoid further controversy. The recent political strife notwithstanding, it did not help that in his final thesis on the natural order of things, T'Ralo painted an unflattering portrayal of where people of the world fit into the designs of the omniverse. The Sayzr Order preferred to do without the further contumely certain to be sparked by any dissemination of T'Ralo's thesis, particularly where it was likely to be received by their human allies and other civilizations whose cultural and social order was built upon the self-important glorification of their own existence.

Mainly, however, the council of sayzrs thought the best hope for T'Ralo's development was to allow him to continue on his path of void beliefs and social alienation. Since a life of hardship could yield a great poet, the Sayzrs

Order saw no wisdom in interfering with the path that had led T'Ralo to transdimension. T'Ralo was stripped of his academic honors and a great many other things in a cruel way.

"Cruelty can be as effective as love when it comes to nurturing abilities," Moshe-djin croaked.

CHAPTER 38

OUTCAST

Sissi was noticeably absent partway through the school day. She was not seen in any of the classes or recess periods that followed fractals class.

T'Ralo, like the rest of the student body, was aware the Sayzr Order had something special in store for its most special new master of psychetropes, the child prodigy Magistra Haanna. Exactly what that would be—and the nature of her role among the master sayzrs—was yet unknown.

School let out well ahead of his last academy-sanctioned sword fighting lesson with Karmin Porris. The disappointing news about his sword fighting hit him particularly hard. Though it was the kind of disappointment he'd come to expect from his dealings with the academy, he didn't suppose the day could get any worse.

T'Ralo stuffed his hands firmly into his pockets and hunched his shoulders as he walked the deserted hallways of the school on his way to the main outer courtyard. *"Ask your sword."* Karmin's last words to him echoed through his mind. It hadn't sounded as if Karmin would be willing to take him on as a student now that the school year was over—at least, not yet. Supposedly that could change, the way Karmin had put it. But why and when?

"Ask your sword."

He looked down at his sword again, searching for answers along its slender length as he stepped into the forward outer courtyard. Was it not of a high enough quality? That didn't seem to match with Karmin's philosophies.

The sword was just old, dull, and pitted. Did he need to show more respect for his blade? It wasn't his fault the blade had been neglected and left to rust.

He was still left to ask, even after asking, but he decided he'd have his lonely walk home to ponder it further. But, to his surprise, when he stepped outside the archway, there sat Rasilla. She was uncharacteristically alone and still hanging around the yard.

Of course he immediately walked over to her. With no one else around, this would be his greatest opportunity to approach Rasilla and possibly walk her home.

To his surprise, Rasilla revealed she had been waiting for him. Before he could think of what to say, she was already smiling warmly and addressing him. "You should be proud of yourself," she said as he sat beside her. "I always knew you were destined for greatness. You succeeded at the Chambers Challenge." She tilted her head slightly. "What are your plans for the future?"

Rasilla, having failed at the Chambers Challenge and with Glimmer moving on, seemed desperately lost. T'Ralo felt bad for her, seeing her struggle to cope with an uncomfortable turn of events. "I'm no master like Glimmer Trezpin," he said with a shrug. "I heard he's going to be invited to work on the dimensions project to chronicle other dimensions of existence and chart the parallel universes."

"So you're the first nonmaster in history to transdimension," she said. "What does that mean?"

"Besides my not graduating, I have no idea. And it doesn't seem as though the prefects know, either. Do you know what happened to Sissi?"

Rasilla rolled her eyes. "Please don't mention her name. Last I heard, they took her home to meet with her parents. Beyond that, I prefer not to even think about her. They're probably going to crown her queen of all glory, when what they *should* do is put her on trial for usurping my free will. In fact, I wish I could forget all about her—and you should, too. She's no good for you, T'Ralo, and is probably even dangerous. Besides, she can't appreciate you the way I do. You need to follow your heart and be with those who truly care about you. You should be with the people you love." Rasilla, while holding his hand, leaned over and kissed him on the cheek.

Dumfounded, T'Ralo chuckled softly.

"Well?" Rasilla said, raising her eyebrows. "Aren't you going to ask to walk me home?"

"Huh? Oh yeah. I guess I should. Or I think I should. I mean—I know I should." He was surprised by his own feelings. "Sorry. This is weird, but for some strange reason, things aren't the way I expected them to be. Nothing is."

"You mean you really didn't know I was sweet on you? I was just playing hard to get. Perhaps I just played it too well."

T'Ralo gave her a peck on the cheek and stood to leave. "Thank you, Rasilla, for you have opened my eyes. I can't believe what a fool I have been."

"Where are you going?"

"To do as you suggested!" T'Ralo shouted over his shoulder. "To be with the one I love!"

He took off down the road and didn't bother to look back, but he had a hunch Rasilla wasn't smiling sweetly at him anymore. Surely she wanted to shout something nasty at him. But by the time Rasilla overcame the shock of her wounded pride, T'Ralo must have been too far away for her to convey anything she could work out to say.

At the Haanna residence, T'Ralo found several village watch guards, political leaders, and academy prefects gathered outside. It looked as though they had brought all the people of governing importance to honor Sissi and her family. There was even a full troop of boundarymen to guard and protect the area.

But something didn't seem right. Everyone was outside their home, and Sissi's mother had the wrong kind of tears in her eyes.

T'Ralo hurried to Mrs. Haanna's side. "What's going on?"

"They say they need to take her away for her own protection," said Mrs. Haanna.

T'Ralo spotted Sissi in the middle of the crowd, suspended in some kind of energy globe. He wanted to go to her, but the security wardens blocked his way.

The prefects and the governor were discussing Sissi's capture and their plans for her isolation.

Sparzd stood alongside the energy globe. "Careful what you say, Governor. She is contained but can still hear you. May Nature's will forgive us if she is ever freed and does not look favorably upon what we have done this day."

Everything was happening too quickly for T'Ralo. Everyone was rushing off to depart with Sissi as their prisoner.

Then Sissi's eyes discovered T'Ralo's. Her gaze was foreign—the monster revealed.

His feelings of love combatted the doubt. The Sissi he knew was sweet, innocent, and favored him. She was always helping him, not manipulating him. Did the villagers see that differently? Did Rasilla? Sissi seemed to be on T'Ralo's side. But for how long? Would she ever turn against him? What would happen if they had a disagreement? Did she really pose a threat to anybody? There was Sparzd. There was Rasilla. There was Morris Multhrobe . . . and who knew who else. When she did it right, her victims never knew they were under attack.

Nonsense, he thought. It all had to be an overreaction, a misunderstanding. Did they fear Sissi or just her omnipotence?

"Wait!" shouted T'Ralo.

Where there was Sissi, there was love and friendship. Where there was her power, there was uncertainty and terror.

Sissi placed her hands against the inside wall of the bubble and spoke. The bubble muted her words, but it was obvious what she was trying to say. "T'Ralo, help me."

T'Ralo couldn't think what to do. He knew he should at least speak up, that he should do something to fight for his friend and beloved.

"You have to help me."

T'Ralo owed her. He owed her for everything.

Sissi's plea became a demand and then an outright order.

He felt powerless. He did nothing.

Three boundarymen remained standing firm with arms crossed facing T'Ralo and Sissi's family, whilst the rest of the troop carted her away inside the bubble.

T'Ralo was angry. His face and ears burned red. Faced with a barrier of powerful security wardens and the will of the village, he felt helpless—and afraid to act. He was angry with the academy, angry with the prefects, angry at his entire village community.

It was then that he made up his mind to leave the village. He would no longer remain to continue any training. No magic, not even sword fighting, would keep him here, for that, he reasoned, was what they wanted. They, who took away his friend and beloved. They, who guided and controlled no less than Sissi ever did. And he would not join the outcasts at the outpost. He could not, in this moment, abide the social order of his community nor fathom its justice.

As if reading his anger, Mrs. Haanna invited T'Ralo to walk with her to the rooster pen at the back side of the cottage. He could see that she was deeply troubled and trying to keep up a brave face for his benefit.

Mrs. Haanna slid back her shawl from where she had it draped over her arms and pulled out of her shirtsleeve a cylindrical tube wrapped in leather.

"When they went through our home, the prefects were extremely disturbed to learn that Sissi had been recreating their maps outside of school. They said it was a security risk, and the boundarymen were ordered to confiscate all of her drawings. But I think Sissi would have wanted you to have this." Mrs. Haanna handed the leather scroll case to T'Ralo, who removed the cap and peered into its opening.

"It's empty," T'Ralo said.

"Her father made it for her to store her drawings in," she said. "It didn't matter that she had them all memorized. She would still spend hours a day fixated on them. It just didn't seem healthy."

"That sounds like our Sissi, all right," said T'Ralo.

"Yes. So, in order to prevent her from getting stuck like that, we wrapped the case in an extra layer to hide her maps from her whenever we needed to." Mrs. Haanna smiled and unfastened some of the leather laces. She then peeled away an outer layer to reveal several papers tucked within the leather covering itself. "It worked," Mrs. Haanna said. "And it worked against the boundarymen as well." She then pointed to the scroll case. "They may have taken most of Sissi's drawings, but I believe these were the ones that you and she studied together." She rolled it closed and refastened it. "Our little secret," she added.

T'Ralo agreed and grinned appreciatively, though still with more bitterness than sweetness.

"Everything will be all right," Mrs. Haanna said to him in a reassuring voice. "The prefects know best. As painful as this is, it's necessary to help

Sissi." She bent down and handed T'Ralo the little bunny rabbit that had been Sissi's latest pet. "Will you take care of her for Sissi?"

T'Ralo was surprised to see it. "Is this . . .?"

Sissi's mother smiled behind her tears and nodded. "The same one," she confirmed. "Over five weeks and going strong."

—— CHAPTER 39 ——

THE SKY BELOW

Like triangular columns supporting the School in the Sky, the Great Ore Mountains rose above the clouds concealing the school within the sky. Beneath the base of the mountains, miles below, the chilling silence of the subterranean caverns was as palpable as sound.

Galar's heavy footsteps echoed down the maze of catacombs that twisted an obscure path to where he had been summoned. The disrupted quietude only served to heighten his already self-conscious feelings about his sizable mass. The most unlikely of errand boys straightened his shirt around his bloated trunk and secured the loose opening by tucking its slack under his belt. The faded tunic matched Galar's jaundiced skin, his sunken eyes, and gloomy sense of futility.

As a younger man, his natural strength served him to great advantage. When he first earned an invitation to join the guard at the School in the Sky, he actually worked up high in the sky; he actually worked at the school. The ghostly memories of emotions past teased him as he wandered the dim corners of his mind in search of days once filled with the fresh faces of optimistic students and service to a warm, congenial staff. He had even once known the school's most prized and most powerful of all magicians, the famed Potash the Magnificent. The everyday energy and excitement throughout the school in those days was infectious to lift the general spirit.

But as the years went on and Galar was tasked with greater responsibilities, he learned more about the darker side of the school, the so-called Lord of Light who founded it, and his kingship over all of wizardkind. He had come to know things that even the great Potash the Magnificent could not be allowed to know. By the time he had come to realize that everything he had enjoyed about his job was no longer part of his job, it was too late. He knew only too well that for security reasons he would never be permitted to hold any other occupation. Galar himself had been tasked with enforcing that same rule against some of his former associates who sought to abandon service to the Warlock King after having been entrusted with too much sensitive information.

The dirty work that had to be done was Galar's work. Extract information, Galar. Dispose of the bodies, Galar. Acquire the unholiest of ingredients, Galar. All the original reasons for serving the security interests of the School in the Sky, such as status, money, friends, family, and a good woman, were gone. But not gone because he didn't have the position or resources to gain these things, rather, gone because for so many years he could never find the time or place to enjoy them until one day he no longer remembered how. During his many years of service, he had become estranged from his past and outlived his friends until he no longer had any. He couldn't remember the last time he'd laughed. He knew only that he had lost the desire to laugh, or love, or play. He understood now that he didn't miss people or doing things for fun, rather, he missed being able to miss them. But in order to do his job well, he had to be cold and detached from caring or feeling. Indeed, he was good at his job. So good was he at being bad that he eventually became cold and detached from himself, the man with aspirations, the man he used to be.

Galar cursed himself when he ran into a dead end. A projection of Warlock Zixhal sitting at a table against a cave wall stared up at him with a deflated sigh.

"You're going the wrong way, Galar."

"Forgive me, my lord, for I am your humble servant." Galar struggled to make it look like less of a chore for him to bend his heavy frame at the waist in respect. But for all his efforts, the image of Beru Zixhal was gone by the time he'd managed to straighten up. He lumbered back the way he had come and chose a different direction—the correct direction, he hoped.

"Wrong way, Galar," said Warlock Zixhal. This time Zixhal stood wearing a cape and a long black cloak with his arms crossed. This time his stern voice was sounding more impatient.

"Your humble servant, m'lord," said Galar, embarrassed for having repeated the same mistake. He tried to compensate for his error by making an extra effort to bow deeply with more distinguished control. By the time he incurred the soreness in his back and labored breathing from completing the maneuver, Zixhal's image had once again disappeared.

The warm whisper of torch flames dancing about the drafty corridors informed Galar that he was getting close to his destination. He unlocked the sealed gate and dutifully entered the lair where Warlock Zixhal had been waiting for him to deliver a message.

In the dark recesses of the lair, Galar was aware that somewhere back there sat the Warlock King, cloaked in shadow, upon his throne. He had to be careful not to divert his eyes in search of the King. Galar's job was to report directly to the warlock high priest, and that was Zixhal.

"His majesty the Lord of Light's plan to do nothing has paid off," Galar reported. "Just as he had foreseen, the prefects from his village have made the mistake of turning against one of their own in the capture and imprisonment of Sissishal."

"Thank you, Galar," said High Priest Zixhal. "Remain here by the doorway and await my further instructions. Try not to get lost."

Galar understood Zixhal's disappointment with him. Though he had managed to maintain his solid reputation up until now, there was no hiding the fact that his wits and senses had been fading of late. Notwithstanding the dark powers that prolonged his life, even the Warlock King could not forever ward off the effects of entropy on his joints and his decaying mind.

He stood just inside the entrance to the throne room and reminded himself not to leave.

The flames of two cauldrons flared up on either side of the throne, casting away the shadows and permitting Galar, from the other side of the room, a distant view of the Warlock King. He watched as his master and high priest, Zixhal, turned to face the grandmaster of masters.

"As you have foreseen it, your majesty," Zixhal said, "we can now take advantage of their mistake by assuming the role of liberator, and in freeing Sissishal, gain her loyalty in the service of the Lord of Light."

The King remained still and stared at Zixhal as if he were studying the high priest. Galar wondered if the King noticed when Zixhal's attention appeared to drift to the enormous statue that made up the throne, and what he might have to say about it. Galar had also wondered about the sculpted scene depicted on the elaborate throne, and if it was intentionally designed to enthrall.

The backrest of the throne was set between the legs of a great and powerful being carved in giant-sized proportion. Its headdress was magestified with outwardly flowing tendrils in every direction, each of them ruby-tipped, with two of the tendrils terminating in the front such that their glowing ends suggested the pupils of an otherwise blank face.

Muscular, steer-horned creatures double the size of a normal man were depicted climbing up the legs of the great being. Some of the horned creatures were clinging to its greatness while others were shown in active servitude, reaching out from the enormous legs whilst wielding a chain wrapped like a whip around the necks of smaller beings on the edge of the pedestal, as if to prevent any escape from the social order.

Below the feet of the god-like sculpture and comprising its pedestal were masses of people upon people. At its lowest levels, bodies of the crushed and dead lay as ruins, and above them, men and women set firmly on their hands and knees, as if forming tables, braced to support all the people on their backs. Three layers of these tablemen supported a bustling crowd clamoring toward the feet of their god—their ruler. The hand of one man in the face of another signified the adversarial conditions of their existence. A woman whose torso was arched back with chest pointing to the heavens, her arms dangling off the pedestal, and her face crossed out as dead, revealed the casualties of competition. Even among those shown as achieving a higher success, some were still subjected to the crushing weight of the god-like figure. Around each firmly planted leg, outlining the footprint of the glorious being, were the dead and broken bodies of privileged nobles who had struggled and toiled to reach such top ranks.

"I have watched you ponder this throne for many years," said the Warlock King.

"There's . . . something about it," said Zixhal.

"Yes. It speaks to you, much like the Djin, as if it were something universally familiar."

Galar watched Zixhal nodding in agreement.

"You were hoping I'd tell you more about it, perhaps?" asked the King.

"Only when you felt the time was right, my master."

"Indeed. And that time is now."

Galar strained to listen intently for he, too, had found the throne sculptures strangely compelling, and yearned to understand more about them.

The Warlock King's low, regal tone filled the chamber. "The story being told is a story as old as stories. It is in recognition of the Oracle of the Djin." He pointed up to the faceless sculpture of the god-like being towering over them and dominating the throne room. "Though the powers of Nature cannot forever be contained, the question becomes, how will they be distributed and to whom? Among the greatest masters and leaders meted out by Nature's hand, those fated to occupy certain stations in life fall in tune with the Djin at just the right moment bearing just the right skills and behaviors. What scares the greatest powers of the world about these windows of opportunity is the untamed randomness of the selection, and the possibility that no matter how hard we may try to rule and control all things around us, that the next Oracle of the Djin is chosen out of the ordinary—a peasant, a vagrant, or a vagabond. But by occupying all positions, by ruling a population or keeping it down, the chances can be greatly increased that either that honor will befall the wealthy and powerful, or someone who serves us."

Zixhal's eyes must have brightened or done something to give away his sudden realization, because Galar could see that the Lord of Light had relaxed his shoulders and donned a self-satisfied smile.

"You are speaking about Sissishal," Zixhal surmised.

"She possesses the oddest of unique qualities," said the Warlock King. "And has managed to unlock powers never before seen. If she is fated to become the next Oracle, we cannot simply erase and replace her. For, it is beyond my powers to mimic her bizarre nature."

"But we might use her and control her enough to place her in your majesty's service."

"We might," agreed the Warlock King, stroking his chin. "But she is too peculiar to be mapped with what we've learned so far of the psychetropic spheres. She remains . . . unpredictable."

"So unpredictable?" asked Zixhal.

"If we are not careful, the next Oracle could control us." The Wizard King tapped a finger against his armrest. "We need to send someone who can gain the initiative on her, someone who is least susceptible to being read, someone who is . . . dead inside." The Warlock King leaned to one side and spoke more loudly, as if intending for his words to reach Galar. "She will join us or die."

CHAPTER 40

WHICH SIDE OF THE BARS?

T'Ralo stood alone among the border pines and gazed out on the open plains as he pondered his next move. He was equipped for the trip and of the mind to break free from parents, prefects, and the village rule.

Yet good plan and good purpose, however well justified, were far removed from the stark realities of action. Leaving the Black Forest meant leaving the only home he'd ever known. And for what? The dangers of strangers and the unknown? What was freedom, he wondered, and what was freedom worth? So much of his time and energies had been spent rebelling against the control of his community that he'd never really had the chance to contemplate the alternative.

A sleek hawk on a thermal breeze glided gracefully over the fruit trees that graced the plains beyond the forest's edge. It floated by like a dream, the way the entire scene took T'Ralo back to *A Time Before*.

END
BOOK ONE

Please look for more books in the *Wizard's Ruse* series available now at your local bookstore or coming soon!

COPYRIGHTS AND CONTACTING THE AUTHOR

Please be sure to obtain written permission from the author before using this book in a manner protected by copyright law. Depending on the project, it may not cost you any money for a license to use these works, but written permission is still required.

If you happen to be a writer interested in obtaining legal permission to add to the series or to co-author a work with Brian Smallbrook, please do not hesitate to contact the author or his designated agent. Other artistic expressions and mediums are also welcome, such as comic books, films, video games, role-playing games, scripts, screenplays, or converting your fan art to an official, commercially licensed product. If you are not an artist but wish to contribute in some other fashion, please let us know.

Do you think this book could be a good fundraising tool to raise money for your school, charitable organization, or other good cause? Please inquire about fundraising programs where all sales profits and royalties go to support your cause.

You may contact Brian Smallbrook online through social media or his websites:

www.briansmallbrook.com
www.wizardsruse.com

www.ingramcontent.com/pod-product-compliance
Lightning Source LLC
Chambersburg PA
CBHW030239200626
46816CB00002BA/436